I squirmed in my seat. It had been five long years since he'd taken the job overseas and yet sometimes it still felt like yesterday. And while I could turn off the TV, turning off the memories had proven a lot more difficult. Memories of those large strong hands of his, touching me in all the right places. His warm body moving over mine. The way those piercing blue eyes would lock onto me—making me feel, for one brief moment—that I was the center of the universe. His universe.

Of course that had not actually been the case. I hadn't been the center of his universe at all. Turned out, I wasn't even a distant star. But he remained the sun—his brilliance and passion and confidence radiating from halfway across the world. While I had been reduced to a black hole of misery, perfect for sucking in solar systems of hurt. (Or pints of Ben and Jerry's, as the case might be.)

"Oh my god. Sarah, are you even kidding me right now?"

I looked up, my face reddening as my neighbor, Stephanie, walked into my beach cottage without bothering to knock, catching me in the shameful act of spying on my ex on TV. I cringed. I was so busted.

At First Light

MARI MADISON

BERKLEY SENSATION
New York

BERKLEY SENSATION
Published by Berkley
An imprint of Penguin Random House LLC
375 Hudson Street, New York, New York 10014

Copyright © 2017 by Marianne Mancusi Beach
Excerpt from *Just This Night* by Mari Madison copyright © 2017 by Marianne Mancusi Beach
Penguin Random House supports copyright. Copyright fuels creativity, encourages
diverse voices, promotes free speech, and creates a vibrant culture. Thank you for buying
an authorized edition of this book and for complying with copyright laws by not
reproducing, scanning, or distributing any part of it in any form without permission.
You are supporting writers and allowing Penguin Random House to continue to
publish books for every reader.

BERKLEY and BERKLEY SENSATION are registered trademarks and the B colophon
is a trademark of Penguin Random House LLC.

ISBN: 9780425283158

First Edition: March 2017

Printed in the United States of America
1   3   5   7   9   10   8   6   4   2

Cover photo of couple embracing on beach © Flying Colours/Getty Images
Back cover photo: Beach © T. Dallas/Shutterstock
Cover design by Alana Colucci
Book design by Kristin del Rosario

one

SARAH MARTIN

In a perfect world, once you broke up with someone, you would no longer be required to see them on a daily basis. You could move out of their apartment, block them on Facebook, pick a different Starbucks so you don't end up waiting in line together for your Triple Venti Skinny Vanilla Lattes (you) and Grande Java Chip Frappuccinos (yes, I'm that confident in my masculinity [and metabolism]—him).

Sure, once in a while you might find yourself at the same wedding (no one ever scores the perfect friendship split in these sorts of things) but no bride in her right mind would sit the two of you at the same table. And hey, if you got drunk enough you wouldn't care if she did.

In a perfect world, once you broke up with someone, they slipped away from your life like rain down a gutter—exactly where they belonged—and you never had to deal with them again.

Unless, that was, that someone happened to have a job on network TV.

"I'm Troy Young, reporting live from Damascus. . . ."

Seriously, it was enough to turn a girl to Netflix. Every time I turned on my television and flipped the channel, Troy Young, ex-boyfriend extraordinaire and former love of my life, reentered my living room once more with feeling. Usually looking annoyingly hot in the process with his clipped, sandy brown hair and piercing eyes that were so blue they caused my TV settings to look over saturated. Add in a deep, baritone voice that made even the driest of politics sound absurdly sexy and you could start to see why the guy was responsible for launching a thousand fan girl tweets.

And don't even get me started on his wardrobe. As always, Troy seemed to be allergic to the traditional shirt-and-tie motif of most respectable reporters, choosing instead to wear completely inappropriate short-sleeve T-shirts that emphasized his broad shoulders and chiseled chest, paired with dark-rinse jeans that hung low on his narrow hips. Emphasizing, well, other things.

Forget Netflix. It was enough to drive a girl to drink. And I'm not talking Triple Venti Skinny Vanilla Lattes, either.

And yes, I am completely aware I had the power to change the channel. Skip the news, go on a reality TV show binge or start a *House Hunters* marathon. Or hell, maybe even turn off the TV entirely and go to the beach or something. One single click of a button and Troy Young could be blasted into oblivion, banished from my living room forever.

But sometimes, for some reason, that seemed the hardest thing to do—even if it was the smartest. And instead I found myself stupidly lingering on the broadcast, finger hovering over the remote as I tried to will myself to keep up with some Kardashians instead of Kuwait. In fact, on really bad days, I sometimes surrendered to my pathetic nature entirely, curling up in my recliner, closing my eyes and letting that sweet honeyed voice of his roll over me like a wave. Remembering how husky it would get when he used to lean in and whisper naughty things in my ear. (Oh, Twitter, you have no idea!)

I squirmed in my seat. It had been five long years since he'd gone overseas and yet sometimes it still felt like yesterday. And while I could turn off the TV, turning off the memories had proven a lot more difficult. Memories of those large strong hands of his, touching me in all the right places. His warm body moving over mine. The way those piercing blue eyes would lock onto me—making me feel, for one brief moment—that I was the center of the universe. His universe.

Of course that had not actually been the case. I hadn't been the center of his universe at all. Turned out, I wasn't even a distant star. But he remained the sun—his brilliance and passion and confidence radiating from halfway across the world. While I had been reduced to a black hole of misery, perfect for sucking in solar systems of hurt. (Or pints of Ben and Jerry's, as the case might be.)

"Oh my god. Sarah, are you even kidding me right now?"

I looked up, my face reddening as my neighbor Stephanie walked into my beach cottage without bothering to knock, catching me in the shameful act of spying on my ex on TV. I cringed. I was so busted. Stephanie shook her head in disapproval, as I could have predicted she would.

"Seriously, if you looked up *glutton for punishment* on the Internet, I'm positive the Wiki would have your picture." She pushed a glass of champagne into my hand, still holding the open bottle in her own. "Now, down the hatch, girl," she commanded. "And stay focused. We've got major celebrating to take care of tonight and I refuse to accept anything less than full-blown party-pony-level enthusiasm from my bestie."

I straightened up in my seat and did as I was told, tipping back the glass and swallowing down the sparkling wine in one long gulp. A moment later, my stomach warmed, already feeling a little better as I prepared to party-pony up as best I could.

We were celebrating Stephanie's triumphant return to News 9 tonight, and I didn't need to rain on her parade. It had taken her over a year to get back in the game after being wrongfully accused of sabotaging another reporter's career, and she'd been slaving away as a waitress ever since.

But now she was back—like a heart attack (her words)—and we were about to head to Rain, one of our favorite nightclubs, to mark the occasion—Tinder apps locked and loaded and ready to go.

I had to admit, the two of us looked pretty swipe-rightable tonight, too. Stephanie stunning in her short sequined dress and stiletto heels. Me in my cute cropped top and red maxi skirt ensemble, a color Stephanie had insisted perfectly accented my blue eyes and long blond hair. No doubt we'd at least be attracting a few of the society photographers tonight, if not any hot men. Which, to be honest, would be fine by me. I didn't really need a hookup. It was just . . . something I did sometimes, to pass the time. And it pissed off my dad, too, as an added bonus. Somehow he had it in his head that twenty-seven was a ripe old age to settle down and start popping out grandbabies. Future voters of America and all that.

For a while my dad had really pinned his hopes on this guy Asher who used to do the weather for News 9, where I now worked as an entertainment reporter. Asher was fun. He was super hot, too. And for a brief moment I actually had entertained the idea of getting serious with him. After all, on paper it was a match made in society heaven. Asher's mother was the owner of News 9. And my dad was the new mayor of San Diego—and one of News 9's biggest advertisers.

But Asher wasn't in love with me. He was in love with his producer. Some girl from the wrong side of the proverbial tracks who was completely wrong for him—yet somehow completely right. Which I understood—truly. After all, hadn't that been the way with Troy and me, back when we were in college? My dad had hated Troy and his outspoken left-wing ideals and save-the-world causes. At one point I think he was convinced Troy would turn me into a socialist. Which wouldn't have jived very well with his Campaign O' Hate and Misogyny™ he'd been preparing to unleash on the world. (Troy's description of my dad's politics at the time, which had made me laugh for days.)

My eyes drifted back to the TV. Troy's story had ended and he was back on camera, wrapping things up. I watched, my stomach squirming a little, as it always did when I saw him this close up. It was this weird juxtaposition of him appearing so near—while being halfway across the world.

I scowled. What was I doing? I was more than a glutton for punishment—I was a complete masochist. And all over a guy who didn't deserve a second of my thoughts, especially after how he'd left me. On that day five years ago—the day that should have been our greatest victory—which turned into a nightmare. Changing my life forever.

But what did Troy care about that? He'd been using me from the start.

Feeling a lump in my throat, I reached for the remote again, this time ready to zap him out of my life for good.

But just as I was about to hit the off button, something caught my eye at the back of the screen. I squinted: Was someone coming up behind him? Some kind of man, dressed in black?

I scooted to the edge of my seat, the hairs standing up on my arms, though I wasn't exactly sure why. It was probably nothing, after all, just a random guy, out for a stroll . . .

. . . with something that looked a lot like a gun in his hand.

"Stephanie," I called out. She had gone over to the kitchen to open a new bottle of champagne. "Do you see that?" I asked as she poked her head back in the living room. I pointed at the screen.

"Sarah . . ." She started to lecture, then stopped. Her eyes widened. "Wait. Is that—"

"Troy!" A voice offscreen suddenly broke through the broadcast, sounding tense and worried. His cameraman? His producer? "Troy—I think we need to—"

The sound of gunshots burst through my speakers, popping through the air in quick, sharp bursts. I watched, heart in my throat, as Troy jumped back, his face stark white as he seemed to realize the danger he was in for the first time. Before he could do anything, the man behind him leapt into action, grabbing him and shoving a black hood over his head.

"Oh my god!" I cried.

I watched, paralyzed with shock, as Troy tried to wrestle free and for one brief second I thought he might escape. But then the man placed a gun up against his temple and yelled something unintelligible at him. Troy stopped moving, his shoulders slumping.

"Troy . . ." I gasped. "Oh my God, Troy!"

I wanted to crawl into the TV. To rescue him myself,

against all odds. Instead, I could only sit there, helpless and horrified, watching the scene unfold. Stephanie stood behind me, her hand squeezing down on my shoulder so hard it would have hurt had I not been completely numb.

The man turned to the camera. He was wearing a mask, but it didn't hide the ugly smirk on his face.

"We have your journalist, America," he spit out in a halting accent. "Tomorrow morning, unless you comply with our demands, he will be beheaded."

Oh my God. Oh my God.

I rose to my feet, my knees buckling out from under me. Stephanie grabbed me, holding me close, tears falling down her face.

But I couldn't cry. I could only stare blankly at the screen as the feed cut back to the newsroom. Back to where the anchors were sitting safe and sound behind their desk, their faces mirroring the fear and horror on my own.

For a moment, no one said anything. And the silence stretched out, sharp as razor wire. Then, finally, after what seemed an eternity, the female anchor opened her mouth to speak.

"We're not sure what just happened," she said in a shaky voice. "We have lost contract with the crew. We will continue to update you as we learn more about this . . . situation."

Her voice broke. The station cut to commercial. A small cry escaped my lips and I staggered, black spots swimming before my eyes. Stephanie caught me before I collapsed, pulling me back down to the couch and holding me close.

"He'll be okay," she whispered in my ear. "I know it looks bad, but . . . You know Troy." She attempted a smile that didn't quite reach her eyes. "He can get out of anything."

It was true. Or it had been true, at least, once upon a time.

Troy was a master of escaping tight situations—that was part of the reason he was so good at his job.

But this time . . . This time . . .

I swallowed hard, trying to come to terms with the truth. That suddenly the one man I'd wanted so desperately to exorcise from my life was now the one man I needed to see again—more than anyone else in the world.

The one man I wasn't sure that I would.

two

TROY YOUNG

four months later ...

"Let me go! Let me go, goddamn it!"
Rough hands grab me by the back of the neck, slamming my face down onto the cold stone floor. My vision spins, but I force myself to keep conscious, though half of me isn't sure why I bother. After all, if I pass out, the pain will end, right? Or at least I won't be feeling it.

But no. Fuck that. I'm not letting these bastards win. I'm not giving them the satisfaction of seeing me willingly retreat into oblivion.

"Go to hell," I growl, wondering if my sudden defiance surprises them. After all, I've been a good little boy for the most part these last months. Mostly because until recently I'd held on to this inane hope of some miraculous rescue. Of a sliver of light cracking through the darkness, voices speaking English ringing through my prison cell.

But that hope has long since been shredded. And now I just want it all to end. They've won. They've broken me. I'm a shell of my former self. I wonder now: If I piss them off enough can I make them finish me? Quick, easy, no regrets.

Okay, so I have one regret. With long blond hair and wide blue eyes. The girl I walked away from five years ago—choosing this nightmare world over a paradise with her.

Where would I be now if I had made the other choice? If I had agreed to run away with her, instead of taking this job? Would we be married, have kids? Would we be living a simple life in a run-down cottage on the shores of a Mexican beach as she'd described, towheaded little boys and girls running barefoot and wild up and down the sands?

It sounded like hell at the time. A tiny life. Wasted in selfish pursuit of happiness instead of the greater good. I had wanted to make a difference. To save the world.

Yet in the end, I hadn't even managed to save myself.

Angry now, I push her from my mind. Concentrate on the brute behind me, his dirty nails digging into my flesh.

"Just fucking do it," I growl, trying to turn my head. "I'm done here!"

My captor ignores me, yanking me to my feet instead, dragging me toward the door. My pulse kicks up and my heart slams against my ribcage. He's taking me outside? Why is he taking me outside?

To kill me?

Or . . .

I haven't been out of the hole in three months, by my rough count, and the sunlight nearly blinds me as it hits me full on. I blink and I squint and I stumble, my body weak from near starvation. When I finally do manage to right myself, I realize I'm standing in front of the man who cap-

tured me that first day. He is unshaven, a wicked scar down his cheek.

"Your government has met our demands," he tells me in halting English. "You are free to go."

You are free to go.

I shot up in bed, eyes wide. Sweat pooling down my chest, my breaths coming in short gasps. I swallowed hard, blinking my eyes a few times, then reached over for the bedside lamp, the idea of on-demand electricity still feeling like a miracle after months in the dark. The first couple weeks back I'd slept with the lights on. But it had felt like a pussy move and I'd turned them all off the night before.

Inviting the nightmares back with a vengeance.

"Get a grip, Troy," I muttered under my breath as I flicked on the switch, prompting the room to flood with warm, golden light. I exhaled. Kicking my legs out from under the covers, I swung them to the side of the bed then stood up, walking across the cold hardwood floor to the bedroom window. I pulled back the curtain and stared outside.

From here, in this little apartment on the hill, I could see downtown San Diego in the distance, sparkling with light. It was only one AM according to my bedside clock, which meant there were probably people still out there, drinking, dancing—without a care in the world. Without a thought in their empty heads of those stuck in dark holes, being tortured . . . or worse . . .

No, those people out there, those dancers, those drinkers—they were too busy Instagramming and Snapchatting and selfie-ing or whatever the hell else kids did these days. Content to live their small lives with blinders on—oblivious to the rest of the planet.

I didn't know whether I hated them . . . or envied them.

I groaned, raking a hand through my hair. I'd gotten it

all shaved off when I'd first set foot back on US soil, but it was already growing back. I'd need another haircut soon to wrestle it back into shape, but that would require calling a salon and making an appointment. To sit down at the mercy of some hairdresser who might have secretly wished they'd left me in that hole.

Oh God. I needed to pull myself together. Tomorrow I'd be officially reentering society, starting my new job as a reporter at News 9 San Diego, and I couldn't let them see me sweat. I needed this job and I knew I was lucky to have gotten it, given the circumstances. But still, it was hard to get excited. Mostly because it felt a lot like a pity gig—the news director doing me a favor.

Not that I wasn't experienced enough for the position— if anything my five years as a national news foreign corre- spondent made me overqualified for some local news gig. Hell, covering fires and car chases and other mundane first- world-problem news should be a cakewalk after what I'd done. What I'd been through.

Should being the operative word here.

I walked to the living room and turned on the TV, mind- lessly flipping through the channels, trying to settle on a station. But they all seemed too loud, the characters yelling at me over the airwaves until I turned the volume down so low I couldn't hear them at all. The light was too bright, too. Hurting my eyes. Eventually I just turned if off altogether. Grabbed a beer from the fridge and slugged it down. Then I lay down on the couch and pulled a pillow over my head, waiting for dawn.

I t seemed I'd just fallen asleep when the alarm woke me up, announcing the start of the day. Or the middle of the day, as the case might be. Thankfully my shift didn't start until noon. I rolled off the couch feeling sore and exhausted, my knee twanging as my foot hit the floor a little too hard. They'd dislocated it when I'd first been captured, and it never did set right. I'd gone to a doctor when I first got back and he said I'd need surgery to get it fixed. Add it to my list.

I worked to get dressed, then got into my car and headed to my job. It still felt strange to be driving down the street not looking over my shoulder to see if anyone was following. To watch others go about their lives, pumping gas, dropping off kids, living this weird, surreal normal life that for so long had felt like an impossible dream. My car itself felt impossible, too. Back-up cameras, air-conditioning, GPS. Luxuries I had once taken for granted, but since forgotten all about. Of course you didn't need a ton of air conditioning in San Diego. The weather was perfect. No more breaking out into a sweat the second I walked out my front door.

I pulled into the TV station a few minutes later, parking the car and getting out, slamming the door behind me. I stood there for a moment, surveying the building, my eyes darting to each perimeter, observing and recording each exit, even though I knew that wasn't necessary anymore. Just a habit left over from the last five years of going into buildings where it was.

Inside the front door, a pretty brunette greeted me at the front desk. I informed her who I was and showed my ID, and she buzzed me in. I took note of the bulletproof glass and double-door entry and felt a little better as I stepped through.

"There you are! You made it!"

I looked up. A Latino man with a short, trim beard stepped toward me as I entered the newsroom, holding out his hand. When I gave him what must have looked like a doubtful expression he grinned. "Sorry. I'm Javier. Your new photographer."

My first instinct was to ask how he knew who I was. But that was stupid. The entire country knew my face at this point. I took his hand and shook it.

"Good to meet you, man," he said. "And thanks for your service."

I nodded stiffly, feeling my face heat. People had been saying shit like that to me since I'd gotten back. Thanks for your service. Missing the fact that I was a journalist, not a soldier. I felt guilty accepting their misplaced gratitude, but knew it would be even worse to try to argue that I wasn't worthy of it.

We walked into the newsroom together and I tried not to wince at all the bright lights and loud noises assaulting my senses. The place looked like a deranged nightclub with TVs hanging from every available surface and neon lights flashing everywhere else. It was open concept with little pods of desks for the producers and writers of the newscast scattered throughout. On the far walls were doors presumably leading to the executive offices and special projects department. I wondered if it would sound too prima donna to ask for an office of my own. Because working out here in the open was going to drive me completely crazy on day one.

I realized everyone's eyes were on me now and I found myself breaking out into a cold sweat, despite the cool air conditioning. I tried to pretend it was all my imagination—that they weren't actually looking at me—but that was ridiculous. After all, I was one of the most famous people in the country right now. #AmericasHero or #ShouldaLetHimDie, depending on your point of view. For weeks I'd been courted by all the networks—including my former employer—to tell my story. I was hotter than Ryan Reynolds.

I swallowed hard. Maybe this was a mistake.

Thankfully Javier seemed to sense my unease. "Come on, man," he said. "Let me show you the photographer's lounge. It's a lot quieter there."

I followed him gratefully through the newsroom, trying my best to ignore the stares. We headed down a hall and into a small room, just off the editing bays. It was filled with ragged armchairs and threadbare couches and a small TV hung from a wall, broadcasting the news. It was quiet, too. At the moment, no one else was there. As Javier went straight to the coffeemaker and grabbed two cups, I settled down into a chair and let out a long sigh. Much better.

Javier loaded up the Keurig and turned back to me, his eyes shining. He shook his head. "I can't believe you're actually here," he said with a low whistle. "You are a fucking legend, man. I can't believe I actually get to work with you."

I felt my cheeks redden. "I'm really not a big deal," I muttered.

"Are you kidding? What about that time you were on the front lines, reporting live from the hood of a freaking tank? That was so hard-core."

I stifled a grimace. Hard-core, maybe. Stupid and ridiculous, definitely. Back then I'd fancied myself as some kind of superhero cowboy reporter. Made of Teflon—nothing could touch me.

"Well, that was my old life," I said. "And it didn't exactly end well."

Javier blushed. "Yeah. Sorry, man. I can't even imagine." He trailed off, catching my expression. "Sorry," he said again. "You probably don't want to talk about it, huh? That's cool with me. I have a cousin who was in the service. He never says a word about his time over there. In fact, every time some idiot brings it up he has to leave the room."

I nodded absently, kind of wanting to leave the room myself. Or maybe the entire building. This had clearly been a mistake. I was so not ready for this. I hadn't even started working yet and my skin was prickling and my heart was beating a mile a minute.

Come on, Troy. Pull it together.

I forced my eyes to meet the television set on the wall, trying to focus on something besides the room. The noon anchors were announcing the entertainment block—a new movie review of some mindless rom-com I had never heard of. I started to turn back to Javier. But then something stopped me in my tracks.

Make that *someone* . . .

My eyes widened. I stared at the screen. At the beautiful blonde talking into the camera. "Who is that?" I asked, though I was pretty sure I had already made a positive identification.

Sure enough, Javier confirmed it. "That's Sarah Martin," he said. "Our entertainment reporter. Her dad's our mayor and a big advertiser, too. Not that I'm sure that had anything to do with her getting the gig." He rolled his eyes. "She's hot, though, I'll give her that. And she seems to know her stuff. Though how hard can it be to watch movies for a living?"

I didn't answer and instead attempted to pull in a breath. But the air was suddenly ice-cold, and made my lungs ache. Oh God. Sarah Martin. Sarah Martin working here? As an entertainment reporter?

Swallowing hard, I turned back to the TV where Sarah was now sitting, interviewing some celebrity I didn't recognize. She was dressed in a silky sky-blue blouse that, in my opinion, was cut way too low for TV. And her skirt? It was so short it made her legs look as if they went on forever. She completed the look with a pair of red-soled shoes, and her hair was smooth and long and perfect, styled within an inch of its life.

No. This wasn't my Sarah. My Sarah with her ripped jeans and ratty political T-shirts and Converse sneakers on her feet. With her messy ponytail and fresh face, devoid of any makeup.

I sighed. I guess we all had changed. And not necessarily for the better.

A sudden voice broke out into the room and it made me almost jump out of my skin. "Desk to Javier. Are you loaded up?"

I dropped my shoulders. Right. It was just the walkie-talkie.

Javier shot me a look. "You okay, man?" he asked.

"I'm fine." I gritted my teeth. "Just . . . startled me is all."

He nodded, pulling out his walkie. "Yeah, I'm loaded. And I've got Troy here." He let his finger off the button. "Are you good to go?" he asked. When I nodded, he pressed the button again. "Where do you need us?"

"We're getting reports of some kind of robbery and police pursuit just south of downtown," the assignment desk editor informed us. "Do you want to head down there and see if there's anything to it?"

"Roger that," Javier said, looking pleased. "We're on it." He stuffed the walkie into his pocket and crossed the room, over to a set of lockers. I watched him, curious. Especially when he pulled out a bulletproof vest and threw it at me.

I caught it, giving him a questioning look. He grinned. "I know it's silly," he said. "But I love wearing them. Makes me feel like a badass." He shoved his arms into the vest and strapped it up. Then he laughed. "That probably sounds lame to someone like you."

"No. It's smart," I admitted, reaching out to take the other vest and strapping it to myself. Just like old times. Not that the vest had done me any good during those old times.

And the way my heart was pounding in my chest? I wasn't sure it was going be much help now, either.

three

SARAH

I stepped out of the studio after finishing my live intro to the Liam Hemsworth interview I'd done a couple days before. Now I had to work on my actual movie review, which would air on Thursday, the night before the film's opening. I'd gone to the press screening last week where I had struggled to not fall asleep in the middle of the film, which was basically packed with mindless action, little plot, and a lot of gratuitous Hemsworth ab close-ups. (So, you know, not a total waste.)

In the end, I'd decided to give it a B+, rounded up from the C- I'd originally planned after being reminded by News 9's owner, Mrs. Anderson, that in addition to being in the business of making crappy movies, this particular studio was also a major News 9 advertiser. And therefore it would be . . . appropriate . . . for us to be generous.

It was funny; when I had first been offered this job I'd been over the moon. After all, I'd started as a film major in college and had seen just about every movie made from back in the Golden Age of Hollywood and had a special place in my heart for foreign films as well. I spent my twenty-first birthday at a Fellini Film Festival and had once watched all of Kieslowski's Decalogue films in one sitting. (That's over nine hours of English subtitles, people! I was pretty sure I was going to go blind by the end.)

Of course that was all before I'd gotten involved with Troy and his do-gooder friends. Switched my major to Environmental Studies and attempted to save the world. To Troy, movies were a waste of time. A diversion to lull us into complacency and distract us from what was truly going on in the world—not to mention in our own backyards. Troy didn't even own a television set—in fact he had a bumper sticker on his car that read *Kill Your TV*—something at the time I thought was so rebellious and cool.

And when, in the end, he left me high and dry? When instead of killing his TV he decided to become a network star? I ordered every single cable station imaginable just out of spite. Binge watching the most mindless reality shows—which, oddly enough, were not nearly as fake as our relationship had turned out to be.

At that point it was too late to go back to film. And after the Troy debacle I had lost all faith in the idea of saving the world. So I bounced around for a while doing social media and public relations gigs for art galleries and small businesses, ultimately going to work for my father and his mayoral bid.

So when this job opened up, just after my dad's election, I jumped at it, seeing it as a chance to return to my roots. Instead, it had turned out to be just another PR job for big Hollywood films that didn't really need it.

Case in point, this particular blockbuster.

A month ago I had begged the executive producer to send

me out to the SXSW film festival in Austin, Texas, to report for a week on all the smart, innovative indie film selections for the show. Instead, I'd been dragged to L.A. for a press junket and a bunch of red carpet crap for a slew of "reimaginings" of old eighties films—the only thing they seemed to make anymore in Hollywood.

Everyone likes a good do-over, I guess.

"Hey, Sarah!" My producer, Ben, greeted me at the doorway to the entertainment center, pushing his thick, black-rimmed glasses up his nose. Ben was my salvation at News 9. The only guy whose appreciation for old movies rivaled my own. "Did you hear about the noir film festival they're holding this weekend?"

I grinned. "I already have my full access pass," I assured him.

"Oh my God. Jealous," he pronounced. "Who are you going with?"

"No one, actually. I'm just going by myself."

"Seriously?"

"What's wrong with that?"

"Nothing. I mean, I go to the movies by myself all the time," he admitted. "It's just . . . I didn't think someone like you would have to."

I choked out a laugh, even though I wanted to scowl. It was the kind of comment I got all the time from people. People who thought they knew me, just from a quick glance. A good-looking blonde. A rich chick. That was all they needed to know before making their assumptions.

"Maybe I enjoy going to movies by myself," I said. "Ever think of that?"

He gave me a skeptical look. Of course. "Well," he said, "if you change your mind and would like a noir-loving nerd to share your popcorn with, just let me know."

I gave him a smile. "I may take you up on that, actually."

He paused and I watched him shuffle from foot to foot. "Is something wrong?" I asked.

He shook his head. "I was just . . . wondering. Have you heard who they're going to put in the new He Said, She Said movie review segment yet? I mean, obviously you're the *she*. But I didn't know if . . ." He trailed off, looking sheepish.

"I'm sorry," I said. "I haven't heard anything." I gave him a rueful look. "Fingers crossed though, right?"

He nodded, holding up both hands with crossed fingers. Then he turned back to his work. I watched him for a moment, feeling kind of bad for him. I knew how much he wanted to be on air. To do this segment. Heck, it was his idea to begin with and there was no doubt he'd be amazing at the job. But I wasn't sure the studio brass was going to care about that when they selected their talent. The way things went around here, looks trumped skill almost every time. And Ben, well, he wasn't exactly suave, to say the least, with his wrinkled shirts and high-water jeans and unkempt hair.

After grabbing my purse, I headed back out of the entertainment office, glancing at my watch as I left. I had to be across town by one to attend the screening of yet another blockbuster film: *Depressed Yet Gifted Teenager Saves the World from the Vampire Apocalypse While Choosing between Two Hot Guys*. (Okay, fine, that wasn't the official title, but it might as well have been.)

As I walked down the hall, my cell phone buzzed and I looked down to see who was texting me. Stephanie wanted to know if I wanted to go out tonight. As I pushed through the door, typing my reply, I managed to smack into someone full force.

"Oh! Sorry!" I cried, nearly dropping my phone. "I wasn't—"

I stopped short. Unable to speak. Unable to know if I was ever going to be able to speak again as I stared at the man I had just literally walked into. The man I thought I'd never see in real life again.

"Oh my God. Troy," I breathed.

He stared back at me, his face stark white. A muscle twitched at his jaw. For a moment I wondered if he was literally going to turn around and run the other direction, far away from me. Then, he straightened himself and squared his shoulders. As if this were no big deal.

"Sarah," he said, giving me a slight nod. "Good to see you. It's been . . . a while."

I gaped at him, still unable to form words, my mind racing a thousand miles a minute as I tried to convince myself that this was really happening. Right here, right now in my very own workplace.

Troy Young in the flesh.

It was funny: Back during those months he had been captured, I'd spent long hours trying to imagine what I'd say to him if I ever saw him again. I even wrote a lot of it down, letter style, though of course I'd never sent any of it. I still had them, though, tucked away in a small shoe box under my bed. Never to see the light of day.

Once he was freed and had returned home I'd thought about calling him. In fact, for a while that was all I thought about, and I could barely resist the urge. Thankfully common sense had won out in the end, however. I had managed to keep a little dignity. Stay far away.

But now, not so much.

"I heard you were back," I stammered, even knowing as I said it that it was the stupidest thing to say. I mean, the entire world had heard he was back. He was front-page news. In the A block of every newscast for weeks. There was even this crazy Twitter debate going on about whether the President should have bargained with the men who took him—or stuck to the policy of not negotiating with terror groups. I suddenly wondered if Troy knew about this debate. And how it would feel to know. That some people's politics (including my dad's) would have preferred he get his head chopped from his shoulders than back down on political policy.

"So, uh, what are you doing here?" I asked. "Are you here to be interviewed?" I knew all the networks had been after him since he'd been back. But far as I knew he'd turned down every one. It'd be a huge deal if News 9 had scored the exclusive.

He gave me a weird look. "Actually . . ."

Before he could finish his sentence, Javier stepped through the door. He smiled at me, then at Troy. "Ready to go?"

"Go where?" I asked, confused. "I have a screening."

"Not you, darling," Javier interjected. "My man Troy here."

Wait, what?

I watched as Troy's face turned bright red. "I'm, uh, working here for a bit," he said in a gruff voice. "Just . . . filling in and stuff for a while. Until I can get on my feet again."

I stared at him, shocked beyond belief. Troy was working here? At News 9? As a reporter? But that was so beneath him! He was a network star. A national celebrity. Publishers had offered him millions in book-deal money. Why on earth would he choose to slum it here with us instead?

He caught my look. "Sorry," he said, clearly misinterpreting my expression. "I had no idea you were working here too when I took the job." He shrugged. "Don't worry. I'm sure we won't cross paths much."

My heart panged in my chest at the look I saw on his

face. "No! I mean, that's cool! I'm glad you got a job. That you're . . . back on your feet. And so soon. And . . ." I realized I was rambling, but I couldn't help it.

He gave me a strange look. "Yeah. I'm . . . glad, too," he said in a clipped voice. "I guess I'll see you around."

And with that, he turned abruptly. "Are you ready to go?" he asked Javier. Javier nodded and the two of them walked out the door, while I stood there staring after them, hardly sure what had just happened.

All that was clear to me were two simple things:

One, Troy Young was really back.

And two, he was definitely not happy to see me.

four

TROY

God, I was happy to see her.

Okay, maybe *happy* wasn't the right word. In fact, if anything I felt somewhat physically ill as I followed Javier to the truck and hopped in. As if I'd been sucker-punched in the stomach. But in a good way, if you know what I mean. Just to see her! Standing in front of me. In the flesh. Half of me wanted to poke her—just to make sure she was real. That she was the real flesh and blood Sarah—instead of the construct I'd created down in that hole.

You gotta understand: After I was captured, I thought I'd never see anyone from back home again, never mind her. Hell, I knew it was unlikely I'd ever see anything outside the walls of my prison. I wasn't some naïve tourist. I'd reported on half a dozen stories of journalists getting beheaded so jihadist groups could prove a point. People didn't usually get out of this kind of thing alive and unscathed. My best hope was that they wouldn't leave me hanging too long.

Which, of course, was the kind of non-hope that could drive a guy insane (which probably, I realized, was half the point). And so, in an attempt to keep some thread of sanity in my life, some small good in my dark world, I ended up spending a lot of time in that prison thinking of her. Talking to her. Pretending she was there with me, like some blond guardian angel, watching over me and keeping me safe.

Sarah Martin. Love of my life. The girl I quite literally left behind.

I had met Sarah on the UCSD campus when we were both undergrads. She was standing on the lawn with her girlfriends, selling cookies as some kind of fundraiser for her film studies group. But to be honest, she could have been peddling dog shit and I would have stopped and signed up for a lifetime supply. I was too chicken to ask her out on the spot so I asked her if she wanted to bring her cookies to sell at my Environmental Club meeting the next evening. That's where I first introduced her to Ryan. Ryan who had dismissed her as a dumb blonde with no redeeming qualities—until he discovered who her father was.

And . . . things started to get complicated.

But I didn't want to think about that. In the end it was irrelevant anyway. Maybe things between us had started less by chance than most relationships did, but that didn't mean I didn't believe Sarah was the one in the end.

And who could blame me? There was no other girl in the universe like her. It wasn't just that she was drop-dead gorgeous, though God help me she was always stunning, even in her ripped jeans and Converse. But in the end it had been her passion that had truly sucked me into her world. Her drive, her dedication. Whatever Sarah decided to do, she did it so fully. Throwing everything she had into the endeavor. Never holding back.

Even when, in the end, she probably should have.

Her dad hated me. He called me a socialist when he was in a good mood. Communist when he was mad, even though in reality I was neither. He hated the idea that I had opened his little girl's eyes to the atrocities that were going on in the world—and right here in San Diego. He wanted a debutante, a future politician's wife. Not some hippie hipster with big eyes and bigger dreams of changing the world. The world that he and his cronies had helped create.

I sighed. From the look of Sarah now, he may have gotten what he wanted in the end. Though possibly that was largely due to my actions, not his.

"Here we are," Javier announced, pulling the truck to the side of the road. I peered out the window, police lights flashing in my eyes. Opening the car door, I jumped out of the truck, running around back to help Javier with the gear. Soon we were all set up and interviewing police officers about the crime and getting interviews from a few passersby. The story seemed pretty straightforward. Guy robs a convenience store. The clerk presses the emergency button. Police show up and the guy runs away. They pursue him down the streets of San Diego until he high-speed smashes his car into a tree and dies.

"Drugs!" an older woman witness shouted as I held the microphone to her face. "He was clearly on drugs. PCP. Meth. Maybe both. You know kids today. Always on drugs."

"Did you know this man?" I asked.

She shook her head. "I don't need to know him. I know his type. Druggie thug. A menace to our neighborhood." She glanced over at the wrecked car. "He got what he deserved."

I swallowed hard, finding the hatred flashing in her eyes a little unnerving. I'd seen that kind of look far too often overseas. It was even harder to see it here.

Shaking it off, I walked back to the truck to start writing the piece. On a whim, I typed the victim's name into Facebook, figuring maybe I could find a picture to use in the report. A moment later a man's profile popped up. Bingo. I scanned his bio quickly and read a few posts on his (thankfully public) wall.

Turned out his name was Luke—though his friends called him Bub—and he was a married father of two living in Mira Mesa. It appeared he'd been laid off from work a few months ago from a city job due to budget cuts. Hadn't been able to find new work since. He had tried to start a GoFundMe campaign to raise money to feed his kids and pay the back rent on his apartment. But when I clicked on the campaign I saw it had ended. No one had given him a goddamned dime.

"Sorry, man, that sucks," I muttered, downloading a few pictures, then switching back to my interview, listening for useable sound bites.

"Drugs!" the woman on the screen shouted at me.

"This guy couldn't afford drugs if he wanted them," I shot back at her, now more irritated than ever. I shook my head, stopping the video and jumping out of the truck to approach Javier, who was shooting more of the car crash for the piece. "Do we have time to head over to the family's apartment?" I asked. "Or maybe see if we can get his former employer to talk? I want to get some more information on what brought him to this point. That he felt the need to steal."

Javier raised his eyebrows, looking at me as if I'd just suggested we collect some neighborhood kittens and get them together for a playdate. "We're live in an hour," he reminded me. "I can't just break down the truck and drive somewhere else. This is a car crash story, not an I-Team investigation."

I screwed up my face. Of course. What was I thinking?
This wasn't journalism. This was TV news. Wham, bam,
thank you ma'am reporting.

After all, no one at home cared that this man was probably
part of a bigger problem. A modern day Jean Valjean, steal-
ing bread to feed his family and paying the ultimate price.
As a news station we should be looking at the bigger picture.
The breakdown in the system that left people desperate
enough to do things they never would have done. Why was
his job eliminated? Who benefited from these budget cuts?
What fat cat was sitting back on his yacht now, smoking a
cigar, while this man lay dead in a smoking ruin?

But no. No one wanted to put in the work on that kind of
story. It was much easier to fill the time slot with good car
crash video for people to rubberneck from the comfort of
their own homes. At the end of the day our broadcast was
nothing more than a glorified reality TV show. Where anyone could achieve their fifteen minutes of fame if they were
willing to screw up their lives for all to see.

I sighed, remembering how naïve I had been back in the
day. When I switched my major to journalism, truly believ-
ing I could save the world. Expose wrongs, bring bad guys
to justice. Change laws. Back then I felt so powerful. King
of the world, giving it to the man.

Now I wasn't much better off than the guy in the smoking car.

Feeling defeated, I walked back over to the editing deck.
I wrote up a quick script, picked some sound bites, and
handed it all to Javier so he could get to work. Then I went
and sat back in the passenger seat of the truck, staring out
onto the accident scene. The police lights reflected in the
mirror, an endless repeating pattern of blue and red and
white.

Feeling restless, I got out of the car again. A small crowd had gathered around the accident scene, behind the police tape, watching eagerly. I wasn't sure what they expected to see—the guy wasn't going to suddenly get up and walk away. It made me a little sick to see their excited faces. One man's tragedy, as seen on TV.

"Hey! Look! That's that guy! That reporter that was kidnapped."

Oh crap. I tried to make a move back into the shadows, but it was too late. Accident forgotten, they'd all turned their attentions to me.

"You coward!" one of them yelled.

"You should have died like a man!" another cried. "Pathetic."

"You think your life is more important than all those who are going to die now because that jihadist was freed?"

I staggered backward as if I'd been shot, their anger and screams worse than any bullet. My heart thudded in my chest and I felt as if I was going to throw up. I wanted to say something. To tell them it wasn't my fault. I didn't ask to be rescued. I didn't even know a deal was on the table. That I was stuck in a hole while this was all going on, praying they'd let me die.

But I knew all the rationality in the world couldn't cauterize the hatred radiating from their eyes. I was the face of all their frustrations. It was easier to blame a person than a public policy, after all.

And so, feeling like the worst coward, I retreated to the news truck, climbing inside and locking the door. Javier looked up from editing, catching my face. "You okay, man?" he asked.

I bit my lower lip. "Peachy. Just had to deal with some fans out there."

Javier nodded, taking me literally. I didn't have the heart to tell him the truth. Instead, I turned to my script, reading it over, trying to memorize the live hit and move forward. To forget the people outside.

Come on, Troy, I scolded myself. *Man up. Do your fucking job.*

But try as I might I couldn't stop my heart from racing in my chest. And as the live shot loomed ever closer, so did my dread.

five

SARAH

I had just settled onto my couch that evening, a glass of wine in my hand, when I heard a banging at my door.

"Come in," I cried. "It's open."

I knew who it would be before she pushed the door open. No one ever banged on a door with as much enthusiasm as Stephanie. Sure enough, a moment later she came bursting into the room.

"Aha!" she cried. "You are so busted!" She pointed to the TV, which, of course, was tuned in to News 9 at the start of the evening news.

"What?" I asked, feigning innocence, even as I was unable to help the guilty smile playing at the corner of my lips. "I taped a segment earlier today. I wanted to watch it on air."

"Yeah, well, I might actually believe that ridiculous lie if you didn't once tell me that you never watched your pieces live," Stephanie reminded me. "In fact, I believe you told me it was nothing short of cringe worthy to watch oneself on TV."

I sighed. That sounded like something I would say. And it was true as well. To watch myself on TV, as a regular viewer would. To listen to the vapid bullshit spewing from my lips about which celebrities had hooked up, who had cheated on whom with what nanny, whether Gwen Stefani was pregnant again—or had just eaten a few too many tacos. Oh, and don't forget that crazy thing Kanye had posted to Twitter the day before. Can't go to bed without knowing that.

Seriously, if you watched me on TV, you'd probably decide I cared less about the state of the world than the state of Chris Pratt's (or Chris Pine's) last haircut. Which was one of the reasons I'd made it a policy never to tune in.

"Okay, fine," I said, realizing I was busted. "I was just checking in on him. It is his first day, you know. I was curious how he was going to do. I mean it can't be easy. Going back to work after . . . well, you know." I cringed a little.

My mind flashed back to our encounter earlier that day. I'd been so flustered, so ridiculous—leading him to believe I wasn't happy to see him. When in fact, nothing could have been further from the truth. After all those months of not knowing for sure whether he was alive or dead . . . then seeing him in real life again . . . I wanted to say everything at once. But instead I found myself unable to say anything at all.

You can talk to him tomorrow, I told myself. *Try to straighten everything out. I'm sure he'll understand. It has to be hard for him, too. After all, it wasn't exactly as if you parted on good terms. At the very least he probably feels pretty awkward about everything he did to you. Not to mention the way he left.*

The thought made me frown. Because that was exactly

why I shouldn't have been thinking of any of this at all. Why I should have been letting sleeping dogs lie—not trying to wake them to start things over again. I mean, what was my end game here, anyway? After what he did to me? After how he used me and spit me out like so much garbage? Why should I be the one to go back like a wounded puppy dog, whimpering for another chance? Was I that eager to open up old wounds? I had finally moved on with my life. I was doing well. I didn't need to backtrack.

Stephanie plopped down on the couch next to me, plucking the glass of wine from my hand and taking a long, large slug. "So when's he on?" she asked.

"After this break, I think," I told her. "He's covering some kind of convenience store robbery and car chase. Fatality, I think."

"I remember seeing that on the AP wire earlier," Stephanie replied. "And I'm pretty sure that's why traffic was so crappy on the way home." She rolled her eyes. "Ah, criminals. Always messing up the commute for the rest of us." She took another sip of my wine.

I grabbed my glass back from her and pointed to the fridge. "You want more, you get your own glass," I scolded, just as the broadcast came back on. After all, I needed all the liquid courage I could get to watch my ex-boyfriend on TV. Not that I'd been able to drink a drop yet.

Stephanie laughed and kissed me on the top of the head before climbing off the couch backward and dancing toward the kitchen. I turned back to the TV, trying to shake the weird feeling of déjà vu that had just hit me hard and fast. Stephanie and I drinking wine, watching the news . . . just as we had been doing the night Troy had been kidnapped by the jihadist group.

But he's here now, I reminded myself. In America, safe

and sound. Surrounded by police. Nothing bad could possibly happen to him here.

But did he know that? I thought back again to our unexpected run-in that morning. The haunted look I'd seen in his eyes. So different from the Troy I remembered. The Troy who had been so cocky and confident and carefree. Instead he had looked completely troubled. Almost scared. Hell, half of me had wanted to grab him and lock him in a closet and throw away the key—in an effort to keep him safe forever.

Which would probably be a bit awkward. Not to mention super creepy.

I turned my focus back to the TV. Troy's story was on the air now, his voice talking over the video, explaining the robbery, the chase, the crash. After about a minute of overview, he came back full screen. I gulped, almost alarmed at his sudden presence in my living room. While I knew for a fact he was just staring into a camera, I couldn't help but feel he was staring straight at me.

Maybe watching this was a bad idea.

"Police have not given a motive," he said. "But according to his Facebook page and a recent failed GoFundMe campaign, it appears the crime may have been financially motivated. Wilder was laid off from his government job six months ago and behind on his rent."

I squirmed in my seat, catching the judgmental look flashing in Troy's eyes. I wondered if he knew that it was my dad that had cut ten percent of government jobs six months ago, in an effort to give new tax breaks to his buddies in the one percent. I had told him it was a terrible idea when the bill was first put forward. But he had just rolled his eyes at me and told me to go back to my little movies. Leave the politics to the professionals.

And now a man was dead. And two children had lost their father. A wife had lost her husband.

I grabbed my phone, taking down the man's name. I'd do some research tomorrow. Find the family. Help out if I could. It wouldn't fix what my dad had done. But maybe it would ease the pain a little.

The camera cut from Troy back to the studio, where Beth, the new nighttime anchor, was sitting behind the desk. "So, Troy," she said, "do you have any idea what might have—"

Before she could finish her question, a large bang echoed over the airwaves. I frowned as the camera cut back to Troy. To my surprise, he had gone stark white. He dropped the microphone he'd been holding and it clattered to the ground. A moment later he dropped out of frame. I waited for a moment; maybe he was just grabbing the mic? But he didn't reappear.

"Troy?" Beth tried again. "Did we lose you? Are you still there?"

But there was no answer.

"Troy!" I cried, even though of course he couldn't hear me. I turned to Stephanie, my heart thrumming in my chest, déjà vu now hitting me hard and fast. "What's going on? Where did he go?"

But Stephanie just looked at me, shaking her head. She clearly had no idea, either.

I turned back to the TV. They had cut back to the studio. Beth was still looking a little puzzled. Then she turned face the camera again.

"Sorry about that. It appears we lost the feed," she said. "We'll see if we can get him back after the break. But first— stay tuned for your local weather forecast. It's going to be another sunny one in SoCal this week." She grinned. "What a shock, right?"

As the station cut to commercial, I flipped off the TV. I rose to my feet. Set my wine down on the breakfast bar and grabbed my shoes.

"Where are you going?" Stephanie called to me, looking even more puzzled now.

I turned back to her. "I'm going to head over there and make sure he's okay."

SIX

TROY

Hey, man, you okay?"
I could vaguely feel Javier's hand on my shoulder, jerking me back to reality. I looked up, horrified, trying to remember what had just happened. I'd been answering a question. There was some kind of noise. My heart had leapt so hard I was half-sure it was going to explode from my chest. My vision spun. I couldn't breathe. When I came to, I was on the ground.

I shook my head, blinking. I turned to the camera. "The live shot," I started. Javier shook his head.

"I shut it off when you stopped responding," he said. "I told them we had technical difficulties."

"Right." I sank down onto the curb, trying to catch my breath. Technical difficulties indeed. But not with the camera equipment. Rather my own head. "I heard a noise," I said, trying to put it all together.

"A car backfiring, I think," Javier said. He paused, then added, "Did you think it was . . ." He trailed off, obviously not sure if he should continue.

I didn't answer. I couldn't answer. I didn't know what I thought. I wasn't thinking at all. It was like my body had jumped in and taken over my brain without asking permission first. Super-charging every nerve, just in case.

The shrinks had warned this could happen. That any situation might trigger the trauma I'd experienced in Syria. I had been in the middle of a live shot when I was first captured, after all, just like this one. There had been a sound then, too. Not a car backfiring, of course. But actual gunfire.

Clearly my mind wasn't taking any chances though.

Fucking hell. This was not good.

The network had offered to pay for psychiatric services when I'd first gotten back. The kind of thing soldiers went through when coming back home. I'd been to a couple of sessions, but stopped going after the doctor had tried to repeatedly force pills down my throat to ease the "transition." I'd tried to explain to him I didn't want the easy way out. The idea that they would dull the edges of what had happened to me seemed wrong somehow. Taking away something that was inherently mine, even if it wasn't a good thing. I wanted to stay sharp. In control. To make sure no one could ever do what they'd done to me ever again.

Of course I didn't feel very in control at the moment . . .

I could feel Javier giving me a pitying look, and anger burned in my gut. I wondered if the protesters were still here. If they'd gotten to witness my epic freak-out. That would be sure to make their day. They could go balls to the wall on Twitter. #America'sIdiot. #Pathetic. #Weak. #ShouldaLetHimDie.

"It's okay, man," Javier interjected. "They've given us another live hit in the E Block. You can make it up to them then."

"Right." I rose to my feet and began pacing the sidewalk. Trying to purge the adrenaline still pumping through my veins. To come back down to earth. To act like a normal person again. "Absolutely," I added. "I can make it up then."

It was no big deal, I told myself. It wasn't as if anyone was expecting perfection my first day on the job. And who knows? Maybe they did buy the whole technical difficulties thing. All I had to do was nail this next hit and everything would be fine.

I was Troy Young and I was strong and there was no way I'd let those bastards break me.

I glanced down at my notes. The words seemed to swim on the page, in and out of focus. I blinked a few times, held the paper farther away, but it only made it worse. God, was I losing my vision on top of everything else?

My mind flashed back to my dark prison cell. That debilitating feeling of sightlessness. My other senses overcompensating, allowing my ears to lock onto tiny scratching sounds in the distance—rodents, insects crawling over rocks. Crawling toward me. On me.

My skin began to itch. That phantom itch that try as I might had never completely gone away. Even now I would lie in bed at night sometimes and scratch my skin until it bled, unable to stop focusing on the parasites of my nightmares.

I collapsed down on the pavement again, breathing heavily. The pressure in my chest was back and my left arm alternated between feeling prickly and numb. Was I having a heart attack? Should I skip the live shot and head straight to the hospital instead? But then I wouldn't have a chance to redeem myself. Of course if I was really having a heart attack, that might not matter in the end.

"Five minutes," Javier said, calling over to me. He squinted in concern. "You gonna be okay, man? You look really white."

"Yeah. I'll be fine."

"Cause I can tell them to just run the package. Kill the live shot."

"No!" I almost shouted, then gave him a sorry look. "I'm fine. Really." I rose to my feet, trying to give off the appearance of someone who was fine. Rather than someone who wasn't entirely convinced his heart wasn't about to give out at any moment. I walked over to the camera and took my position in front of it. I looked down at my notes again, drawing in a long breath.

"I'm fine," I muttered, more to myself this time. "I'm Troy Young and I'm reporting live and I'm absolutely, totally fine."

"Two minutes," Javier said, getting into position. I gave him a thumbs-up. My vision had cleared enough to read my notes. I read over my intro, concentrating on it and ignoring the exterior noise. I could get through this. I could do this.

"One minute."

But what if I couldn't? What if this was it, I was done? What if I screwed this up and they fired me on my very first day back on the job? If I couldn't do this—this crappy local news stuff—how was I ever going to get back to the network? Back overseas? And if I wasn't a reporter, what did I have left? I was nothing, no one without TV news.

"Ten seconds."

I swallowed hard, my mind racing. My stomach churning. My heart squeezed by the pressure in my chest. I looked up at the camera. The red light turned on. Javier pointed at me.

Go time.

Except . . . I couldn't go. I opened my mouth, but no sound came out. I looked down at my notes, my pulse racing, but they started to swim again, unreadable. I looked up at the camera. Like a fish, my mouth opening and closing—but no sound coming out.

Javier sighed. He switched off the camera. I closed my eyes, my stomach so nauseated for a moment I thought I would throw up. I sank to the ground, not even bothering to find the sidewalk this time, scrubbing my face with my hands.

Fuck. FUCK, FUCK, FUCK.

"Troy!"

I looked up, my eyes widening as they caught the angel in patterned leggings running in my direction fast as her legs could carry her, her face bright with concern. I frowned, at first half-convinced she was another hallucination. Like the ones my brain used to conjure up in my cell. Back then I'd spent hours talking to pretend Sarah. Some days she was the only thing to keep me going. So it would make sense for her to show up again now. I mean, hey, I'd already acted like a complete jackass on live TV. Why not move forward into full-on delusion mode? Javier could speed-dial the men in white coats for me. Maybe I'd even make the news.

But then she reached me. Dropped down to her knees and pulled me into her arms. Her hair smelled like sunshine and cinnamon and I could feel the rough threads of her jacket against my hands, the fierce pressure of her fingers against my back. This wasn't pretend Sarah—the construct of my starved imagination. This was real-life Sarah. And she was holding me against her chest, whispering in my ear. Holy crap.

"Are you okay?' she asked in a low voice. Probably so Javier couldn't hear.

Ugh. My momentary elation dampened as reality waved

its ugly flag. She must have seen me on TV. Witnessed my pitiful collapse. She'd come here feeling sorry for me and I knew if I looked up I'd see pity written on her face. Pity and maybe a small flutter of triumph. She'd been right. I'd been wrong all along. Hell, it was probably all she could do not to tell me she told me so.

I didn't answer, just stared down at the ground. She sighed and stepped out of the embrace. Leaving me feeling empty and cold. I could feel her eyes, burning into my back. Big, blue, endless eyes that I used to love to get lost in, now the eyes of a stranger.

"What happened?" I heard her asking Javier.

"I don't know," he said. "He just kind of . . . froze. I didn't know what to do so I just turned off the camera." He paused and I imagined him shrugging helplessly. "Poor guy. I guess it makes sense though. I mean, after all he's been through? I'd be a quivering pile of Jell-O for the next fifty years. And here he is, trying to pick up where he left off."

Anger shot through my gut and I clenched my hands into fists. The way he was talking about me—as if I wasn't standing right there. They were probably all talking about me like this. Probably had been all day. In the newsroom. In living rooms back home.

#Can'tHackIt. #DoneFor. #ShouldThrowInTheTowel. #ShoudaLetHimDie.

"Troy . . ." I could feel Sarah come up behind me again. I could always feel her approach even back in the old days. Or maybe it was my nose, able to pick up her sweet, floral scent. She stopped just before reaching me, though, I guess not wanting to invade my space. I sucked in a breath. It would be so easy to turn around. To reach out and touch her like I used to. To seek out the comfort she seemed to want to give.

But if I did, would I be able to ever let go again?

"I'm fine," I growled. "What are you doing here anyway? Don't you have, like, a red carpet to go stand on or something?"

"I was watching the broadcast," she said, ignoring the jab. "And I saw your first live hit. I was . . . worried. I wanted to make sure you were okay."

I whirled around, forcing myself to face her. To stand my ground like a man. "Well, like I said, I'm fine. Not that it's any business of yours."

Her face faltered. My stomach wrenched at the pain I saw in her eyes. Pain that I had just put there, intentionally hurting the one person who might actually give a shit about me. What was I doing? She had come down here worried about me and here I was being a total dick. But at the same time the rage was burning through me now like a fire and if I didn't release it somehow I was afraid I would explode. And she had put herself directly in my path.

This was why it was better I had walked away five years ago. A girl like her deserved so much better than a guy like me.

"You're right," she said after a long pause. Her voice sounded too high, a little hysterical. "It isn't my business. I'm . . . sorry I came. Old habits, I guess." She gave a brittle laugh. "Don't worry. It won't happen again."

And with that, she turned, keeping her steps slow and deliberate as she walked back to her car. Away from me. I watched her skinny legs wobble a little, as if they could barely hold her body upright. Something tore inside of me.

"Sarah," I called out after her, my own voice sounding strange in my ears as my lips formed the name. How many times had I called out to her in that dark hole? How many fantasies had I indulged of her appearing out of thin air?

And now she was here. In front of me in real life. Not

pretend Sarah from my imagination. But the real girl who I'd once loved. And yet, instead of reaching out, I'd all but shoved her away.

"Sarah," I said again, softer this time. Because I knew her well enough to know she wasn't going to turn around. It was something I used to love about her, actually. How stubborn and strong she could be. Everyone assumed she was some beautiful delicate flower, but she would never, ever let anyone crush her under their heels.

Not her father. Not even me.

I watched as she got into her car. Some kind of luxury BMW convertible she once would have refused to drive. Revving the engine, she drove away, head held high, not once looking back in my direction. I sighed, dropping down on the pavement, scrubbing my face with my hands. The earlier panic from the live shot had dulled to nothing, replaced by an impossibly heavy feeling of regret.

Javier gave me a disapproving look. Guess I no longer warranted his pity. Then he shook his head and started packing up his gear. We were going back to the station, evidently.

I'd lost my last chance.

seven

SARAH

I was an idiot. An absolute idiot.

What had I been thinking, going down there like that? Checking in to make sure he was okay, as if he were still my freaking boyfriend. We hadn't spoken in five years prior to that day and now suddenly I was butting my nose into his private business as if I still had a right to do so.

I had no right. In fact, I probably never did, seeing as our entire relationship had been built on lies.

I drew in a breath, trying to calm the nerves pricking at the surface of my skin. Trying to swallow down the ridiculous lump that had formed in my throat. Tears welled in my eyes as I drove down the freeway, not sure where I was going, and I quickly swiped them away.

"Get a grip, Martin," I scolded myself. But that was easier said than done.

It had been a hell of a lot easier to pretend I was over Troy when he was halfway across the world. Sure, I'd peek at him during broadcasts from time to time, but that was where it ended. It wasn't as if I'd been waiting on him, either—I'd dated plenty of other guys. I'd had a great time. I'd even almost gotten serious with Asher. Who would have made a really cool boyfriend if he'd liked me back.

In fact, I'd almost been free of Troy Young forever, until that fateful day. Until I watched helplessly as he was captured by the jihadi and everyone said he would be killed.

The three months that followed had been absolute torture for me—waking up each morning, not knowing whether he was dead or alive. I stopped going clubbing. I stopped dating guys. I started drinking a lot more at home by myself. I prayed every night that somehow, someway they'd be able to bring him home. Even if I never saw him again myself. Just to know he was out there, alive and okay. That would be enough.

And now, here he was. Alive and well, though maybe not unscathed. But who could blame him for that? According to the news reports (and I had scoured them all) Troy had been kept in a dark cave of a prison for three months. Beaten and barely kept alive. His cameraman and producer had been killed and he had been next on the list. If not for the president negotiating with the terrorist group and freeing one of their people in exchange, Troy would have never seen another sunrise.

There was a lot of controversy over that, of course. Many people—even other politicians—didn't think the exchange was a good idea. They said we shouldn't negotiate with terrorist groups no matter what. They said Troy put himself in harm's way by reporting in that sector. And he got what he deserved.

God. Did he know that? He had to know that, right? How did he deal with that knowledge? To see your very existence on the planet endlessly debated online. It had to hurt, right? It hurt me—and it wasn't even about me.

Of course he was having panic attacks. It would be crazy if he didn't have panic attacks after what he'd been through. What he was still going through.

But that still doesn't mean you get to be the one to save him, a voice inside me nagged. *No matter how much you might want to.*

My thoughts were interrupted by my phone ringing. I glanced at my car's dashboard computer to see who it was before answering. For one brief moment, I held out the hope that it was Troy, calling to apologize. But that was ridiculous. He probably didn't even have my phone number anymore.

No. It wasn't Troy on the phone. It was Dad.

I groaned, debating whether or not to hit the ignore button. Finally, I forced myself to answer the call. If I didn't, he'd just call me back anyway. Then send Carl to my apartment to "make sure I was okay." And I so didn't need to see my good old bestie Carl today.

"Hi, Dad," I said as I connected the call, feigning a cheerfulness I didn't feel. "How's it going?"

"Hey, baby girl," he replied. "I saw your interview on News 9 this morning with that Hemsworth kid. Sounds like a wonderful film."

I rolled my eyes. "It was a shitty film," I wanted to say. "So you'll probably love it."

"Oh, yes," I said instead. "It opens Friday. Hope you get a chance to go see it."

He laughed. "Well, the good people of San Diego are keeping me quite busy at the moment. But you never know." He paused for a moment, then added, "Honey, I'm down at City Hall right now. I was wondering if you could swing by. There's something I want to talk to you about."

I resisted the urge to smack my head against the steering wheel. Of course. As if my day hadn't already been crappy enough. I glanced at my watch. "I'm, uh, actually kind of busy this evening," I tried.

"Oh, sweetie. You can reschedule your nail appointment," he said with a laugh, making me cringe with annoyance. I was really getting sick of this pervasive image of me as this vapid little socialite, flittering around town, nothing important to do.

Not that, at the moment, I had anything important to do. Well, except play knight in shining armor to an uninterested ex-boyfriend. But I definitely wasn't going to go there. Let's just say Dad wasn't exactly a Troy Young superfan by any definition. Not that anyone would blame him.

"Fine," I said, giving in, taking the next exit and turning the car around. I could have fought harder, I supposed, but it would always be a losing battle. When Dad said "jump," he expected everyone to ask "how high?" His daughter was no exception. "I'll be there in twenty minutes."

"Excellent. I'll call out for dinner. We can eat in my office."

Can't wait.

eight

TROY

We had just gotten back to the station after the failed live shot when the assignment editor called me over to her desk. I approached, giving her a wary smile. According to Javier, Ana was the one who ran things around here. She gave out the story assignments, assigned photographers to reporters, made sure everything went smoothly for each newscast. In other words, you wanted to be on her good side.

After today, I was probably not.

"Hey, sugar," she said as I approached. "Are you okay? We were all worried about you out there today."

I swallowed hard, resisting the urge to hang my head in shame. Now that I'd put distance between the accident scene and myself the whole thing felt a little ridiculous. Why the hell had I reacted like I had? It was just a stupid live shot. I'd done hundreds over the years without a problem—what made me freak out now?

Okay, yes, sure I'd gotten abducted during my last live

shot—I hadn't forgotten that little detail. But that was in enemy territory—a place I wasn't even supposed to be. This was downtown San Diego. I probably had more chance of being run over by an antique VW Bus.

But all the rationality in the world couldn't make my body see reality. And because of it, I had embarrassed myself on live TV—and screwed up an important news story in the process—my very first day back on the job.

"I'm fine," I said gruffly. "Just a little rusty is all. I'll be back on my feet tomorrow. No big deal."

Ana didn't reply at first. And I caught her worrying her lower lip. Uh-oh.

"What?" I demanded.

"Um. It's just . . . well . . ." She shrugged. "Richard wanted to see you in his office when you got back," she finished, giving me an apologetic look.

My heart stuttered in my chest. The news director wanted to see me? In his office?

Shit. I was getting fired. Already.

I thanked Ana and turned back to the newsroom. My feet feeling heavy as lead as I trudged around the pods of desks, I was a dead man walking as I made my way to Richard's office. I could feel the curious stares of the other employees on me as I passed, but refused to look in their direction. I imagined they'd had quite a field day this evening at my expense.

"Troy!" Richard cried as I entered the office. He rose from his seat, holding out his hand. I shook it, giving him a rueful smile. God, this was so humiliating. I only hoped he wouldn't drag it out longer than it needed to be.

"Have a seat," he said instead, gesturing to a nearby chair. I slumped down onto it, scrubbing my face with my hands. Then I looked up at him.

"Look, I know I messed up today," I said. "And I have no problem if you need to let me go. Just make it quick, okay? I don't need to hear what a hero I am. Or how I need time to heal. I've heard that all before."

Richard sighed. He ran a hand through his thinning hair. "Did you know I was in the war?" he asked after a brief pause. "Operation Desert Storm. Two years. I had joined the National Guard and got sent overseas. Ended up with an honorable discharge after a bomb went off in our tent and busted me up. Got a metal plate in my head and a ticket home. Took the GI Bill money and went to college to become a journalist."

"That's . . . cool," I said, not sure what to say. "I mean, not the bomb. Or the metal plate." I gave a brittle laugh.

Richard smiled. "I know what you meant," he assured me. "Point is, I got out. But the whole experience screwed me up for years. I had nightmares, panic attacks. I couldn't be alone or I'd start seeing things. PTSD. Trust me, it's a real thing. And it can really mess up your life."

I stiffened, my heart picking up its pace. I glanced back at the door behind me, wondering if I should just get up and leave. Walk away and not come back. That was just as good as being fired, right?

"Look, Troy. I'm not going to pretend I understand what you went through. My story is a walk in the park compared to yours. It's going to suck for you for a while. I mean, you'll have your good days. You'll think everything's getting back to normal. Then something will trigger you and you'll end up starting over at square one."

I sighed. "I know," I said, my stomach twisting into knots. Why couldn't he just come out with it? Tell me this wasn't going to work. Couldn't he see? I didn't need his understanding. His pity.

"Look." Richard's gaze settled on me. His eyes were

stern, but kind. "Maybe you aren't ready for live news just yet. Maybe you need to consider something a little less triggering until you've had time to work things through."

"Sure," I said. "Maybe I can finally fulfill my lifelong dream of underwater basket weaving while I'm at it."

He snorted. "I was thinking more along the lines of entertainment reporting, actually."

"Excuse me?" I sat up in my seat, not quite sure I'd heard him right.

"Hear me out. Cathy, our owner, has been talking about starting up this new franchise. Some kind of 'He Said, She Said' movie review thing. Says it's more interactive and interesting than just one person giving out reviews. And there's more chance of the segment going viral if you get some good banter going on."

Now my gut was burning, as if on fire. "Richard, I am a multiple Emmy Award–winning foreign correspondent," I scraped out. "I have three Edward R. Murrow Awards to my name. I am a national goddamned reporter who—"

"—needs a job," Richard finished for me, giving me a look. "And I'm guessing a paycheck, too." He paused then added, "Unless you've decided to go work on that book?"

I cringed, his words nailing me straight in the heart. Ever since I'd been back home I'd been hounded by publishers, agents—begging me to write my story. They'd even offered me a ghostwriter, meaning I'd just have to tell the stories and have someone else write them down. They'd offered me huge sums of money, too. Staggering amounts. The kind of money that would mean never having to work again.

But every time I tried to sit down at the keyboard, fear paralyzed my fingers. And I knew I couldn't do it. Even for all the money in the world. What had happened to me—well, it had happened to me. And I felt weirdly possessive of the experience. I didn't want it to be debated on the national news stations. Didn't want my personal tragedy hung out to dry like dirty laundry. Hell, this was why I didn't even grant interviews to journalists.

But Richard was right about one thing. By saying no to the book, I'd limited my options. After all, who wanted to hire a burned-out reporter who couldn't even complete a simple live shot without completely freaking out? Richard had taken a chance on me. And now I was being an asshole to him, out of some misplaced crappy pride. Yes, I might have once been a nationally recognized, award-winning foreign correspondent. But now I was a broke bastard, lucky to have a job.

"I'm sorry," I said. "I don't mean to sound ungrateful."

"And I don't mean to sound condescending," Richard replied, not missing a beat. "Believe me, I know your résumé. I've watched you for years. I know what a rock star reporter you are." His eyes locked on me. "But I also know you're in transition at the moment. And that daily news reporting isn't going to work for you—at least in the short term." He paused, then asked, "Am I wrong?"

"No." I swallowed hard. "You're not wrong."

"But you need a job."

"Yes. I do."

"Okay then. Well, I am offering you a job. As an entertainment reporter. No live shots in the field. All studio based. You watch a movie. You give your opinion. You pass go. You collect a paycheck. And then, later, when you're ready—you can go back to live shots. Or whatever it is you decide you want to do. No matter what, you'll always have a place here at News 9."

I nodded stiffly, feeling the lump form in my throat. He made it sound so simple. And maybe it was. Maybe this was exactly what I needed to do.

But then I remembered the real complication. I looked up at him. "You said it's a 'He Said, She Said' segment," I said. "Who's the 'she' in this scenario?"

Even as I asked the question, I realized I already knew the answer. Because fate was a damn right little bitch.

"A girl named Sarah Martin—the mayor's kid. She just started as our entertainment reporter not too long ago." He paused, catching my look. "I know, I know," he said, waving a hand. "But she's a good kid. A real sweetheart. Smart, too, for a socialite. I think you'll like her. And if you don't?" He shrugged. "All the better for your banter on set. We want you guys to disagree. That's sort of the whole point. Get the audience to take sides. Feel invested in the segment. Tune in to hear what crazy thing Sarah will call you next." He grinned, looking proud of himself.

"Sounds . . . fun?" I stammered. Which was exactly the opposite of the word I really wanted to use. I thought back to seeing her earlier today. When she'd driven out to the freeway, just to find me. To make sure I was okay. And I had yelled at her. I had told her I was none of her business.

Not exactly true anymore.

I forced myself to draw a steadying breath. Maybe this wasn't a big thing. Maybe this would be a way for us to get past what I'd done five years ago. Give us an excuse to start talking—but not about anything personal. And maybe someday she would forgive me for what I'd done to her. And maybe that would help me move forward, too.

If I had any chance of healing, I had to start sewing up these old wounds. The ones that started this whole thing.

The ones that came from what I'd done to Sarah.

nine

SARAH

Dad had a full dinner spread laid out on the conference room table when I arrived. Mostly of the meat-filled variety. He'd never fully accepted the fact that I'd become a vegetarian at seventeen and liked to make snide comments whenever I brought it up. Usually jokes about kale even though I'd only ever eaten the vegetable once in my life and didn't really care for it when I had.

But meat was for men. Red-blooded American men. Men like my father.

Whatever. I'd hit the In-N-Out drive-through on the way home. For a burger joint they made a mean meatless sandwich. Maybe I'd even go all out and have it animal style.

"Sweetie!" Dad cried, crossing the room as I stepped inside, pulling me into one of his traditional giant bear hugs that always felt as if he was trying to squeeze the life out of me. I hugged him back best I could then extracted myself and slipped into a nearby seat. A seat far away from his campaign manager, Carl, at the far end of the room.

"What's he doing here?" I muttered.

Carl smirked. "Nice to see you, too, princess," he sneered. Carl didn't like me. However, he did like making it his life's mission to let me know how much he didn't like me. I suppose he had good reason—I hadn't exactly been a model daughter back in the day and he'd been the sucker tasked with getting me back in line. As much as I hated the guy, he had been the one to keep me out of jail five years ago after the Water World fiasco. I guess he felt I still owed him something for that.

Water World was a marine life theme park franchise that had opened in San Diego a few years before that. Touted as a SeaWorld competitor with cheaper prices and more thrill rides, it had been an instant commercial success. Less successful, however, was the marine life it had accumulated as exhibits, and there were rumors from opening day onward of the mistreatment of animals and unhygienic living conditions for them and the staff.

In other words, the perfect company for Ryan and the rest of the UCSD Environmental Club to target for protest.

I had joined them enthusiastically after my very first meeting; after all, who didn't want to save the whales? Not to mention I was crushing hardcore on Troy, the VP of the club and Ryan's right-hand man. Troy was so passionate. So driven by the crusade. For the first time in my sheltered life I didn't want to play it safe. I wanted to rebel. I wanted to save the world. And with Troy by my side, I truly thought it would be possible to do.

Soon I was spending every Saturday outside the theme park, waving signs and warning tourists that this "family" experience was actually more Manson than Disney. We even went undercover with a whistleblower we'd met, posing as employees and getting video footage of some of the abuses. We planned to gather them together and put out an exposé on YouTube. So everyone could see the atrocities for themselves. So we could get the place shut down for good.

At first I couldn't understand why Carl and my father objected so vocally to me rallying against this particular institution—after all, it didn't seem all that controversial to want to save animals being abused. It wasn't until later on that Ryan revealed the truth: that my father's companies were secret financial partners in the Water World enterprise and had been from the beginning. That every manicure I got, every college class I took, every fancy dinner I ate could have come from the proceeds earned from those dead dolphins.

It had made me sick at the time. Furious. Which was exactly what Ryan had been counting on all along. After that it was just a matter of Troy making a simple suggestion . . . And I, the sucker in love with him, agreeing to strike against my own family.

I shook my head, feeling a little sick to my stomach. To remember how badly I'd been played. How stupid I felt when it all came to a head. When Ryan was arrested. When Troy ran away overseas. When half my dad's IT department, including the man I'd tricked into giving me passwords, got fired all because of me.

The moment I realized no one actually cared about saving the whales—they only cared about saving themselves.

I realized my father was talking. "Sorry, sweetheart," he said. "But I needed Carl here for this one. I'm afraid we have a bit of a . . . situation."

"Oh?" I quirked my head, wondering if I was coming off as interested or bored. "Did the people of San Diego finally come to their senses and kick you out of office?"

Dad snorted. "Sorry to disappoint you, but no. And actually it's more serious than that. Carl has intercepted a few possible threats from an unknown source."

"So, it's like Tuesday then," I said with a shrug. Let's just say my dad was really popular with those who liked him. And really not with those who didn't.

"Maybe before you roll those pretty little eyes of yours you should hear your father out," Carl interjected. "These threats concern you."

That got my attention. "Me? Why me?"

"We don't know," my dad replied. "But I have Carl and his best men looking into it. In the meantime, I think it's best if you lay low. Maybe take an extended trip. You were talking about missing Paris last week, right? What about a month in Paris? I could book you a flight out tomorrow."

I frowned. "Dad, you do remember I have a job, right? I can't just jump on a plane at a moment's notice and take off for a month. They're relying on me."

Carl gave a gruff laugh. "You will be quite a loss, I'm sure. Still, I'm confident they'll be able to find someone to fill in on the grueling assignment of watching movies for you."

I shot him a glare, my stomach twisting with annoyance. God, I hated his arrogant, dismissive attitude. Yes, on the surface my job might have seemed easy. Frivolous. But it was actually a very vital part of the newscast and took a lot of work behind the scenes to make it appear so effortless.

"I'm sorry. But that's out of the question," I said, trying to sound firm. "I'm not going away. And I'm not leaving my job. I will keep an eye out for anything weird. And I'll let you know if anything happens."

"You mean like you let me know about your little boyfriend being back?" my father asked, raising an eyebrow. "I watched the news, Sarah. I knew he was back in the States. But I had no idea they'd hired him at News 9."

"Yeah, well, trust me I didn't ask them to," I muttered, my mind flashing back to Troy on the side of the road. The way he'd snapped at me like a wounded dog when I'd offered him help. "I only found out myself this morning."

My dad frowned. "I should talk to Cathy about this."

"No!" I looked up. Cathy was Asher's mother and the owner of News 9, and my dad did a lot of dealings with her, mostly advertising stuff for his business and his campaigns. In short, he was a big financial backer to the station, which somehow led him to believe he should have a say in how things were run on a day-to-day basis. "Leave him alone. He's going through enough. He doesn't need your shit on top of everything else."

"I don't like it," Carl interjected needlessly. His eyes glittered coldly as he spoke and I knew he was remembering five years ago. "Where he goes, trouble always follows."

"Well, maybe it'll follow him then and leave me alone," I shot back. Then I turned to my father. "Look, I know what you're worried about, but there's no reason to be. I hadn't talked to Troy in five years until today. And I doubt I'll see him much at News 9, either—we're on completely opposite beats."

I frowned, flashing back to the way Troy had practically pushed me away when I had attempted to talk to him. If only my father could have seen that little display of affection, he might be less concerned.

I looked him dead in the eye. "Trust me. In the immortal words of Taylor Swift, Troy and I are never, ever, ever getting back together."

My father sighed. "You know I'm only trying to look out for you, right?"

"I know," I assured him. "And I do appreciate that. You don't have to worry though—I'm not jumping back into bed with Troy—politically or otherwise. I just want to do my job, watch movies, and work the red carpet in cute shoes. And the only real threat I'm going to face is blisters from the aforementioned cute shoes. Okay?"

My father gave me a small laugh at this, telling me I'd convinced him. It was sort of sad how easy it was. How little they all expected from me these days. "Okay," he said. "Just . . . promise me two things."

"What's that?"

"That you'll stay out of trouble . . . and stay away from Troy Young."

I nodded. "No problem. On both accounts."

ten

SARAH

I arrived to work slightly late the next morning, thanks to an accident on I-5 that turned a fifteen-minute commute into a fifty-minute one. Lately it seemed as if there were more accident days than non-accident days, and I was beginning to wonder if I should sell my cute and cozy beach cottage and move downtown so I could walk to work. Of course doing something like that would basically be saying this job was going to stick and since I'd pretty much never had a job stick in the last five years, well, maybe I didn't need to be calling a Realtor just yet.

Walking quickly through the newsroom, I caught Stephanie waving at me from the little pod she shared with a couple other reporters. I waved back, wondering how she'd managed to get here before me, considering we lived next door to each other. She waved again, this time beckoning me over. But I shook my head: I was already late. I didn't have time to chat.

Instead, I turned left, heading out of the main newsroom area and into the entertainment studio—a space Mrs. Anderson had designed especially for me after giving me the job. I think it might have been a consolation prize when her son, Asher, went all rogue, disowning his mother and choosing his producer, Piper, over me. Like I'd lost my chance at the prince, but I'd got the kingdom anyway.

To be honest, it was a little embarrassing. To have this luxurious little corner of the newsroom, a real office with a door and separate studio to film in, while the rest of the reporters sat out on the floor in a noisy, chaotic communal setting—no privacy at all. It was the kind of thing that practically begged other employees to resent me and not want to be friends. From what Stephanie had inferred they already thought I'd gotten the job as a favor to my dad, rather than for any real skill.

Of course I *had* gotten the job as a favor, so they weren't wrong.

I sighed. *Poor little rich girl. Feeling sorry for yourself, once more with feeling.*

I entered the entertainment center, stopping short as I realized someone was already there. And not my producer, Ben, either. Sitting in my chair, his feet propped up on my desk, was none other than Troy himself.

A flurry of emotions stormed through me. And for a moment I could do nothing but stare, the happiness in seeing him warring with the impulse to just kick him out.

"Did you come here to apologize?" I spit out, finding my voice at last. "If so do it and get out. I've got a lot of work to do today."

He looked up. His expression was neutral, almost guarded, but I thought I caught unease in the depths of his eyes. God, why did he have to look so good? Dressed casually in a button-down shirt, his hair cropped short against his head, his eyes as blue in real life as they'd been shining from my TV. It was all I could do not to jump him where he sat.

"Well?" I demanded instead, clamping down on the ridiculous urge.

He pursed his lips. "I do want to apologize," he said in a slow voice. "But that's not why I'm here."

What the hell was that supposed to mean? My pulse kicked up, warning bells going off in my head. I tried to ignore them, dropping my jacket on the back of another chair. "Well, then why are you here? Am I supposed to guess? I never was very good at guessing games."

"No," he said, his lip curling into a small smile. 'You never were, were you?"

I felt my face flush, sudden heat rippling through my entire body. God, I'd forgotten what presence he had. What that presence had always done to my insides. Some people— you meet them and there's nothing between you, even if they're hot as hell. Like Asher had been. Asher had been super fun and ridiculously good-looking. But he was never able to make my toes curl like Troy could, with a single look.

"So then how about we skip the whole game and you tell me?" I said.

He shrugged. "You know that new segment they've got going? He Said, She Said?"

I stared at him. He gave me a pointed look. My mouth dropped open. "You've got to be kidding me," I said.

"Afraid not," he drawled. I watched as he kicked his feet off of my desk and sat up straighter. "As you might have noticed yesterday, I'm not exactly firing on all four cylinders just yet. Not ready for prime time, if you know what I mean. So your big boss decided this would be a good place for me to lay low until I get my head screwed on right again."

Oh God. I grabbed a chair for balance, pretty sure my knees were about to give out on me altogether. I had figured after his performance yesterday—or lack of it, as the case might be—they'd bring him back in house. But I'd assumed that meant to write copy for the newscast or maybe work the assignment desk, monitoring police scanners and such. Never did I think for a second they'd put Troy Young here with me. On my brand-new franchise, no less.

Also, Ben was going to be so pissed. He'd been practically begging them to give him the job since he'd presented the idea at one of our meetings. But evidently the station's brass was being true to form. They didn't want someone smart and capable and knowledgeable. They wanted someone hot.

And they didn't get any hotter than Troy Young.

"But you don't even like movies," I stammered, not sure what else to say. This was beyond crazy. Three days ago, I had assumed I'd never see Troy in person again. Now not only had I seen him two days in a row, but he was to become my new coworker?

He shrugged. "I like some movies."

"None made after 1955."

His mouth curled. "You remembered."

Troy, I remember everything, I wanted to say, but didn't. Instead, I blustered on. "You don't know anything about celebrities," I added. "You thought Joseph Gordon-Levitt was Heath Ledger."

He held up his hands in innocence. "What can I say? They look alike."

"Not really. Since one of them has been a corpse for ten years."

He sighed. "What do you want me to say, Sarah? Do you think I like this anymore than you do? Do you think I want to be some . . . entertainment reporter?" He spit out the job title as if it were poison, which only served to infuriate me further.

"There's nothing wrong with being an entertainment reporter," I shot back. "It's an important part of our newscast."

He turned, his eyes locking onto mine, pinning me where I stood. My heart leapt to my throat and for a moment I couldn't move. Couldn't think.

"There was a time you didn't believe that," he said in a soft voice. Then he dropped my gaze.

I staggered backward, as if I'd been shot. I wanted to scream at him. To tell him he didn't have any idea what he was talking about. But I didn't—because that wasn't true. There was a time when something this silly and frivolous would have disgusted me. Would have made me roll my eyes. And, of all people, Troy knew that.

He . . . remembered.

I scowled. But that was the old me. The naïve girl who believed it was possible to change the world. Who believed people were genuinely good. That the ones you loved weren't out to lie and scam and use you.

Troy may have remembered me. But he didn't know me now.

"Look, I know it's a silly job," I said. "But it's my silly job. And I take it very seriously. And if you don't want to do the same, I suggest you march right down to Richard's office and let him know. I don't need you screwing up my life any more than you already have."

The last part came out before I could stop it. And I cringed, feeling my face turn bright red as he turned to look at me, eyebrows raised. I waited for him to say something . . . anything . . . to relieve the sudden tension. The elephant I'd led into the room.

Instead, he said, "Okay."

"What?"

"Okay." He nodded. "Fair enough."

"So you . . . won't take the job?" I was so confused at this point.

He shook his head. "I have to take the job," he corrected. "Trust me, I have very few options right now and I can't afford to turn my back on any of them. But," he added, "I will take it seriously."

I nodded slowly. "I appreciate that," I said, knowing my voice still sounded a little stiff. (Though who could blame me?) I forced myself to hold out my hand. "Welcome to the entertainment beat, Troy Young. Where all the magic happens."

His mouth quirked. His hand closed over mine. Shockwaves of heat spasmed through me and it was all I could do to force myself not to react. Not to let him know just how much the touch of his skin skimming across my own could still reduce me to a shivery puddle of goo.

Troy, you are seriously going to send me to an early grave, I thought.

The question was, would I die happy?

eleven

TROY

"Thanks for joining me," I said to Griffin, after taking a slug of my beer. "It's been a helluva day. And I don't like drinking alone."

Griffin held up his own beer in salute. He had been my mentor back when I'd first gone overseas—a senior war reporter with whom I'd shared many drinks at local dive bars. He'd taken early retirement two years ago after a bomb had blown up during one of his broadcasts—taking most of his right leg with it. Now he had a prosthetic, though you could barely tell by the way he walked. But I knew the phantom pain still kept him up late. The memory of the bomb even later.

"Nothing wrong with drinking alone," he teased after swallowing a generous sip of his own pint. "But I've had my share of helluva days and I'm happy to have an excuse to partake. This way if my old lady bitches at me, I can blame it on you." He smirked.

I rolled my eyes. "Whatever works," I said.

"How you doing, kid?" Griffin asked, peering at me closely. "You holding up?"

I sighed. "I thought I was. Until I tried to get back in the field." I quickly related all that had happened the day before. Griffin listened patiently, without interrupting.

"Can't say I'm surprised," he said once I had finished. "Those kinds of intense situations can be very triggering."

I scowled. I hated words like *triggering*. Nothing more than excuses for people who couldn't handle what life threw at them, used to get them out of whatever it was they didn't want to do or didn't want to face.

"You sound like a shrink," I muttered.

He gave me a lazy smile. "I've been to my share. I can quote the lingo like a boss when given the opportunity." Then he gave me a sympathetic look. "Look, this is not uncommon, you know," he assured me. "It's just part of your body's fight or flight mechanism, working overtime. Back overseas you needed those heightened reflexes to stay alive. They kept you safe. Now your body still thinks they're necessary, even though you're back home. It'll be a while, probably, before you stop overreacting to things. Stop assuming every little noise is the beginning of the end of the world."

"Yeah, well, it may be normal. But it's embarrassing as hell. You should have seen all the people in the newsroom when I got back. They were all staring at me. Probably laughing at me behind my back."

"You gotta give yourself a break, man," Griffin scolded. "I mean, you come home from something like that— something most people would never even survive—and you jump right back into work? Now, I know you need the job and the money and all that," he added, holding up a hand before I could object. "Believe me, I understand that more than most. But you gotta be kind to yourself. Don't push yourself into more than you're ready to handle." He shook his head. "You should have seen me when I first got back from overseas. Filled with piss and vinegar—ready to prove to every fucking person on Earth that I was still a man. That they hadn't broken me—even if I was missing a leg. But you know what I learned in the end? You can never convince anyone of anything—and there's no damn good reason to even try. Let 'em think what they want to think. Doesn't mean shit in the end."

I sighed. "Easier said than done."

"I know, man. And like I said, it's going to take time. It took me a year before I could sleep through the night. I'd wake up with nightmares and I'd hear stuff outside my window. It was rough." He gave me a sorry look. "It's going to be rough for you, too. But trust me, it will get better. You may not believe that now, but someday you're going to meet me back here at this bar. And you're going to say, 'Griffin, you were right.'" He cocked a crooked grin. "And then you're going to buy me a beer."

"That will be the best beer I've ever bought," I declared.

"Damn straight. And I'll enjoy every sip of it."

"In any case, it doesn't matter," I replied. "No more live shots for me. I'm on the celebrity beat now, don't you know? Just wait 'til you hear what those crazy Kardashians are up to now!"

He snorted. "Not exactly your dream job, huh?"

"To say the least. And if that's not bad enough you won't believe who they paired me with."

"Sarah Martin?"

I looked at him, surprised.

He shrugged. "What can I say? I'm a News 9 superfan. I know all about cute little Sarah and her entertainment

show. But why is that a problem for you? Hell, I'd be counting my lucky stars to be paired with a hottie like her."

"Even if that hottie is an ex-girlfriend who despises the
ground you walk on?"

Griffin raised an eyebrow. Clearly he was not expecting
this. "Do tell," he said with an eager gleam in his eyes.

I hedged. "It's a long story . . ."

"Long stories mean an excuse for more beer."

I sighed. I wasn't sure if I wanted to talk about this. But
then again, maybe it would help to explain to someone who
wasn't involved. And at the moment I needed all the help I
could get.

"It all started back in college. I was involved in this activ-
ist group, started by a grad student named Ryan. He was kind
of a hero to me. To a lot of us, I guess. A crusader for human
rights, animal rights, environmental rights. You name it. If
there was a cause, Ryan was probably fighting for it." I paused,
then added, "And he wasn't afraid to fight dirty."

"Okay . . ."

"When I first introduced him to Sarah he didn't really
care about her. Until, that was, he found out who her father
was. He wasn't mayor back then, of course. Just a big-time
businessman with his fingers in a lot of pies. One being
Water World."

"The amusement park with the whales?"

"Yup. The same one Ryan had been wanting to get shut
down for some animal abuse allegations. So he got this idea
in his head and told me to ask Sarah out. To get on her good
side. Make her fall in love with me." I made a face. "At the
time it seemed like an easy assignment. After all, I was half
in love with her already. So we started dating. And I got her
to trust me. And then Ryan swept in and got her to go to her

father's IT guy and use her feminine wiles to score some passwords to her father's network.

"It wasn't hard. He had a really crappy network back then. And the IT guy, Johnny I think his name was, was a sucker for a pretty face. So we got the passwords and the idea was to go in and hack Water World's website—and some of the other business accounts. Post the truth about what was really going there, along with photos and video of the abuses. Hold them for ransom, if you will, until they agreed to reform their policies or shut down for good. 'High-tech protesting,' Ryan called it. It seemed like a great idea at the time."

"I take it things didn't go to plan?"

"Oh. They did all right. To Ryan's plan anyway." I shook my head, remembering. "You see it turned out Ryan wasn't actually interested in saving the animals at all. All of this was just a smoke screen to get us idiots to pitch in and get him access to what he needed. The access to so much more."

"Like . . . ?"

"Like bank accounts. Financial data. With the passwords Sarah got him, he was able to strip her father's accounts of almost a million dollars. And he would have gotten away with it, too. But he was too cocky. He bragged about it to me before leaving the country and Sarah overheard."

"Ouch."

"Of course he had this whole story. How Sarah's father had stolen all this money from everyday people and he was going to be some big Robin Hood and give it back. I almost thought he was going to convince her—that was Ryan. He could sell ice cubes to Eskimos. But in the end, she went to her father and confessed everything. Then they went to the police. Ryan was stopped at the border and arrested."

"He was crazy to think he would get away with something like that to begin with."

"Ryan was always crazy. We just thought it was the good kind of crazy. Not the criminal kind. Anyway, everything started moving fast after that. The police trying to figure it all out. Who was involved, et cetera. Sarah's father was considering a political career even then and couldn't afford to have his princess affiliated with what the media had dubbed a domestic terrorist cell. So he worked his connections and got her immunity. Then he turned his attentions to me. Handed me the chance of a lifetime—the job of my dreams on a silver platter, halfway across the world. Told me in life you got one 'get out of jail free' card and this was mine. Take it or go down with the proverbial ship."

Griffin gave a low whistle. "So he made you an offer you couldn't refuse."

"Sarah wanted me to refuse it when she found out. She begged me not to go. She wanted to run away to Mexico. Get away from all the crazy of her father and the situation. She had this idea that we could just live a simple life on the beach together." I scowled. "But I couldn't do it. I had determined I was meant for something bigger. Something important. Man, was I a fool."

"So you decided to go overseas."

"I did. Except I almost changed my mind at the last minute. I realized I loved Sarah, and I didn't want to leave her behind. I went and bought a ring. And I was on my way to find her and ask her to marry me. But before I could, she learned the truth."

"That you were in on it all along."

I nodded grimly. "That the only reason I was dating her was because Ryan told me to. That it was all part of a setup to get her to betray her family. That I had played her like a fool from the very start. She was"—I made a face—"pissed off to say the least."

"Ain't no fury like a woman scorned."

"Right." I shrugged. "So I took the job. What else could I do? I went overseas and never looked back. I loved being over there, until the end. It was a dream come true. But I could never quite leave the memory of Sarah behind. Even though I knew full well I didn't deserve a girl like her after what I did."

I stared down at my beer, my stomach churning as I remembered those lonely years away. I'd had plenty of adventures. I'd hooked up with plenty of other women. But nothing had ever compared to how I'd felt with Sarah in my arms.

"So now I'm back. And Sarah—she's not so happy about that. At least she doesn't appear to be. And I don't blame her, of course. She has every right to hate me for what I did to her. But at the same time, I still care about her like crazy. And I have no idea how I'm going to work side by side with her every single day."

Griffin nodded. "That's rough, man," he said, taking a swig of his beer. "I don't know what to tell you, either. All I know is you need to be careful. You've got a lot on your plate right now as it is. Stuff you have to swallow before you can take on any new problems."

"I know," I said glumly. "Believe me, I know. But what can I do? I need this job. I have to work with her."

"Then work with her. And try to be her friend. But there's no need to take it any further than that. To push her too hard. Or too fast. You have five years of pent-up feelings—but remember, she does, too. You come on too fast—even if you mean well, you're going to scare her away forever."

I nodded, knowing he was right. If I ever wanted the

chance to get Sarah to forgive me, I'd have to take my time. Get her to trust me again. Show her I could be a good friend. And then maybe, someday, we could explore the idea of being more than that. Maybe.

Maybe . . .

I set my empty beer on the table. "I got to get going," I told Griffin. "Big day tomorrow. Can you believe I'm getting paid to sit in a theater and watch a movie all day?"

Griffin grinned. "Sounds like nice work if you can get it." Then he turned serious. "Look, Troy. I know things may seem grim now, but I promise you, hang in there and it's going to get better. Trust me, I've been there. I know."

"Thanks," I said. "I appreciate that."

"And if you need me? Call me. I don't care what time it is, I sleep with the phone by my bed. I will answer. I'll come by. I'll bring beer."

I nodded, the huge lump in my throat making it impossible, at first, to speak. "Thank you," I managed to say again in a croaky voice after a pause. "That means a lot."

"And good luck with Sarah!" he added with a wink. "I'll be rooting for a reunion . . . and lots of hot make-up sex!"

I rolled my eyes. "Don't hold your breath on that one," I said with a smirk. "At this point I'll settle for not being strangled to death in my sleep."

"Aim high, my friend. Aim high."

twelve

TROY

In my old life, I'd start a typical day on my computer, scouring Reuters, the AP, BBC News—to get a sense of the overall picture of what was going on in the world that day, and specifically my corner of it. Then, I'd call my list of contacts or meet up with them in various cafes and bars—to see if they'd heard anything, seen anything, thought anything was worth checking out.

Of course it wasn't always up to me. The network was always asking me to go here or there, to cover whatever the big story of the day might be. In fact, it could be a real juggling act—to balance between reacting to news that had already happened (a bombing, an invasion, a flare-up in a refugee camp) and seeking out less obvious stories that I thought were important, like exploring the cultural or social issues behind the conflicts.

Turned out entertainment reporting wasn't all that different, at least when it came to process. Sarah had me start the morning of my second day on the job by scouring the Hollywood trade publications, Deadline.com, and the gossip magazines while she fielded calls from movie PR firms which offered her interview ops with various stars who were coming to town.

We were halfway through our morning research when the executive producer came in to make sure we would include the big *Real Housewives* meltdown that had happened off-camera at some swanky San Diego bar the night before. One of our viewers evidently shot some "good fighting video" from his iPhone they wanted to air. Sarah, God bless her, took it with a smile and promised to make sure it made her show.

"Okay," she said, turning to me and looking down at her notes. "So for the five o'clock newscast we'll lead with the *Real Housewives* thing—that's the best video anyway. Then we'll cut to the Kim Kardashian selfie snafu. We'll need to send the photo to graphics—so they blur out the naughty bits. Oh and I'll pull a few funny Twitter reactions to follow the actual picture. Does she look hot? Is it too much? Is she ruining the future lives of young girls as we know it by taking her clothes off so often? That kind of thing." She scribbled something down on her notepad. "Then we'll use the second part of my Hemsworth interview. That's already edited so we're good there. And we'll close with a tease to our new franchise. I doubt they'll have the beta open ready yet—they'll probably need to get a few shots of you to insert into it before it's final. You'll want to check with the promo department on that." She looked down at her notes. "And I think that should do it."

I gave a low whistle. I didn't know whether to be disgusted by what garbage was going into the newscast or impressed by the way Sarah had artfully arranged that garbage. Origami out of ashes.

"That's quite a bit. How much time do you get for your slot anyway?" I asked.

"The whole D block if I want it," she said, looking a little sheepish. "That's about five to seven minutes. Of course the new He Said, She Said may get a little more time since it's airing in the four PM newscast. There's not as much news at four. Most reporters save their big packages for the five or six PM when we have a bigger audience."

"Right." I raked a hand through my hair, staring down at her notes.

"What?" she asked, cocking her head. "You don't approve?"

I shrugged. "It's just . . . there's so many things going on in the world. People here have no idea. We could be broadcasting all day long and we'd never even scratch the surface of what people need to know. And yet—we're devoting twenty percent of the newscast to celebrity selfies and bar fights?" I paused. "Doesn't that bother you at all?"

She frowned. "Of course it does," she said. "But what am I supposed to do? I don't run this place."

"Right. Construction worker on the Death Star . . ."

She stared at me for a moment. Then her eyes sparkled. "Keep your eyes down," she said, finishing our old joke. "Jedis don't have 401(k)s."

I looked up at her. She met my eyes with her own. God, she looked so different than my Sarah. But it was her. Deep down it was still her. Something inside me twisted a little.

"Look," she said. "If it makes you feel any better? There's a method to this madness. Entertainment stories bring people in. They're like live bait to lure the fish. Melted cheese on a kid's Brussels sprouts. You want people to hear the important stuff? What's going on in the world? Well, you have to get them to tune in first. These mindless entertainment stories serve that purpose."

I nodded slowly. While I hated the idea that people out there were so content to be ill-informed of what was going on around them, I knew what she said was true. And if what we did here got them to turn on their TV and hear the rest? Well, that was something. In fact, it was a lot.

"Fair enough," I said. Then I shot her a wicked grin. "Now let's see that selfie again. I might need to be the judge of whether it's hot enough to reel people in."

She laughed. "How about I take care of the selfie?" she suggested. "You go ahead and check in with the promo department about getting your mug into the beta open. You won't have time later with the screening."

"The screening?"

"Yeah, sorry. There's a screening for this new thriller starring Kristin Stewart at one. I have us down to check it out. I figure it can be our first He Said, She Said review film. Does that work for you?"

"Sure, I guess." I paused, then added, "So News 9 is literally paying us to go to the movies?"

She laughed. "We can't review it if we haven't seen it."

"Good point." I shook my head. Spending the day at the movies. And getting paid to do it.

"Don't get too excited," Sarah added. "It'll be a small theater. Just press, most of them probably only half paying attention. And make sure you eat a big lunch. They never serve popcorn at these things. Which, in my opinion, is a damn shame."

"A travesty," I agreed. "You should seriously protest."

Her smile faltered at this and I winced as I realized what I'd just said. What I'd inadvertently inferred. But hey—now that I'd led the gigantic elephant into the room, I figured I might as well introduce it around and let it ask for peanuts.

"Do you ever, uh, do that anymore?" I asked, trying to tread carefully. "Protest, I mean."

Her face turned bright red. "No," she replied in a clipped voice. "Not since . . . well, you know." She turned away, staring at the wall.

"Right." I sucked in a breath, pausing before adding, "Well, that's too bad. You were really good. A real advocate for those whales."

"Yeah. Well, evidently I was the only one."

Silence fell over us, as her words dug like a dull knife into my stomach. I opened my mouth to say something. Anything—to clear the air. But what could I say? What had happened had happened and nothing could change that now, no matter how much I wanted it to. I could apologize again—and maybe this time she'd be willing to listen. But then again, maybe not. She'd certainly never listened before. And maybe I deserved that.

"Whatever happened to the undercover footage?" I asked instead. "All the stuff we shot back then? We could still do something with that if we had it, don't you think? I mean, I know it's old. But it's proof we were right about what they were up to. What they probably still are up to."

She stared at me, as if I had two heads. "I don't know," she said at last. "Ryan had it last I knew. And obviously he isn't around to give it back."

"Right." I sighed. Of course everything came back to Ryan in the end. That bastard. If only I could get my hands on him again. He'd be the one needing to be saved.

But Ryan was locked away in prison, which was probably for the best. And the rest of us were forced to pick up the pieces of our lives best we could.

I rose to my feet, clearing my throat. "Anyway, I'll go check in with promotions. See you back here when I'm done."

She nodded but didn't reply. I watched her for a moment, the way her shoulders slumped. Her head bowed. Cracks in a perfectly polished façade. It hurt my heart to see her like this. Especially when I knew much of her pain had to do with me.

But while I couldn't do anything about that—at least not right away—I realized I could do one simple thing. I could take this job and work it like it was the most important job I'd ever had in my life. Prove to her I could take it seriously. That I could take her seriously.

That wasn't nearly enough to make up for the past. But it would be a start. And once I got started? Well, who knew how far I'd be able to go?

thirteen

SARAH

"Wow," Troy said as we walked out of the film screening later that afternoon. "So that was . . . something."

I glanced over at him. "You didn't like it?"

We stepped out into the parking lot and I shrugged on my jacket. There was a strong ocean breeze today, making it a bit chilly outside. Unlike inside the theater, which had felt almost boiling. Though possibly that had been less to do with the actual temperature and more to do with my proximity to Troy.

Okay, fine, that was definitely it.

When we'd first arrived at the theater I'd assumed it would be no big deal. We'd sit down, watch the movie, and we'd go on our merry ways. But I hadn't taken into account the way my traitorous body would react when Troy sat down beside me—sending me into an instant tailspin, my skin practically humming from his nearness, goosebumps breaking out up and down my arms. At one point, when his right thigh accidentally brushed mine as he moved to get comfortable I was pretty sure I was going to spontaneously combust on the spot.

It had been five years, but clearly my body had a great memory. And I found it nearly impossible to concentrate on the film while my mind was hell-bent on rolling flashback reels of our shared past through my brain. I would catch a glimpse of his hands and remember how they used to rove over my body. See his mouth and be reminded of how it was never content to leave one inch of me unexplored. And how could I forget the one time we'd actually gone to the movies together—and we'd been the only ones in the theater? Let's just say I'm still not certain what that particular film was about.

I watched now as he tapped a finger to his chin. "Let's just say it's a good thing I was born an overly intelligent man. Because I'm pretty sure I lost a measurable amount of brain cells in the last two hours, just from sitting in the theater."

I started to laugh, then sobered as I caught a couple of the studio PR people lingering outside the theater, handing out press packets.

"I mean seriously," Troy continued, "I'd say it was a train wreck, but that would be an insult to trains."

"Shh," I scolded, poking him in the arm. "Keep your voice down!"

"Why?"

I gestured around the parking lot. "Uh, because we're still standing amongst the people who made the movie?"

He followed my gaze then shrugged. "So? I thought the whole point of this was for us to tell people what we thought. We are doing a film review segment, right? Which requires, I assumed, us to review the film? I'm just practicing in advance."

I sighed. "Yes, yes. Of course. And you can. But you have to remember these companies are also our advertisers. So maybe try to be a little more . . . diplomatic with your criticism?"

"Wait one second." Troy stopped in his tracks, turning to stare at me. "Are you saying I can't say the film sucks—for fear of pissing off advertisers?"

"Of course not. I'm just saying when it comes to reviews you need to think glass half-full," I explained. "For example, saying, 'the plot didn't exactly work for me,' is nicer than saying 'the plot had so many holes it resembled Swiss cheese.'"

"Please. Swiss cheese is delicious. This film made me want to throw up a little in my mouth."

I groaned, shaking my head.

He held up his hands in innocence. "Okay, okay! Positive! Right." His mouth quirked to a mischievous grin. He cleared his throat. "Swiss cheese lovers unite!" he declared in an overly dramatic movie-announcer-style voice. "This is the film you've been waiting for. So holey, it'll make your favorite *fromage* feel frumpy!"

I giggled. I couldn't help it. "I'm not sure that's any better."

"Okay, okay. How about this?" he asked, obviously now on a roll. "Sick of always feeling like the smartest person in the room? Then you'll definitely want to catch this film. Guaranteed to make your friends seem like little Einsteins in comparison."

I laughed. "Fine. You've made your point. Now save the rest for your review!"

We reached my car and I slipped into the driver's seat, Troy getting in beside me. I reached down to activate the convertible top, then pulled out of the parking space. I glanced over, surprised to see him writing something down into his Moleskine notebook.

"What are you doing?" I asked curiously.

He looked up. "Just taking some notes for my review. It was hard to write anything when I was in the theater, it was so dark. But I didn't want to wait too long and forget what I wanted to say."

I nodded, feeling an unexpected rush of appreciation whoosh through me. He was living up to his promise to me to take the job seriously—even if the film itself was a joke. Which, to be honest, was even hotter than his six-pack abs.

I watched for a moment before pulling out onto the street. The way his eyelashes swept across his cheeks as he intently scribbled on the page. The way his mouth set into a firm line, as I remembered it used to always do when he was concentrating.

Oh God. I swallowed hard as my body unnecessarily started to rev its engines all over again. *Calm down, girl. We are coworkers. Nothing more than coworkers.*

And . . . maybe, possibly friends?

"Look," I said, after he finished his notes and put the notebook away. "I was thinking . . ."

He glanced over at me. "Yes?"

"If you wanted to see some real movies. . . . There's this big film noir thing happening this weekend. Four films each afternoon, many of them rare prints from the foundation's private collection that haven't been publically shown in decades."

He raised an eyebrow. "Sounds interesting. Are you going?"

"Yes," I said. "I've got an all-weekend pass. It's just for fun, though. Not something I'm covering for News 9."

"Yeah, no advertising bucks in old movies, I'm guessing."

"Not exactly. But a nice palate cleanser after digesting the Hollywood trash buffet all week."

"Makes sense." His eyes zeroed in on me. "Who are you going with?"

I kept my eyes glued to the road, feeling my face suddenly flush. Oh right. Of course he would ask me that. Problem was, I didn't have a good answer.

"I was . . . uh, thinking of taking Ben," I stammered, my heart fluttering in my chest. When I had started explaining this, I hadn't meant it to sound like I was asking Troy on a date. "He loves all those old movies."

Troy's mouth quirked. "Of course he does."

I sighed. Ben and Troy had met briefly on his first day. And let's just say it hadn't gone too well. And by *hadn't gone too well* I mean it was amazing Troy had the patience not to punch Ben in the face. I tried to explain to him later where Ben was coming from. How disappointed he was that he didn't get the He Said, She Said job. That he was really a good guy, despite his open hostility to Troy, and was sure to come around in the end. Troy, at least, seemed to accept this.

My talk with Ben, on the other hand, didn't go quite so well. And so I'd ended up blurting out the only consolation prize I had at my disposal. For him to come to the festival with me.

And now, somehow, I'd gone and managed to invite Troy to come, too. This was sure to work out great . . . or not.

The silence stretched out between us, long and insufferable. I bit my lower lip, trying to focus on the road. Trying to focus on anything except Troy's presence at my side. Why had I even brought this up? Did I want him to come with me? To sit by my side all weekend long—when I'd barely been able to stand his presence for one lousy screening today? It had been all I could do in that theater not to grab him and jump his bones. Now I was suggesting eight more hours in the dark?

At last he laughed. "So?"

"So what?"

"Are you ever going to ask me if I want to come, too?"

Oh God. My face burned. "What, you need a formal invitation?" I barked back, with a little more force than necessary.

He shrugged. "Not really. I just like the way you blush when I pretend that I do."

Oh my god. Oh. *My. God.*

"Well?" He waggled his eyebrows at me. "I'm waiting . . ."

I sucked in a breath. He was going to be the death of me. "Hey, Troy, want to go to a film festival?"

"See? That wasn't so hard, was it? Now, let me check my busy social schedule. . . ." He reached down and grabbed his phone, making a big show of looking through his calendar. Then he looked up. "Well, what do you know? I'm free for the next forever." His eyes sparkled. "Miss Martin, it looks like you have yourself a date."

fourteen

SARAH

The week went by in a blur, and before I knew it the weekend had rolled around and with it the film festival. Troy was good to his word, waiting by the concession stand as I rolled into the theater with Ben. Ben had insisted on driving, saying my house was totally on the way anyway. And me, still feeling guilty about him getting passed over for the He Said, She Said job, reluctantly agreed.

I'd tried to get Stephanie and some of my other girl-friends to join us as well—safety in numbers and all that. But they had looked at me as if I was suggesting we cut off the heads of puppy dogs and eat them raw when I used the words *film noir* and *uncovered prints* in the same sentence while inviting them to go. Evidently the only prints these girls were interested in uncovering were the fingerprints of the hot guys at Bar West after they ravaged their bodies.

Besides, Ben had wanted to go so badly. And he deserved to go, as well. He knew more about the noir genre than anyone I'd ever met. In fact, the entire trip over he'd been peppering our conversation with little-known trivia.

"Did you know in *Double Indemnity* Fred MacMurray wears his real-life wedding ring throughout the film? Even though his character in the movie is single?"

"Did you know an uncredited second-unit cameraman was the first to use the now-famous dolly zoom in Alfred Hitchcock's *Vertigo*? It cost nineteen thousand dollars to film that staircase scene alone."

"Did you know the photos of the young Norma Desmond in *Sunset Boulevard* were actual, genuine publicity photos from Gloria Swanson's younger years?"

And so it went. And as we walked up to Troy I was relieved beyond belief at the possibility of new, non-noir related conversation. Ben, on the other hand, looked displeased.

"What's he doing here?" he demanded.

"He works with us now," I reminded him.

"I didn't know this was a work trip."

I shot him a look. "Be nice," I scolded. "You're lucky I didn't decide to go solo."

As I approached Troy, I couldn't help but give him a quick once-over. He looked freshly showered, his hair still a little damp and his cheeks clean-shaven. He was dressed casually, in a tight black T-shirt that nicely accentuated his abs, and a pair of well-worn jeans. I sighed. Why did he have to be so cute? It only made this whole thing harder.

His blue eyes locked on me, sparkling in a way that should by all rights have been illegal. "There you are," he said. "I was beginning to think you stood me up."

"Sorry. Ben had to stop at the store on the way here to grab some contraband candy bars to smuggle in."

Something flickered in Troy's eyes as he looked over at

my producer. But all he said was, "Hello, Ben. It's good to see you."

Ben made a face. "Are you sure you're ready for this, Young?" he asked. "I mean, you do know the Rock isn't starring in a single one of these films right?"

"Are you serious?" Troy feigned horror. "Next you're going to tell me Taylor Swift isn't doing the soundtracks!"

I laughed. "Don't worry, Ben. Troy may not know as much about noir as you do, but I think he'll hold his own. Right, Troy?

"Only if you hold the popcorn," Troy shot back with a grin. He pushed the tub into my hands. It was practically as big as my head. "To make up for that terrible popcorn-free screening," he explained. "Extra butter. Extra salt."

My heart squeezed a little more than it should have as I realized he remembered my popcorn order. Something so small yet so impressive, all at the same time. This man standing before me was practically a stranger. Except he once knew everything about me—things no one else in the world knew. What else was stored deep down in the recesses of his brain beyond my favorite popcorn? My mind flashed back to that thing he used to do with his tongue and I felt my face heat.

Get your mind out of the gutter, I scolded myself.

Suddenly I was very happy to have Ben as my chaperone. At least he could play third wheel and keep anything from happening when the lights went low. His little trivia could be the social equivalent of a cold shower.

"Shit," Ben muttered, looking at his phone.

"What?" I frowned.

"I'm sorry." He looked up. "I completely forgot. I'm supposed to take care of my grandmother today."

"Wait, what?" I stared at him, incredulous. "You've been

asking to go to this thing for like three weeks now. I got you an all-access pass. You're just going to bail?"

Leave me alone in the dark with Troy? I thought but didn't add.

Ben shot Troy a withering look before answering. "It's not like you'll be alone," he sneered.

I swallowed hard. Was Ben jealous of Troy? Had he thought this was some kind of date? But no, I'd been very clear that this was just a favor for a friend. And besides, he genuinely loved noir. He'd been talking about the festival for weeks. Surely he wasn't that petty.

"Okay," I said doubtfully. "If you're sure . . ."

"I can pick you up later. Just call me and I'll come by."

"That's okay, I can Uber it," I replied. "Thanks for the offer though. And I'll see you . . ."

I trailed off, realizing Ben was no longer listening. Instead, he was hurrying out of the theater as if the devil himself was on his heels. I shook my head, puzzled.

"That was . . . odd," Troy remarked.

"Yeah." I bit my lower lip. "I worry he has a little crush on me."

Troy's lips quirked. "Is there any red-blooded man alive who doesn't?" he teased.

"I can think of a few . . ." I said, then immediately felt my skin flush. I had been thinking of Asher, of course, when I said it, but I realized the statement could be taken very differently, given Troy and my shared past.

Sure enough, the teasing expression faded from his face. "Come on," he said gruffly. "I think the first movie's about to begin."

I nodded and accompanied him through the theater doors, trying to balance the huge popcorn in my hands. The screenings were being shown in an old-fashioned movie house, complete with a top balcony overlooking the main seats. I had tried to score balcony tickets—there was something romantic about being up there in the rafters, looking down on the world—but they had long been sold out by the time I'd inquired.

We took our seats, which weren't terrible, then settled in to watch the first show. A moment later the stage lights came on and the spokesperson from the Southern California Film Noir Foundation stepped onto the stage to talk about the first film. A restored edition of a 1940s noir with a science fiction twist called *Repeat Performance*—where a young woman who may or may not have shot her husband goes back in time to live the year over again. Will she make different choices this time around? Or was everything predestined to happen all over again?

I had to admit, the subject matter rang a little close to home.

I glanced over at Troy. His attention was locked on the speaker. Absently, he reached over, without looking, to grab a handful of popcorn from the tub on my lap. I watched as he brought his hand to his mouth, my stomach twisting a little. That definitely shouldn't have been as erotic as it felt.

Easy, girl, I scolded myself. *You do not want to go back there.*

And yet, I realized, in some ways I did. And that was becoming a big, big problem. After all, the last thing I needed was to go back to the days when I was hopelessly in love with this man. Ready to do anything to see that look of approval in his eyes. Even betray my own family.

The host walked offstage and I shook my head, pushing thoughts of the past away as I tried to focus on the film. I loved movies like this—rare prints dug up from some archives and carefully restored. In a world like ours, where everything was cataloged and backed up on the cloud, there was something special about these lost little gems you couldn't just Google and stream via YouTube.

I settled into my seat, taking another bite of popcorn. Soon I was so immersed in the story I almost forgot the man who was sitting by my side. It wasn't until nature called that I realized I needed a break. Those damn extra-large sodas . . .

I leaned over to Troy. "I'll be right back," I whispered. Then I started rising from my seat.

Whoosh!

Something hard and heavy flew by my face, missing me by inches. I screamed. *What the hell?*

For a moment, I had no idea what had just happened. I looked around, confused, as the theater erupted in chaos. Glancing above me, I caught sight of a lone figure up in the balcony, pushing by people to get out in a hurry. From there I couldn't catch his or her face, and at first I assumed it was some kid who thought it would be funny to throw his popcorn or drink down on the audience below.

But then I looked down at my feet.

It was a rock. A large rock.

"Oh my God!" I cried, alarm rioting through me. My mind raced with horrifying possibilities. If I hadn't picked that moment to get up, it would have hit me square on the head.

That couldn't have been an accident, right?

I turned to Troy, but he was already on his feet. He pushed past me, running out of the theater. I could feel the eyes of everyone else staring at me, horrified, as the film played on with no one watching. For a moment I felt frozen in place, a deer in headlights, not sure what to do. Then, somehow, I found my feet and excused myself down the aisle, my whole body shaking as I ran to the exit.

A moment later I burst into the lobby. The manager met me, his face as ashen as mine probably was. "Are you okay?" he asked.

I tried to swallow past the huge lump that had formed in my throat. "I'm fine," I assured him. "Did you . . . find him? The guy who dropped the rock?"

Before the manager could answer, Troy was back. His face was grave. His forehead sweaty from running. "I'm sorry," he said. "I tried to catch up with him, but he was too quick. He must have had a car waiting for him outside."

I collapsed against a nearby wall, trying to still my racing heart. My breath came in short gasps and I struggled to wrestle it under control. Someone had tried to hurt me. Maybe kill me. Dad's warning echoed through my ears—suddenly not seeming as silly as it had back in his office.

Troy's eyes locked on me. "Are you okay?" he asked.

I opened my mouth, but no sound came out. He looked at me for a moment, then grabbed me, pulling me into a strong embrace.

And suddenly I was in his arms again—for the first time in five years.

My heart beat wildly in my chest and for a moment I panicked, wondering if I should try to break free. But his grip was so strong and so warm and so clear in its intention to not let me go. And so, in the end, I forced myself to relax into him, to absorb his strength as if it were my own. To collapse into this body that was so familiar, yet so foreign all at the same time. And as he ran his hands up and down my back, whispering soothing noises in my ear, I could feel the tears slip down my cheeks.

"I'm sorry," I stammered, feeling lame and pathetic and useless, all at the same time.

He pulled away, just enough to reach up to cup my chin

in his hands. He tilted my face until I met his eyes with my own. "Why are you apologizing?" he demanded.

I laughed weakly. "I don't know. I just—I mean, I can't believe . . . If I hadn't moved when I did . . ."

He pulled me back into him and I could feel his heart also racing in his chest, like mine. It had scared him, too. But he'd gone after the guy, just the same. My hero.

"Well," I said with a sigh, shaking my head. "I guess my dad will now get to say his favorite words. *I told you so.*"

Troy pulled away from our hug again. He looked at me with confusion. "What do you mean?"

"Oh. He called me in a couple days ago, to say he'd been receiving some strange threats—maybe having to do with me. He wanted me to lay low, maybe leave the country for a while."

"Wait. You think the rock was meant for you?" Troy looked surprised.

I frowned. "Of course. Who else?"

He shrugged. "What about me?" he asked. "After all, you may have noticed I'm a bit of a persona non grata around here these days." He said it lightly, but I could hear the pain in his voice all the same. I gave him a rueful look.

"Anyone who thinks that is an idiot."

"I'm not sure about that, actually," he muttered. Then he shook his head. "Anyway, in either case we need to file a police report. Get it all on record in case this guy strikes again—no matter who he's targeted." He pointed outside the theater where two cruisers had just pulled up. "It won't take long, I'm sure."

It did, actually, take pretty long. Especially once the reporters came. They were practically salivating when they realized who had been the target of this "terrorism." (Their words not mine.) The beautiful mayor's daughter and the celebrity ex-hostage. It was a match made in front-page heaven.

"I know I should be understanding when it comes to these guys," Troy grumbled as we made our way past the line of reporters, yelling no comment as we went. "I mean, technically we're just like them, right?"

"We're not like them," I assured him. "These guys would sell out their own mothers for some sleazy story. You were out there, trying to better the world."

"Lot of good that did the world . . ."

I opened my mouth to argue, but he cut me off. "Look, I'm guessing you don't want go back in there, right?"

"I think I've had enough real-life noir for one day, thank you very much."

"Agreed. So how about I take you home?"

My heart stuttered in my chest. "There's no need. I can call an Uber . . ."

"I'm so not letting you go home in an Uber."

I sighed. "Troy, I'm fine. Really. The whole thing just startled me. I'm perfectly capable of getting myself home."

"I'm sure you are," he said. "I'm also sure you have some great noir films of your own in your video library, yes?"

"Well, sure . . . But I don't see—"

He held up a hand. "You promised me a film festival, Miss Martin," he said with a small smile. "And I plan to collect on that promise."

fifteen

TROY

Okay, Troy. What the actual hell?

Did I just say that? Did that line actually just come from my mouth? Here I'd been trying to put her out of my head and suddenly I was inviting myself over to her house.

I opened my mouth, to take it back, to tell her I was just kidding, ha-ha, have a good day and I'll talk to you in the morning. But before I could utter the words, she looked at me—just looked at me—with those wide blue eyes of hers, filled with a mixture of hope and fear and evidently liquid kryptonite and all at once I was a goner.

"I would like that," she said. And even though I knew I should not like that—not like that one bit—I was only human after all.

And so I put an arm around her shoulder. I led her to my car. I opened the door as if I was some gentleman and allowed her to slip inside, while trying and failing not to notice the way her skirt slipped up her thighs as she sat down.

Five years ago, I would have climbed in after her. Pushed the seat back as far as it could go. At the time I'd taken that privilege for granted. What I wouldn't have given to have it granted again.

Slamming the door shut, I walked around to the other side of the car, my whole body practically vibrating from the memories. Of how I used to climb on top of her, spreading her thighs open to me. Slipping between those thighs, anchoring her to me, locking my hands on her hips. Mouth on mouth, skin on skin. It was never enough—and yet oh so much.

But that was in the past. And unlike in the movies there were no real-life do-overs. Now, I should have considered myself lucky to have even been invited to her house.

As I slipped into the driver's seat, she looked at me, catching my expression. "Are you okay?" she asked.

"Hunky-freaking-dory." I turned on the ignition. Then paused. "I guess I should ask where you live."

The fact that I didn't know crushed me a little. A brutal reminder that she'd lived this entire life lived without me while I was away. Which, of course, should have been obvious. She hadn't been frozen in time. She'd had five years to live and change and grow as a person. From the awkward little college girl who'd been out to save the world—to the poised, polished woman she was today.

A woman who didn't need someone like me in her life.

She lived on the beach now; of course she did. In a cute little cottage that could have been pulled straight from a lifestyle magazine, meticulously decorated in shabby chic, hipster décor. I felt a bit like a giant ogre as I stepped into the overly feminine space. As if my mere presence was going to cause priceless artifacts to fall off the shelves. I thought back to her old college dorm. Its cheerful messiness and patchwork style. Her dad was always offering to send over his decorator to help her out, and she would laugh and assure him she liked it how it was. That there was order to her chaos.

Now there was only order.

"Do you want a drink?" she asked, going straight for the kitchen. "I think I need like ten of them myself at this point."

"Sure," I said, forcing myself to sit down on the couch. "That sounds great."

She bustled around the kitchen for a moment, surprising me by returning with a tumbler of Scotch with one single ice cube, exactly how I used to drink it when we were together. My mouth salivated as the warm, robust scent rose to my nose. I hadn't had a good Scotch since I'd left. Overseas I drank whatever swill was being served at the local dive bars—if it got me drunk it was good enough for me.

I took the glass from her now, trying not to notice how soft her hands were as they connected with mine. I pulled the drink to my lips, breathing it in before taking a sip. I could feel her eyes on me as she slipped down next to me on the couch, glass of wine in her own hands, and I tipped the glass, savoring the tingle and burn on my lips. Goddamn.

"What is this?" I asked, after swallowing. I swirled the liquid in my glass. An amateur move—real Scotch drinkers didn't agitate the spirit. But I couldn't help it.

"Just a Macallan," she said. Then she gave me a mischievous grin. "1964."

I raised an eyebrow. "No way."

"Yes way. One of my dad's little lobbyists gave him the bottle last Christmas to help grease the wheels of his newest Screw the Poor People campaign. I swiped it on principle, of course."

"And you don't even like Scotch."

"Nope. But I do like screwing over rich bastards who think they can buy my dad's support."

"Fair enough." I glanced back to the kitchen, noting the bottle was half-empty. Clearly I wasn't the only man she'd served it to.

The thought made me sober. What the hell was I doing here? Sitting in her living room, drinking her alcohol. As if we were still friends. As if we were more than just friends. Of course back in the old days I wouldn't be content to just be drinking Scotch. I'd be dragging her caveman-style to the bedroom—to satisfy a much different thirst.

I cleared my throat. *Come on, Troy. Keep it together.*

"So do you really think someone might have been targeting you?" I asked, trying to switch my focus to safer territory.

She sighed. "Maybe," she said. "My dad did get that warning, though we don't know who it was from. I mean, he has a ton of enemies. Your guess is as good as mine as to who he pissed off this time."

"But that has nothing to do with you."

"I've made it my life's mission not to," she agreed. "After, well, you know."

I winced a little. I knew all right. After the whole Water World fiasco, dozens of her father's people—mostly in the IT department—had lost their jobs for failing to stop what Sarah had set into motion. I knew how bad she felt about that at the time. That her well-meaning actions to save the whales had ended up ruining so many other people's lives.

She gave a brittle laugh, but her smile didn't quite reach her eyes. The pain on her face made something inside of me ache, and for a moment I had to fight the urge to move closer. To put my arms around her again and tell her everything would be okay.

But who the hell was I to make such an assurance? I thought everything would be okay when I went overseas. But it very nearly wasn't. And who was I to tell her I would do everything in my power to keep her safe? When I couldn't even keep myself safe in the end?

As if on cue, my mind flashed back to the darkness. Blacks spots swimming before my eyes. Angry voices echoing through my head.

If you do not comply with our demands, he will be beheaded.

Beheaded.

We will chop off his head.

If you do not comply . . .

My breath caught in my throat. My heart slammed so hard against my chest I was half-afraid it would crack a rib. I tried to take another sip of Scotch, but it went down the wrong pipe and I choked, spitting it out onto her beautiful, pristine white rug.

"Shit!" I growled, looking around, desperate for a napkin, all the while feeling as if I was going to throw up. My heart was beating faster now, ice seeming to swim through my veins. Sarah was looking at me with worry in her eyes—which only made it worse. I rose to my feet to try to make it to the kitchen, but my legs only buckled out from under me and I was forced to sit back down.

"Are you okay?" she asked.

"The rug . . ."

"The rug is fine. What about you?" She grabbed my jaw and turned me to face her, to stare into those huge, endless blue eyes of hers. I sucked in a breath, forcing myself to focus all my attention on those eyes—to lose myself in the dilated pupils, as I desperately worked overtime to quell the irrational fear swarming inside of me.

This was the worst thing. When these attacks came out of nowhere. The ones that had purpose—when I was in danger or threatened or whatever—those made sense. These random ones? They made me feel like I was going fucking crazy.

"Troy . . ." she whispered, her lips parting in a way that was suddenly so damn erotic and, before I knew what I was doing, I had reached up to touch them, desperate to feel something real. Something solid. I traced a finger along her lower lip, concentrating on the soft plumpness of her skin. The way her lipstick stained my finger red. She gasped, letting out a small sound—a sound that suddenly brought me back to life.

I jerked my finger away. "I'm sorry," I said. I swallowed down the huge lump that had formed in my throat. My stomach was still churning and my heart was still racing, but I was back on earth.

She gave me a look that pretty much melted me where I sat. "It's okay," she said. "Where were you just now?"

I swallowed hard. I didn't want to talk to about it. I didn't want her to know how bad it had been. I wanted her to see me as someone strong and in control. Someone able to protect her when things went wrong. I didn't want her to know what I had been like down in that hole. Broken, sobbing, begging for my life like a fucking coward.

I jerked to my feet. "I need to go."

She frowned. "You just got here. I thought we were going to watch a movie."

"Turns out I'm not in the mood."

She sighed. "Then we won't watch a movie. We'll hang out. Talk."

"I'm not in the mood to talk, either." I scowled, knowing I was being as petulant as a child. But what else could I do?

The walls were closing in on me, and I needed to get out.
Before I was smothered by pity and understanding and all
the other emotions I didn't deserve.

Especially not from her.

She rose to her feet. Took a step toward me. My breath
caught in my throat.

"Then we won't talk," she said, reaching up and making
a motion to zip her lips with her finger. My heart wrenched
at the familiar gesture. The one I remembered all too well.
From my Sarah. My beautiful Sarah.

I turned away, pacing the room like a caged tiger, my
steps eating up the distance between walls. Why had I come
here? I knew it would be hard. I hadn't realized it would be
this hard.

"Don't you see?" I wanted to scream at her. "You should
want me to leave. After what I did to you? How I tricked
you? How I ran away? The last thing you should want is me
back in your life."

I suddenly realized I'd taken a step toward her. The tension in the air so thick you could cut it with a knife. I tried
to turn away, but instead I took another step forward. Then
another until suddenly I was close enough to touch her. I
looked down at her, realizing she was trembling.

"You shouldn't want me to stay," I whispered.

I could see her swallow hard. "I know," she replied.

"You should tell me to leave. Now. And not come back."

"I know," she agreed, her voice wobbling on the words.

I reached out, the air crackling between us as I traced a
finger down her jawline. She shivered, but her skin was flush,
boiling hot to my touch.

"Tell me to walk out that door. Tell me to not come back."

"I . . . can't."

I grabbed her, pulling her to me, until she was flush

against my body, soft and pliant in my hands. I could feel her heart beating fast as a bird's against my chest as she clung to me, her hands gripping my sides. She was so small. So thin. I could probably crush her with little effort, and I tried to relax my grip so as not to hurt her.

Because I didn't want to hurt her. I wanted to kiss her.

Which was the worst idea ever.

And also . . . the best.

I pulled away, just enough to reach up, tipping her face with my hand, meeting her eyes with my own. In one fluid movement, I leaned down, pressing my lips against hers. She let out a small cry, but thank God not one of protest—just surprise. And as I coaxed her mouth open with my tongue she let me in. And something inside of me soared at the familiar taste of her. Mint gum and sunshine.

Sarah. My Sarah.

The memories flooded back to me now, as I hoisted her onto the back of her couch, pushing her thighs open and closing the distance between us. Memories of all those nights in the dark when I couldn't sleep, not knowing if these were my last hours on earth. I'd thought of her then. Imagining the feel of her hot, wet mouth clinging to my own. The way her tongue would swirl around mine in a feverish dance. I'd thought of her arms reaching around to hook at my lower back while my own hands dipped down to tease her perfect ass.

It had been a great fantasy.

But oh my God, reality.

She moaned against my mouth, her tongue greedily flicking against my own and, encouraged, I increased the pressure of the kiss, smashing my face against hers. Her hands grasped my hips, as if hanging on for dear life and for a moment there was no longer a her and me—only an us—only this lost thing that I never thought I'd find again.

So many days in the dark hole. So many nights spent fantasizing about something like this. Sometimes the thought of her sweet body pressing against mine like it was now was the only thing that had kept me going. My dream Sarah, rescuing me over and over again.

And now here was real-life Sarah. In my hands, against my mouth. My groin tightened and I prayed she didn't mind the feel of my desire, rubbing against her like a desperate caged thing with a life of its own.

Yes, I'd had other women overseas. But no relationships. Not one lasting for more than a few nights, a passing fancy. I used to say it was because I was married to my job. But that was a lie. I just couldn't imagine myself with anyone but her.

And now, here she was.

"Oh God, you feel so good," I groaned as her nails dug into my back. I shifted against her, so aroused it was starting to hurt. In my fantasies, clothes had always just disappeared into thin air. Real life was proving to be a bigger struggle.

I reached up, cupping her breast with my hand, dragging a finger over the tip, which sharped in response to my touch. She squirmed, a gasp escaping her lips as she pushed against me, clearly as lost in the moment as I was. Encouraged, I dropped my head, nipping at the nipple beneath the thin fabric of her blouse, cursing the man who had invented bras. I wanted to feel skin on skin. Her skin on my skin.

And I wanted it now.

She nodded, as if I'd said that out loud, her breath now coming in short pants. I reached down to slip my hand under her blouse and skim her smooth, taut stomach and bony hips. She was skinny—far skinnier than I remembered her and for a brief moment I longed for her soft milky curves. But that was ridiculous. She was still Sarah. And Sarah was amazing.

My hands moved upward, her skin feeling alive under my fingertips. Hot and electric and pulsing with desire. I reached up, ready to tear off her bra if I had to so I could really feel her—

Ding-dong.

I froze, the sound echoing through my ears. At first I wasn't sure what it was; then my fuzzy brain managed to pull it together.

It was the doorbell. Someone was at Sarah's door.

sixteen

TROY

I opened my eyes to find Sarah—to tell her to just ignore it and maybe they'd go away. We didn't need any Girl Scout cookies and I didn't need anyone to help me save my soul. And she probably already had a vacuum—or at least a cleaning service that did.

But the jokes caught in my throat as I recognized the fright in her eyes. Eyes that said, with no subtext, *What the hell are we doing?* And while I desperately wanted to answer—to tell her it was all going to be okay—she was already climbing down off of the couch, yanking down her skirt. Smoothing her hair.

Half of me wanted to beat her to the door—cut her off. Open it myself and tell whomever it was to go away. Kick the crap out of them if they refused. After all, this was my Sarah. And I wasn't big on sharing.

But that would be stupid, I scolded my brain. Crazy even. After all, I had no claim on her. She wasn't my girlfriend.

She wasn't the fantasy I'd lived with for three months in a cave. Hell, before this week I hadn't spoken to her in five years. I should probably be grateful we were saved by the bell before we dove into something we would live to regret.

But still. It was tough. Tough to just stand here, half in a daze, as she opened the door. Even tougher to recognize the man on the other side. Carl. Her father's sleazy little lackey. Back in the day he'd been my number one cock block when it came to hooking up with daddy's little princess. It appeared he was still aces at the job.

His eyes flickered to me, narrowing in disapproval, though not surprise. Then he turned back to Sarah. I hid a smile as I suddenly realized how flushed and ravished she looked from our all-too-brief encounter. Carl was an asshole, but he was no fool. He'd realized exactly what we'd been up to.

Take that back to Daddy, you douche bag.

"Sarah," he said. "Your father sent me to retrieve you. He heard the news broadcast about what happened at the theater and is very upset." His mouth twisted into a scowl. "Why didn't you call me immediately? And why haven't you been picking up your phone?"

"Um." Sarah winced, looking like a scolded child as she glanced guiltily back in my direction. I shook my head. She was a grown woman; she had to make those decisions herself. She didn't need to answer to this creep. "I was going to call," she stammered. "But then Troy took me home and . . ." She trailed off, her skin reddening again. It was all I could do not to slam the door in the guy's face.

"We got a little busy," I finished with a smirk, leaning against the doorway. Let him take that as he would.

Carl gave me a disgusted look, clearly realizing how things had gone down. For a split second I wondered if he was going to take me out himself and school me in appropriate manners when it came to the boss's daughter. But he only shook his head, instead. Probably because he knew I'd easily kick his ass if he tried.

Instead he turned back to Sarah. "Princess, you need to start taking this threat seriously. You could have been hurt."

She sighed. "I know, Carl. And we talked to the police. They have no idea whether the guy was even aiming at me. It could have nothing to do with the threat Dad got. It could have been some kid, even. With a bad idea of a practical joke."

"You talked to the police?" Now Carl's voice had taken on an incredulous tone. "Sarah, you know you should never talk to the police without your father's lawyer present."

"Fine. It won't happen again," she shot back. "Now, I think you've made your point. Thank you for stopping by. I'm sure you're a very busy man, what with all that licking of my father's boots you have on your plate. I wouldn't want to keep you."

I burst out laughing. I couldn't help it. Carl glared at her, steam practically coming from his ears. Then he switched his focus back to me, as if I were dog shit, found on the bottom of his shoe. Clearly he blamed my presence for the princess's sudden obstinacy. And hell, maybe he wasn't wrong. After all, back in the day I had helped Sarah stand up to her father many times. Causing Carl no end of annoyance.

Finally, he drew in a breath. "I don't think you understand," he said in clipped voice. "I've come to collect you. I'm supposed to bring you back to the La Jolla house. Go ahead and pack a bag if you like. Or I could send someone to collect your things later if you'd like to get going now."

Sarah froze, the teasing look fading from her eyes. I watched as she bit her lower lip, garnering courage. "I think it's you who doesn't understand," she replied in a cold voice. "I'm not going anywhere. With you or anyone else."

"But your father—"

"Is welcome to come out here and attempt to drag me back himself if he really sees the need," she finished. "Now step back so I don't hit you when I slam this door in your face."

I stifled another grin at this, loving the look on Carl's face. This was the Sarah I remembered. The girl may have been a spoiled socialite but she was also a total badass when the occasion called for it.

Carl stepped forward, looking as if he might try to grab her himself. But I was too quick, stepping in between them. "You heard the lady," I said. "She's staying here. Now, I suggest you get off her property—before I go after you with a lot more than a door." I clenched my fist to my side in case he didn't have enough imagination to catch my meaning.

For a brief moment, he just stood there, then took a hesitant step backward, as I figured he would. He had a reputation for being an asshole to women, but when the boys came out to play? Georgie Porgie ran away.

"Your father is not going to be happy when he hears this," he declared. But he was already backing up, almost tripping over a potted plant in his haste to get the hell out of Dodge.

"Yeah, well, he's used to it," Sarah replied. Then she turned, shooting me a mischievous grin before slamming the door shut. It closed with a satisfying bang.

I laughed. "Now there's the Sarah I know and love," I teased, then blushed as I realized what I'd just said. "Maybe you haven't changed as much as I thought," I added quickly.

She shrugged. "Or maybe you bring it out in me," she replied. "I mean, to be honest, I've actually been a good little girl lately. This is my first act of open rebellion in ages."

"Well, I'm honored to have borne witness to it."

She sighed, her shoulders drooping. Then she walked over to the couch. I watched her go, dying to follow her. To crawl on top of her and continue where we'd left off, this time without interruptions.

But Carl wasn't the only one who had come to the door. Common sense had also barged in. I could see in her eyes that she wasn't going to be up for a replay. And the last thing I wanted to do was push her into something she wasn't ready for.

Something I shouldn't have been ready for, either, as the case might be.

"Look, you're clearly exhausted," I told her. "Why don't you go take a nap? I'll stay out here. Guard the door against any bad guys. Or, you know, your father's men."

"Six of one . . ." She snorted. Then she sobered. "Are you sure? I mean, I'm sure you have better things to do than babysit me."

"Actually I don't," I said simply. It wasn't a lie. "And to be honest, I don't like going home. It's . . . too quiet there. Which . . . brings back a lot of memories."

I let the words hang out there for a moment, hardly able to believe I'd just spoken them. Since I'd been back I'd never said anything close to this out loud to anyone—even the shrinks. And now, here I was, in the home of my ex-girlfriend, a girl who, by all rights, shouldn't have even let me through the door. Stripping myself down, laying myself wide open, naked and vulnerable before her. Allowing her access to a part of me I thought I'd locked up and thrown away the key to.

Was it just because she looked like my dream Sarah? The illusion I'd talked to endlessly in the dark hole? Or was there still some kind of nebulous connection existing between the two of us in real life? A thread that I had somehow managed not to sever five years ago when I broke her heart?

I swallowed hard. She had every right to throw this back in my face. To laugh at me and tell me the tables had turned. That I had gotten what I deserved.

But the look in her eyes now told me that was the furthest thing from her mind. And instead of laughing, she put her arms around me and gave me a hug. Then she handed me the remote and headed off to bed.

seventeen

SARAH

After showing Troy how to work the remote, as if it were normal as anything to have him sitting in my living room watching TV, I headed back into my bedroom, presumably to take a nap. But though I was indeed exhausted by the stress of the day, I knew in my heart there was no way I was getting any sleep. Not knowing that Troy Young, of all people, was playing knight in shining armor in the next room. Hell, it took everything inside me not to walk to my door, open it, and beckon him to come in here with me. To my room.

To my bed.

Oh God. My hand involuntarily flew to my mouth, my fingers tracing the outlines of my still swollen lips. Lips that just minutes before Troy had ravished in a way that was both completely new and all too familiar. It was almost as if I were some amnesia patient who had been offered her memory back. Not all of it, mind you. Just enough to appreciate the way his tongue licked at the seam of my lower lip, the way his hands had hooked onto my hips and dragged me to him. That feeling—that electricity—his erection pressing against my core. That memory of the two of us doing this same dance five years ago, though back then without any clothes on.

We may have had five years apart, but our bodies remembered as if it were yesterday. And they clearly wanted a rematch.

But that couldn't happen. I had moved on. I had become strong. I had worked hard to create this new life. Sure, Troy looked innocent now, almost vulnerable the way he admitted how hard it was to be alone. But deep down he was the same man. The man who had tricked me. Used me. Broken my heart.

And then run away.

It had taken me five long years to get over him. And I wasn't about to throw everything I'd worked for away for some passionate romp in the sack.

But oh, what a romp it would be. I rolled over, staring up at the ceiling, my mind replaying the scene from earlier. I'd hooked up with plenty of guys since he'd been gone. But none had ever made me as crazy as Troy could—with just a simple touch.

It was a good thing Carl had come to the door when he had. Stopped the madness before it went too far.

But oh, how a part of me wished it would go even further. Maybe even all the way.

I eventually did fall asleep somehow, and when I woke I was surprised to see how dark it was outside. I frowned, glancing at the clock, realizing it was past midnight; I'd slept all afternoon and into the night. I must have been more tired than I thought.

Usually I was a terrible sleeper, always waking at the slightest noise. But somehow, for once, I had slept deep and dreamless. I wondered if it had anything to do with knowing Troy was outside my door, keeping me safe.

Troy! He probably wanted to go home. He'd offered to stay for a nap, not the whole night. Guiltily, I swung my legs out from the bed and stepped down onto the floor. Grabbing my bathrobe, I slipped it on and headed out into the living room.

As I entered the room, my eyes darted to the couch. The TV was still on, playing some random infomercial at low volume. Troy was on his back, shirtless, his magnificent chest rising and falling in perfect rhythm. Not going to lie— I watched this for a good long minute, which I told myself was so I could determine whether he was actively sleeping. But let's be honest, I was just ogling that six-pack of his.

Seriously! I drew in a breath, shaking my head. Was this man really once my boyfriend? I mean, sure, he was always good-looking. Lean, toned. But this guy. This guy looked as if he were carved out of freaking marble. Like one of those Greek god statues or Channing Tatum in *Magic Mike*. How many hours did one have to clock in at the gym in order to achieve such a physique?

He was locked in a prison for three months, something inside of me nagged. What else did he have to do but work out?

The thought sobered me and I felt a sudden heaviness in my chest. It was hard to remember sometimes, looking at him now, what he must have gone through over there. He hadn't given many details as to what had happened when he was in that hole—at least not from my Internet research. But

I wasn't stupid. I'd read my share of journalist-kidnapping stories, and I knew what usually went down. Troy would have been interrogated. Maybe tortured. Definitely told he was going to die.

And yet, he had worked out. As if he still believed he had a future. As if he refused to give up hope.

My heart squeezed way too hard in my chest and I forced my eyes away, suddenly feeling guilty about analyzing him while he slept. Instead, I tiptoed into the kitchen, opening up the refrigerator, then wincing at the squeak the door made when it opened. I could hear him shift position, but thankfully he didn't wake up. And so after waiting for a moment, listening for his breathing to steady again, I pulled the bottle of wine out of the fridge. After pouring myself a glass, I left the rest on the counter. I'd deal with it in the morning—when I didn't run the risk of waking him. It'd probably been a long time since Troy had had a good night's sleep, too.

Glass in hand, I started to tiptoe back into my room. But before I could reach the door, Troy let out a loud, sudden cry that made me nearly jump out of my skin. I whirled around, realizing he was still asleep, but no longer slumbering peacefully. Instead, he was thrashing around on the couch. As if he were trying to fight someone.

"Get the fuck off of me," he growled, his hands waving madly in the air. "I told you—I don't know shit. Just kill me if you're going to. Get it over with!"

Oh my God. I froze. My heart wrenched in my chest at the fear and anger that rang in his voice. I shouldn't be hearing this. He would be horrified if he knew I could hear this. But what should I do? Let him sleep through it? Wake him up?

He shifted again, letting out an almost inhuman groan. As if he were in physical pain. I couldn't take it anymore. I had to wake him. I couldn't let him suffer.

I crossed the room. Turned on the light. Then I stomped my feet a few times. Dropped a heavy book on the floor. But he didn't come to. So much for me tiptoeing when I first walked into the room. He was like a hibernating bear.

Finally, not sure what else to do, I approached him. Standing above him, I poked him gently in the shoulder, praying I didn't startle him too much. Once, twice. Harder the third time.

"Wake up, Troy," I begged. "You're . . . having a bad dream."

His hand jutted out, grabbing my leg and squeezing it tight. I cried out in a mixture of pain and surprise, trying to pull away, but his grip was too strong. The pressure increased. Not sure what else to do, I smacked him upside the head.

"Dude! You're hurting me!" I cried. "Let . . . me . . . go!" I belted him again. This time using my fist.

His eyes flew open. He stared at me, at first unseeing. Then his vision seemed to clear. He looked down at his hand, still clamped around my leg, and his expression morphed from confusion to horror. He dropped his hand, revealing a large, ugly red welt that was sure to leave a massive bruise.

"Oh my God," he whispered. He looked up at me and my heart ached at the dismay on his face. "What did I do to you?"

I shook my head, dismissing it quickly. "It's my fault," I assured him, my heart still pounding a gazillion miles a minute. "I tried to wake you. You know what they say—let sleeping dogs lie. Uh, not that you're a dog, obviously. In any case, you were clearly just protecting yourself from a crazy ex-girlfriend."

I tried to keep my voice light, like it was no big deal. But inside I was terrified to the bone. Terrified of Troy, of all people. Of course he'd been asleep. He had no idea he was attacking me. Still, try as I might I couldn't seem to calm my racing pulse or steady my breath.

He rubbed his eyes, sitting up in bed. I could see the torment still warring over his face as he fought for full consciousness. He turned to me. "I'm so sorry," he said. "You know I would never—"

I held out a hand to stop him. "I know," I assured him. "Believe me, I know. You were asleep. You were having a nightmare. It sounded like . . ." I trailed off, not knowing if he'd want to know what he was dreaming about. Maybe he already did.

He hung his head, staring down at his lap. "Thank you for waking me," he said quietly.

I nodded and we sat silent for a moment. Then I bit my lower lip. "Do you have . . . a lot of nightmares?" I asked cautiously. I didn't know if it would be better for him to talk it through or only make things worse.

After a pause, he answered. "Yes."

"About what you went through . . . over there?"

"Yes."

"Well, it makes sense," I concluded. "I mean you went through something horrible. It's going to take you a while to recover."

"Sure." He looked up, his expression grim. "It's perfectly normal. And perfectly fucked up. Here I am trying my best to forget what happened and my dear, sweet brain decides to throw it back in my face every time I close my eyes." His hands balled into fists at his side. Knuckles whitening with bone. "Do you know how long it's been since I've had a decent night's sleep?"

My heart shattered at the pain I heard in his voice. I wanted to tell him I couldn't imagine what he'd gone through—what he was still going through. But I knew that would just sound like empty platitudes. Of course I couldn't imagine. No one who hadn't been there could. And what comfort would it be to remind him that he was basically alone in these memories?

He wasn't a soldier. He didn't have a platoon of brothers who had experienced the same nightmare to exchange stories with. He'd had a producer, a photographer. But they had been killed. I wondered if he felt guilty about that. That he was the only one who'd walked away unscathed.

Well, not completely.

"If it makes you feel any better, I wasn't sleeping well, either," I told him, trying to keep my voice light again. "Do you want a glass of wine?"

"How about water?"

"I think I can manage that."

Rising to my feet, I walked over to the kitchen to fill a new cup. Then I walked back out into the living room. In my absence he'd turned off the TV and put his shirt back on. I didn't know whether to be disappointed or relieved.

"I don't think I'll be going back to sleep anytime soon," he told me, by way of explanation.

"Me neither," I declared, pushing the water into his hands and holding up my wineglass in a toast. "Insomniacs unite!"

We clinked glasses before bringing them to our mouths. Troy swallowed his water then looked at me. "Are you sure?" he asked. "I don't want to keep you up."

"Meh. Beauty sleep is overrated."

"Easy to say when you're already beautiful," he said in a low guttural voice that seemed to reach down and stroke my toes. I swallowed hard. Sweet baby Jesus—this man!

I laughed nervously, tossing my hair over my shoulder. "Yeah, yeah," I said, waving him off. Then my smile faded. "Would it help to . . . talk about things?" I asked.

"Things?" He raised an eyebrow. Then his eyes dropped to my nightgown, which I suddenly realized was dipping very low. "What things did you have in mind?"

My cheeks flushed. I reached to pull my robe closed again. "You know what I mean," I scolded.

He sighed. "They assigned me a shrink to talk to."

"Please. You're in SoCal. We all have shrinks," I teased. Then I gave him a shy smile. "But that doesn't mean we don't need friends."

"Is that what we are?" he asked, peering at me with those crazy blue eyes of his.

I swallowed hard. "It's what we could be," I clarified.

It's all we could be, I added silently.

He nodded slowly, seeming to accept that. I watched as his gaze switched focus to something behind me. A photograph, I realized, hanging on the wall. Taken on the day we'd participated in our first Water World rally together. He wasn't in the photo, of course. I'd purged all those from my house the day he walked away. But you could almost feel his presence, just out of frame, all the same.

"You know I'd actually been thinking of coming home anyway?" he asked suddenly, surprising me with his words. "Before, well, you know." He made a face. "I'd gotten pretty burned out over the past five years living in crappy hotels, reporting on whatever shitty story the network had dug up for me that day." He shook his head. "It's funny. When I first got over there, I really had this idea that I could make a difference, you know? Show America what was really going on behind the scenes, behind the headlines. But in the end, I realized I wasn't much different than one of your entertainment reports—no offense. Just fodder to fill a newscast. To sell soap during commercial breaks. I'd report. The pundits would argue. Viewers would go online and post outraged comments. And then we'd all go about our days. Caring more about who was killed on *The Walking Dead* than the latest suicide bombing in Pakistan."

I nodded slowly, letting his words sink in. I knew all too well that feeling of disillusionment. That exhaustion that seeps into your bones as you realize all your hard work has been for nothing. That no matter how hard you fight, no one will really care in the end.

"It's ironic, really," Troy added with a bitter laugh. "I never made a lick of difference broadcasting overseas. But when I stopped broadcasting—when I got abducted—that was the point people finally started paying attention."

"I suppose that's one way to look at it," I said cautiously. "But Troy, I think you're overstating things. I watched your reports and I . . ."

I trailed off as his gaze swung back to meet mine and my face flushed as I realized what I'd just inadvertently admitted. That I'd been home, sitting in front of the TV, watching my ex-boyfriend deliver the news from halfway around the world.

"You watched my reports?" he asked, meeting my eyes with his own. I shivered at the cold steady fire I saw deep within their depths.

"Oh. Maybe a few. You know, when I happened to catch them as I was flipping the channels," I said, trying to sound nonchalant.

"Right." Something that looked like disappointment flickered in his eyes. But what did he expect? For me to be that pathetic? To hold a torch for him after he left me high and dry?

Of course I *had* done that, but he didn't need to know it.

He gave a long sigh. "Look, I'm sorry," he said, giving me a sheepish look. "Can we . . . talk about something else for a while? I can only take so much of reliving the past in one sitting."

I nodded quickly. Setting down my wineglass, I reached for the remote. "Absolutely," I said. "Besides, I promised you a noir night, right? Maybe we need to get started."

Relief flooded his face. "Good idea," he agreed, watching as I flipped through my DVR menu. "Wow, you have quite a few saved."

"AMC had a marathon a few weeks ago," I explained. "I taped them all." I leaned over to hand him the remote. "Pick one that looks interesting. I need another glass of wine."

"You can pour one for me, too," he said, taking the remote. I tried not to shiver as, for a brief moment, our fingers connected.

"I can do that." Hopping from my seat, I ran back to the kitchen. This time I just grabbed the whole bottle. Clearly it was going to be that kind of night.

When I returned Troy had a smile playing at the corner of his lips. I looked at him in question.

"Ever see *Sunset Boulevard*?" he asked, winking at me.

I grinned, dropping back onto the couch. "As a matter of fact I have," I said, reaching out to fill his glass. "Back in college. There was this guy I was dating. He told me it was his favorite movie. Though I have a feeling he said it just to get in my pants."

"Probably so," Troy agreed, wagging his eyebrows at me. "But that doesn't make the statement untrue."

I giggled, refilling my own wine and placing the bottle on the coffee table. "Well, then, what are we waiting for? I'm ready for my close-up, Mr. DeMille."

eighteen

SARAH

W̶ake up, my sexy little slut!"

I groaned, pulling a pillow over my head as rough hands shook me awake. But the hands refused to give up, only shaking harder and harder until finally I reluctantly gave in, sitting up and opening my eyes.

Troy and I had stayed awake last night for only about half of *Sunset Boulevard* before falling asleep on opposite ends of the couch. (So much for an entire movie marathon.) I had woken up only once, to realize my sleeping self had seen fit to crawl over to his side of the couch and lay my head in his lap. Embarrassed, I had attempted to move back to neutral territory, but he had shifted and so I just stayed there, not wanting to wake him up again. Besides, it was way more comfy this way anyway.

But now Troy was gone. He must have pried himself out from under me somehow to head home to change and shower before work. And in his place was Stephanie, giving me a mischievous look.

"So," she pronounced, her eyes sparkling. "What were you up to last night?"

I groaned. "Nothing," I assured her.

"Nothing? Is that what the kids are calling it these days? Cause to me that piece of tall, dark, and handsome exiting your beach cottage just before dawn definitely qualifies as something."

I grimaced. Busted. "How were you even awake for that? Or," I gave her a skeptical look, "were you still up from the night before?"

"I was headed to Equinox, thank you very much," Stephanie corrected. "For the record, I no longer stay out till the break of dawn on work days. This is the new and improved Stephanie." Her eyes locked onto me. "So what happened? Did you go out last night? I thought you were going to that nerd festival."

"Noir festival," I corrected with a sigh.

She waved a hand, as if to say *same difference*. "Did you meet someone there? Did you bring him home? Did you bump uglies all night long?"

I made a face. "First of all, never, ever call it that again," I said. "And second, no. There was no bumping—ugly or otherwise." When she gave me a skeptical look, I added, "Okay, there might have been a few pre-hookup shenanigans you would have approved of. But we quit while we were ahead."

"Oh, Sarah." She clucked disapprovingly. "Don't you know? A winner never quits. And quitters never win."

"Uh, yeah. Except when it comes to ex-boyfriends."

"Wait what?" Stephanie's eyes widened, as I figured they

would. "Was that Troy? I didn't even recognize him. Oh my God, Sarah Martin, you have completely buried the lede."

"I wasn't burying anything."

"That's what he said," Stephanie giggled. "But I bet he wanted to! Right into that pretty little——"

I groaned. "Do you know how much you are not helping right now?" I asked.

"Aw, come on. I haven't had a good hookup in a month. Let me live vicariously through you."

"You'll only be disappointed. The only reason he was even here was because we had to leave the noir festival." I quickly gave her a summary of the day's events. Her eyes bulged in horror.

"Oh my god! You could have been killed!"

I squirmed a little at this. "I'm fine," I said.

"Yeah, but . . ." She shook her head. Then her face brightened. "And Troy stepped in as knight in shining armor. How romantic is that? Maybe you guys need to get back together."

"Um, I remember you calling me a glutton for punishment for watching him on television. Now you're planning our wedding?"

"Look. I'm just not a fan of the unrequited stuff, that's all. But if he's game to get back in the game, who am I to stand in the way of true love?" She grinned wickedly. "Or at least really good sex!"

I plopped back down onto the couch, my mind flashing back to yesterday when Troy had me pinned against it. His mouth on my mouth. His hands all over my body. What would have happened if Carl hadn't interrupted when he had?

"We did used to have really good sex," I admitted with a sigh.

"And maybe you can again!" Stephanie pronounced. "I mean, why not, right?"

"Trust me, that would be a very bad idea."

"Would it, though? I'm not so sure. I mean, clearly you still carry a torch for this guy, right?" She held up a hand. "Don't even try to deny it, sister," she added. "Maybe you just need to screw him and get it out of your system. Then you'll finally be able to move on with your life."

I pursed my lips. I didn't want to admit it, but maybe she had a point. "I don't know," I hedged. "What if I have sex with him and I get even more obsessed than ever?"

"Come on. It's been five years. You've obviously built him up a lot in your mind. He can't possibly live up to all those expectations, right? So you can consider it . . . immersion therapy. That's what the shrinks call it, right?"

I rolled my eyes. "I'm pretty sure this is not the kind of thing they're talking about. Besides, what if he turns me down?"

"Sarah Martin. Have you ever had a guy turn you down?"

I blushed. "That's really not the point."

"And Troy—he's not gay?"

"No!"

"And he's not impotent?"

I thought back to Troy's erection pressing up against my thigh.

"Definitely not."

"And he's not some alien-race type of man who doesn't think with his dick like every other human man on earth?"

I laughed. "As far as I know."

"Then the verdict is clear, dear Sarah. Troy Young wants to screw the hell out of you. You just have to let him."

She made it seem so simple. And maybe it was. Maybe I had built this whole thing up in my mind too much. Maybe it was as easy as just letting myself go. Casual sex, not a new relationship. Cool my obsession and let me move on with my life.

I realized Stephanie was still waiting for an answer. "I will consider it," I promised her. "Now, get the hell out of my house so I can change for work."

She grinned, then danced to the door. I watched her go, slamming the door behind her. Seriously, she was too much sometimes. But she always made me laugh.

I rose from the couch, stretching my arms above my head. I was just about to head back to the bedroom to shower and change when Stephanie stuck her head back through my doorway.

"You just don't know when to quit, do you?" I started to accuse. But the look on her face caused me to pause. "What?" I asked.

"Sarah? You need to come out here for a moment," she said, her voice deadly serious. An uninvited chill tripped down my back.

"What is it?"

"Just . . . come here. Seriously."

I walked to the door, a feeling of foreboding washing over me. My mind flashed back to the movie theater. The rock whizzing past my head.

What now?

I stepped outside. Stephanie gestured to the right—to the brick wall above my little tomato garden. I gasped as I saw the writing on the wall—literally.

I know where you live, it said in a blood-red spray-paint scrawl.

I staggered backward, knocking into a terra-cotta planter, sending it smashing to the ground. I turned to Stephanie. She was staring at the wall, shaking her head in disbelief.

"What the hell?" she asked.

What the hell, indeed.

nineteen

TROY

It took three cold showers before I was ready to head into work. And I still wasn't sure I was prepared to face her again. I was exhausted from barely sleeping and my resistance was down. If she walked into work wearing anything short of a burka, I was going to have serious problems controlling myself.

Thinking back, the night before had almost felt like a dream. To have her in my hands again, against my mouth. Our bodies pressed against one another's, so close it was hard to tell where one of us ended and the other began. I'd never in a million years imagined that would happen again in real life.

But strangely that wasn't the part I remembered most about that night—and perhaps that was the most troubling thing. Sure, Sarah turned me on. She would turn on any red-blooded American man. But it was what happened after the turning on that stuck out most in my mind now. The way she had sat beside me, listening to me talk after waking me from my nightmare. She hadn't judged me, she hadn't pitied me. She hadn't tried to give me useless platitudes like, *It'll get better* or *You just need to move forward*. She hadn't pretended that she understood what I was going through or tried to relate it to an experience of her own. Instead, she'd just listened as I rambled on. Until I had worked my own way out of my panic.

And then she had put on the movie and poured me a glass of wine as if everything was normal between us. As if I hadn't acted like a complete crazy person in the middle of her living room. Which I knew was a lie, but oh God it felt good to lie at that moment. To just feel, for even a second, that it could be possible for me to have a normal life again. And when I woke up to find her snuggled up against my chest, the tenderness I felt for her almost did me in.

Producer Ben looked up at me when I walked through the door, not bothering to hide his sneer. The guy was pissed at me for moving into his territory, I guess. And to be honest, I didn't blame him. But what could I do? I could tell him I didn't ask for this job. That I would be out of his hair as soon as I was able. That I was no threat to him and his little world. But I knew the words would only fall on deaf ears. I just needed to try to be nice.

"Hey, Ben," I said, holding out my hand. He took it and shook it like a limp fish, his fingers stained with ink. "Where's Sarah?"

"Oh, didn't you hear?" Ben asked, looking happy that he evidently knew something I didn't. "She called in sick."

My gut jerked, though I wasn't sure whether it was out of disappointment or relief. "Is everything okay?" I asked, trying to remember if she had acted unwell the night before.

He gave a dismissive shrug. "I'm sure," he said. "She

probably drank too much. Or was out partying too late. Hashtag rich girl problems."

I frowned. Firstly because I hated people who used the word *hashtag* out loud in actual sentences. And second because that didn't sound like the Sarah I knew. I thought back to the days when we worked together on the Water World campaign. The long hours, the late nights. And still, Sarah never failed to show up with a big smile on her face, bright and early the next day.

I shook my head. Whatever. It wasn't my business. Besides, we had been up pretty late. Maybe she just wanted to catch up on sleep. I could use a sick day myself, if we were being honest. But I wasn't about to call in any favors, being on such thin ice as it was.

"Okay then. Guess it's just me and you," I said to Ben, plopping down in a nearby chair. "What do you have for me to do today?"

Ben looked down at his notes. "There's a junket for that new Davis O. Russell vehicle at noon. I've put on you on the list. It's a J. Law, Cooper thing, duh. Amy Adams is a maybe—she has to jet in from the DiCaprio set so we'll see if she makes it."

I choked out a laugh. "Dude. I have no idea what you just said. Was that even English?"

Ben scowled. He pushed a piece of paper into my hands. "Go here. Read these questions to the actors then pause to let them answer. Oh, and look hot while doing it. Evidently that's the number one thing they care about in this place."

I sighed. "I get the feeling you don't like me too much, do you, Ben?"

"I really couldn't care one way or the other. Now if you'll excuse me, I've got to go write up tonight's piece. Sarah's not here to do it, so you'll have to front it." He paused, then added, "That means get in front of the camera and read what I've written."

"Ben, I'm a multiple Emmy Award–winning reporter. I know how do a live shot. It's the celebrity thing I'm not as familiar with."

"Well, then, you're lucky you have me."

I rose to my feet, looking down at Ben's questions. Guess this would be easy enough. Sit down, read the question, wait for the answer. A monkey could have done it if he was allowed to use sign language.

I groaned. Yes, I had gone from illustrious journalist to entertainment monkey. Awesome.

But it was a job, I scolded myself. One that would allow me to make a paycheck. Keep my apartment, buy groceries, keep the lights on. And it was in my field—sort of. I just had to suck it up and do it the best I could and once this PTSD bullshit was over with I could move on with my life.

I sat down at my desk, feeling a renewed sense of purpose. I logged into IMDb, checking out each star's photo so I wouldn't be confused as to who was who when I got there. I read their bios and then switched over to Deadline.com to see what I could learn about the film itself, as Sarah had shown me how to do. Evidently there had been a major delay when a distribution deal fell through. I made a note to ask the director what that was about and how it had been resolved.

I also changed a few of Ben's questions around. Mostly the ones that were completely sexist. Like asking Jennifer Lawrence how she felt having to gain ten pounds for the role. Or if she was ever going to hook up with Bradley Cooper. As if that were any of our business.

Finally satisfied, I printed out the new questions and my research and headed out the door. I waved to Ben, but he only gave me a dirty look and turned back to his computer. I sighed. He was clearly unhappy with my presence here. I needed to ask Sarah what his deal was the next time I saw her.

The junket went about as well as could be expected. Jennifer Lawrence seemed really pleased when I brought up the new cell phone privacy act that was being introduced. From my research I had discovered it was a subject close to her heart, as a past hack had exposed some naked pictures of her online. She thanked me after the interview, telling me they were the only real questions she'd been asked all day.

I headed back to the station feeling pretty good about myself. Sure, it was a bullshit job. But I was rocking it like a boss, right? And that was all that mattered.

Ben met me at the door. He held out his hand. I stared down at it, puzzled. "The hard drive," he said. "With the video?"

"Oh," I said. "Chris is actually uploading it now. When it's ready I'll go ahead and log it and write my script."

"Oh. You don't have to do that. That's my job," Ben said. "You can just go . . . blow-dry your hair—apply mascara—whatever it is you pretty people do. I'll call you when the piece is ready to voice."

I frowned, feeling suddenly itchy. Was this how things were done around here? I didn't get to write my own pieces? I had spent all day working on this story. I wasn't about to just hand it over to Ben now.

"I don't wear mascara," I told him. "I do, however, write my own stories, thank you very much."

He stared at me. If looks could kill, I'd probably be a

messy puddle on the floor. I waited for him to argue, but he said nothing. Just mumbled something that sounded like, "Hashtag stupid Emmy Award–winning reporters" under his breath as he stormed back to his desk. I sighed. I seriously didn't need this animosity on top of everything else I was dealing with. I had real enemies, thank you very much.

It'll be fine, I told myself. Sarah will be back tomorrow. Everything will be back to normal.

Normal. I snorted. As if I had a prayer of anything ever being normal again.

twenty

SARAH

My cell phone pinged and I rolled over in bed, reaching to the nightstand to grab it. I was surprised to see it was a text from Troy.

Turn on your TV, it read.

I smiled, feeling my heart flutter a little in my chest. I'd felt pretty guilty about bailing on him at work today without letting him know why. But I was worried that if he learned what had happened—about the threat that had been left on my garden wall—he'd want to skip work, too, in some vain knight-in-shining-armor attempt to protect me. And I didn't need him risking his already precarious position at News 9 on my account.

Besides, I was safe and sound, having booked myself into my favorite beachside boutique hotel until my dad's people could check things out. Dad, of course, had wanted me to come to his house, which was, admittedly, protected like Fort Knox. But the thought of spending the day alone with his goons and his housekeepers was far too depressing and, besides, this place had room service. I'd spent half the day sleeping off the night before and the other half watching mindless reality TV—a pint of Ben and Jerry's in my hand.

Not a bad way to spend an afternoon in hiding, all in all.

Still, it was tough to relax completely; not with the threat still emblazoned in my mind in an ugly red scrawl.

I know where you live.

I shivered; what the hell was that supposed to mean? And who would have painted it above my wall? The same person who threw the rock in the theater? This unknown threat that my dad had mentioned? It had been easy to dismiss that whole thing while in the comfort of his office. Even the rock could have been considered a prank or a mistake. But this— this was undeniably a threat, directed at me.

But who would want to threaten me? For the last five years I'd done nothing to piss anyone off as far as I could tell. I'd gone to parties and nightclubs and reported on silly movies. I hadn't even had any bad breakups to speak of. Sure, someone could be using me to get to my father, but if so, why? And what did they want from him in return? If anything they were just giving him more ammunition on that Nazi-like crime bill he was trying to get introduced at the legislature.

I know where you live.

I shuddered. Suddenly the whole moving idea was sounding a lot more tempting . . .

Sighing, I clicked the remote and the TV burst to life. Navigating the menu button, I found and flipped to News 9, assuming that's what Troy was suggesting. They were just finishing up the sports segment—the station had recently hired an ex-NFL player who'd been injured on the job to do their sportscasting, causing Stephanie to suddenly gain a very avid interest in San Diego teams. I had to admit as I watched the broadcast, he was pretty hot. Maybe Stephanie would be able to get out of her slump sooner than she'd thought.

The sports section ended and anchors Beth White and Logan Learner came back on the screen. The graphic for our entertainment segment flashed behind them as they introduced another newcomer to the station, a man who needed even less introduction . . . Troy Young himself.

I watched, my pulse kicking up at my wrists as the camera cut to Troy. I suddenly realized this would be his first live shot since the disaster last week out in the field. Would he freak out again when the lights turned on? Did I doom him to failure by calling in sick?

I turned my thoughts back to the TV.

"Thanks Beth. Logan," Troy was saying, beaming with an easy smile. Then he turned to face the camera. "And good evening, San Diego. My partner in entertainment crime, Sarah Martin, is out sick today. So you guys are stuck with me."

He winked and I couldn't help but laugh. His natural charm radiated from the screen. Troy was so great at hard news, it was easy to forget he also had a natural, playful side when he wanted to—something our viewers were sure to eat up with a spoon. I watched carefully, looking for some kind of unease hidden at the edges—the kind of terror he'd exhibited out in the field. But he only looked confident. Relaxed. (Hot, too, but that was beside the point.) My shoulders dropped in relief. Maybe this was a good idea after all.

I watched as he introduced the film he was profiling before launching into the report itself. Which surprisingly turned out to be a smart, well-thought-out piece rather than the fluffy, vapid Q&A one would expect when it came to this sort of film. Troy's questions were thoughtful, political, and even a little risky, too. And some of the things he got the actors to say—well, I'd seen far more experienced entertainment journalists return with less. The network was so going to want to pick up this piece to air nationally and I bet it'd get a lot of views online as well. It was just . . . good. A rare unicorn in our line of work.

I sighed. Hot as hell, smart, brave, talented—and not a bad entertainment reporter to boot. Was there anything this guy couldn't do?

The segment ended, and the camera cut back to Troy, who finished the piece by giving the movie's release date information. Then, before they cut back to the anchors, he turned directly to the camera again. "Feel better, Sarah!" he said with a grin. And at that moment, I definitely did. In fact, I was beaming from ear to ear.

Okay, Sarah. Relax. It's not that big of a deal.

But it kind of was. Not the shout to me, of course—that was just silly. But the fact that he'd done it. He'd gone on live TV, and he hadn't freaked out. That might not seem like much to some people. But I knew for him it was everything. And a thrill of pride trickled up my back at the thought.

When the station cut to commercial, I rushed to pick up my phone. Great job! I texted. I couldn't have done it better myself.

Thanks! he texted back, adding a smiley emoticon. Not sure your little friend Ben agrees. But I'll take it.

Ben can go jerk off to a Tarantino film. I thought it was awesome. And who's to say I'm wrong?

I waited for a response, but my cell rang instead. "Did I shock you into text stasis?" I teased as I put the phone to my ear.

"I spent the last five years alongside the United States military. You'd have a hard time out-texting any of them, sweetheart."

I laughed. "I suppose that's true."

"I was actually just wondering how you were feeling. Did I keep you up too late last night?"

I felt a shiver trip down my back at the suggestive question. Even though all we'd done was sleep. "Something like that," I said with a nervous laugh. "Sorry to ditch you like that. Won't happen again."

"Not a problem. Actually it was good. Gave me a chance to get over the live shot thing." I could hear the satisfaction in his voice. "Not that I didn't miss you."

My stomach flip-flopped. "Yeah, yeah," I said, trying to keep my voice casual. "I bet you say that to all the reporters."

"Sure I do. I also bring them chicken noodle soup when they're sick. You in the mood? I could pick some up after my shift. Maybe come by in about an hour?"

I bit my lower lip. "Um, I'm actually not . . . home."

"What?" he cried in mock horror. "Do not even tell me you're not actually sick, either. Did you seriously throw me to the wolves because Neiman's was having a shoe sale?"

"I wish that were it." I sighed. "Look, I'm at the Pacific Terrace Hotel if you want to come by. But no chicken soup. I'm a vegetarian, remember?"

"Of course. My bad. How do you feel about tomato? GMO free, of course."

I smiled. "How about I order us both some room service and save you the trouble? They have amazing food here."

"Perfect. You know what I like."

Oh, I know, all right. All too well, unfortunately.

I hung up the phone, setting it down on the nightstand. Then I got up and walked over to the mirror and peered at my reflection. Crap. In my haste to invite him over I'd basically forgotten the fact that I looked like a person who had spent all day in bed. And not a glamorous, lounging-around-in-lingerie-like-a-Playboy-bunny type of day in bed, either. In fact, I was currently modeling a big, fat, attractive splotch of Ben and Jerry's Chunky Monkey across my ratty old T-shirt. To make matters worse, I had left my house so quickly I hadn't grabbed a change of clothes.

I picked up my phone again. This time to make an emergency call. Not to 911 of course. But to Stephanie, who was way better than an EMT when it came to a fashion crisis.

She answered the phone in one ring. "You okay?" she asked. "Did the guy do anything else? I've been sitting here worried about you all day!"

"I'm fine," I assured her. "Are you leaving work soon?"

"Already have. I'm almost home. DVR locked and loaded and ready to ogle Julian from the comfort of my couch," she added, referring to the quarterback turned sportscaster. "Did I tell you I passed him in the hall today and almost got him to smile at me?"

"Clearly you're a match made in heaven. Do you still have the keys to my apartment?"

"Duh. How else would I steal all your champagne?"

"Great. I'm going to text you a list of things I need." I paused, then added, "If you can tear yourself away from your football love, that is. Troy's coming over."

Stephanie squealed in excitement. "Oh, boy," she said. "Don't bother with the list. Leave it to me—you are in good hands."

I wasn't entirely sure what she meant by that, but beggars couldn't be choosers. I had a shower to take and very little time to dry my hair. "Thanks, girl," I said.

"Absolutely. You know I'm always here for you. I will totally hook you up."

I had to give Stephanie credit; she was quick. In fact, I had barely gotten out of the shower and donned my makeup when she was at my door, new wardrobe in hand. It wasn't until I started unwrapping the packages that I realized that perhaps I should have been clearer on where the night was going. Or not going, as the case might be.

"What?" she asked, holding up her hands in innocence as I plucked the feather duster from the bag. "I was a Girl Scout. Our motto was 'Be prepared.'"

"I hardly think this is what their fearless founders had in mind," I said, rolling my eyes and tossing the feather duster on the bed.

"Well then I'm sorry for them. They were clearly missing out."

I snorted, reaching into the bag again, this time finding my favorite green silk cocktail dress. A little fancy for room service in a beach hotel, but I had to admit I did like the way it clung to my barely existent curves and accentuated my (also barely existent) cleavage. Plus the color was great at bringing out my eyes.

"Okay, fine. You did good. Thank you," I said. "Though I would have been just fine with granny panties," I added, pulling out the thong she'd grabbed that was so thin it was practically made of paper.

"Troy has a thing for granny panties?"

"I have no idea. The point is he's not going to see them."

Stephanie groaned. "You're so going to waste this opportunity, aren't you?"

"Pretty much." I slipped the dress over my head and let it drape over me. Then I walked over to the mirror and frowned. "Do I look okay?" I asked.

"Dude, even I would bang you in that," she said. "And I'm about as hetero as you can get."

I sighed, frowning into the mirror. I'd forgotten how short this dress was. And how low cut. Was Troy going to think I was dressing sexy for him on purpose? That I wanted something beyond tomato soup? Maybe I should go down to the gift store and see if they had any—

My phone pinged. Crap. It was Troy. He was already in the lobby and was asking about the room number. Guess the dress would have to do. I shooed Stephanie to the door, stuffing the rest of the lotions and sex toys she'd unnecessarily procured under the bed.

"Go out the back," I told her. "I don't want him to see you and suspect something's up."

"Oh, I see. I'm just your dirty little secret now," she teased. Then she giggled. "Actually, that's kind of hot, right?"

"Get out!" I cried, laughing and shoving her to the door.

She opened it and stood in the doorway, her eyebrows waggling. "Have fun!" she said. "Screw his brains out for me."

Before I could reply she danced down the hall, still cackling manically. I rolled my eyes, shutting the door behind her, then walked over to the mirror again, staring at my reflection. At my red lips. My dark-smudged eyes. My skimpy dress.

What the hell was I doing? This was completely crazy! I started pulling the dress back over my head. I should change. Put my jeans back on. That ice cream stain wasn't that noticeable, was it? Then I could wipe the makeup off and—

There was a knock on the door. Nope. No time.

"Um, I'll be right there!" I cried, running to the bathroom to grab a towel and trying to smear the lipstick off my mouth. But it was no use. Stupid me had used a stain, not a gloss, and that shit wasn't coming off for hours.

"Sarah?" Troy's voice came from the other side. "Is everything okay?"

Everything was *not* okay. But I would have to make the best of it. I looked at myself in the mirror. "It's fine," I told myself. "He's a guy. He probably won't even notice you're overdressed . . . underdressed. Whatever." Sucking in a breath, I forced myself out of the bathroom and back to the front door.

Troy was standing on the other side, still in the suit he had been wearing on TV. It was a little unnerving; he'd never worn suits during his overseas gig, but maybe that was due to the temperature or something. I had to admit, he cleaned up nice. The suit coat emphsasized his broad shoulders and the red tie brought out his eyes. But what I really noticed was the sexy stubble on his cheeks. He clearly hadn't shaved since morning—or maybe the day before. And suddenly it was all I could do not to reach up and drag my fingers along his jawline.

Which was exactly what I needed *not* to be doing in this dress.

"Hey!" I said brightly. "You made it!"

But he wasn't looking at me. Well, not at my face anyway. Damn. He did notice the dress. Or more particularly my girls, unabashedly waving for attention from their poor hiding spots underneath the dress. At first I wondered if I should be offended that he was clearly sexualizing me, but then who could blame him when I'd basically put everything out for show?

Besides, it wasn't as if I had just been admiring his sparkling personality, either.

Troy shook his head, as if he suddenly realized what he was doing. He cleared his throat. "Uh, you look . . . nice," he stammered.

"Oh, this old thing?" I waved a hand over the dress. "It's just kind of comfortable."

He nodded stiffly, looking decidedly uncomfortable, but thankfully stepped into the room all the same. I'd done my best to clean it up, gotten rid of all the room service remnants from earlier, and had even attempted a rush job of making the bed. You know, the bed where nothing would be happening tonight.

I wrung my hands together, not sure what to say. "Um, so the room service. They said they're pretty backed up. Probably won't be here for about an hour."

Troy nodded absently, crossing the room. He shrugged off his suit jacket and loosened his tie then pulled open the balcony door and stepped outside. I watched as he leaned against the railing and took a deep breath of salt air as he gazed out at the sea.

I walked out to join him. "It's a nice view, right?"

He turned to me. "Yes." He said after a pause. "It's . . . beautiful."

His voice was husky. Low. And I suddenly got a distinct impression he wasn't talking about the ocean. I drew in a shaky breath, electricity seeming to spark in the air around us. What was with this guy? It'd been five years. Why did just being around him make me want to melt into a puddle on the floor?

Maybe Stephanie was right. Maybe I did need to just get Troy out of my system. Surely he couldn't be as great as I had built up in my mind, right?

I realized he was still staring at me. At my eyes this time, but so hard that it was kind of obvious he was purposely trying to avoid looking at my breasts.

Because he wanted me. As much . . . if not more . . . than I wanted him.

And in the end, what was really in our way? You know, besides a lifetime of regret and disappointment, that was. But, hey, I'd never let that stop me before. Why start now? I wanted him. He wanted me. We were both single. Hell, it wasn't as if we'd even be adding a notch to our belts since we'd done this before.

Sex with the ex. It was totally a thing, right? Totally a no-big-deal thing.

"Sarah . . ." he started.

But I didn't let him finish. Instead, I took his face in my hands, allowing my fingers to greedily drag across that jaw-line I'd craved, which felt as good as I'd imagined. Then I pulled him to me and I kissed him. With everything that I had.

And thank the stars above . . . Troy Young kissed me back.

twenty-one

TROY

Let's just get one thing straight. I really did mean this to be about chicken noodle soup. Or tomato soup. Whatever. A friendly gesture between two friends. I had no idea what I was walking into when I walked through her hotel room door. But once I saw her in that dress. Oh my God. I knew the night was going in a different direction. And suddenly I wasn't hungry anymore. At least not for soup.

You gotta understand. During all those months I'd spent in that dark hole, that hell on earth, never knowing if I was going to live or die, I'd lie there for endless hours, trying to block out the pain, trying to remember something sweet—like her lips moving over mine. The feel of her mouth against my skin.

But let me tell you, those memories, those fantasies paled in comparison to the reality that was pressing hungrily against me now. Tasting like mints and sunshine and cinnamon and roses all wrapped into one. And suddenly I was a junkie, desperate for more. Nothing else mattered, at that moment, but her mouth against my mouth. My body against hers.

I pushed her back into the hotel room, kicking the balcony door shut behind me. For what I planned to do to her now, I didn't want an audience. Just her and me, against the wall, so I could better deepen my kiss. Better run my hands down her back, cupping that perfect ass of hers. She moaned against my mouth, the soft mewing sound making me instantly rock hard. I ground my knee between her legs and she jerked against me. Somehow my hands found the hem of her dress and I bunched it up around her waist, delighted when I reached underneath and found nothing but a very flimsy thong.

I smiled against her mouth. "Since when do you wear thongs?"

"I don't know. Um, sometimes?"

"Did you wear this one for me?"

Her face turned bright red.

I chuckled, feeling way too pleased for my own good as I dropped to my knees in front of her. Pushed the dress up again and buried my head between her thighs, pulling the thong aside with my teeth. She was clean-shaven under that thong, smooth as silk. Had she been like that back in the day? I couldn't remember, but it didn't matter. Nothing mattered at this moment, in fact, save my desire to taste her down there, too. To see if she tasted as sweet as I remembered. My erection strained against my pants, but I ignored it as best I could. Right now all I wanted to do was make her feel as good as possible. There'd be time for me later.

I heard her gasp as my mouth brushed against her, her hands reaching into my hair, digging into my scalp. I smiled, allowing my tongue to slip between her folds while I grabbed her bottom with both hands, drawing her closer to me. It didn't take more than a moment before she shuddered against me, her whole body practically convulsing as she rocked against my mouth, riding the wave to shore.

When I rose to my feet again, her face shone with sweat. Her mascara had run, blackening her eyes, and her lipstick was smeared. She looked like a fallen angel and it sent another jolt straight to my groin. I needed to get her on the bed pronto.

"This is probably a very bad idea," she whispered, her voice husky and hoarse.

"It probably is."

"Also . . ." Her face flushed. "Pretty cliché."

I gave her a solemn look. "Definitely cliché."

She looked at me. I raised an eyebrow. "Do you want me to stop?" I asked, reaching out and tracing her hipbone with my hand. She closed her eyes and sucked in a shivering breath. Then she opened them again, zeroing in on me.

"Hell. No."

That was all I needed to hear. I scooped her up in my arms and tossed her down on the bed. *Hell, no*, indeed. That was good enough for me.

twenty-two

SARAH

Okay, Sarah. This is it. You've gone there and now you'd better make good. You get a one-time pass. Use it for all its worth. Get him out of your system once and for all.

A thousand thoughts whirled through my brain as Troy laid me down on the bed. But they all fled pretty quickly once he settled above me, straddling my thighs, while unbuttoning his shirt and letting it fall from his broad shoulders, revealing his smooth, muscled chest. The same chest I'd ogled while he was asleep, now granting me an all-access pass to not only look, but to feel. I reached up, dragging my palms down it now, rejoicing in the soft skin inlaid over hard steel.

God, he was beautiful. Even with the ugly scar running down the side of his arm. He was somehow still perfection. I felt a spike of adrenaline shoot through me as my eyes roved his body, unapologetically taking him in. My hands stopped at his hips, anchoring him on top of me. As if I were somehow afraid he would just up and disappear if I were to suddenly let go. Something flickered in his jaw and it caused me to smile. I reached up, running my hand along that jaw-line, loving the feeling of rough stubble scraping against sensitive skin. He leaned into my hand, until his mouth found my fingers. He took one into his mouth and sucked on it, sending shivers all the way to my toes.

He might not have been mine. But he was here. He wanted this, too. And that was good enough for now.

Feeling brave, I reached down with my other hand, tracing the trail of dark hair down past the waistband of his pants, until I was cupping his obvious erection. He gave a small groan, his whole body tightening in response, his teeth biting down on my finger. I smiled lazily, liking the cause and effect, and continued caressing him. Finding the zipper and slowly releasing him into my hand.

God, he was magnificent. I had had no idea when we were first together—I was so innocent, I didn't know good from bad. Large from small. But he was perfect. I reached out, wrapping one hand around him, the other hooking at his waist and pulling him toward me.

At first he came willingly. Then he paused. His face flushed.

"Wait," he said. "I don't have . . ."

"Oh. Right." I smiled and held out a hand. "Hang on."

Rolling off the bed, I reached underneath to the bag Stephanie had left behind. Surely with all the toys she had packed she would have also included some protection as well. The girl was crazy, but also very into being safe. Sure enough, I found a stupidly large bag of condoms and grabbed one before returning to Troy, who had shucked off his pants and boxers while waiting. The relief on his face as his eyes fell on the shiny little package almost made me laugh. He grabbed it from me, tore the wrapper with his teeth and slid it on.

And then, suddenly, there was nothing in our way.

Our mouths came together first, our tongues tangling in a wild, familiar dance. My hands wrapped around his lower back as he propped me up against the pillows. Reaching down, he took his length in his hand, guiding it to my core. At this point, I was soaking wet and so damn ready. For a moment, he hovered at the entrance, then he plunged inside of me and I got this crazy weird sensation of finally being home.

"Sarah," he murmured. "Oh, Sarah."

For a moment neither of us moved. We just lay there absorbing the long-lost feeling of coming together—of two becoming one. It was like a spell had been cast over the both of us and all we needed in the world—at that second—was that feeling of being together. It was almost too much. And I almost told him to stop as the tears began to prick at my eyes. This was supposed to just be about sex, after all. A one-time thing to get him out of my system for good.

So how come it was feeling like so much more?

"Sarah," he said again. And this time it almost sounded like a prayer.

"Fuck me," I commanded. Trying desperately to regain control. To lose the unbearable sweetness and find the fire instead. "As if I'm a stranger."

For a moment he looked at me with uncertainty. Then something feral flashed in his eyes. He rose above me, pulling himself slowly out, then thrust down on me again. Piercing me to the core.

His hand found my breast, roughly squeezing the nipple until it almost hurt. His mouth bit at my jaw, my neck. I arched my back, wrapping my legs around him and locking my ankles at his lower back. He groaned and thrust deeper and harder, as if he was chasing something or maybe running away. As the sensations washed over me like a tidal wave, I dug my nails into his back. My teeth into his shoulder.

"You like that?" he growled in a rough voice, nipping at my ear.

"Oh, yeah," I managed to eke out. "Harder."

He was happy to oblige. His thrusts becoming so intense, so hard and fierce they almost hurt, but at the same time felt ridiculously good. My skin was slick with sweat. My heart beating a thousand beats a minute. For a moment I was pretty sure I saw actual stars. And then I was falling over the cliff. The orgasm tearing through me like a tornado, completely without remorse. Without apology.

A moment later he found his own release. Shuddering against me, a guttural groan escaping his lips before he collapsed on top of me, completely spent.

We lay like that for a moment. Then he rolled over, staring up at the ceiling. I felt a weird emptiness wash over me as I lost the connection between us. I scolded myself for feeling it. This was just supposed to be sex, I reminded myself. Just good sex. Nothing more.

A heaviness seemed to settle on my chest and I scowled, trying to will it away. *Do not go all girly girl on me now, Sarah. You've hooked up with plenty of people in the past and it meant nothing at all—this is exactly the same thing. It's not good or bad or anything. It just is what it has to be. The last thing you need is to fall for Troy again.*

"You okay?" Troy asked, rolling over to face me. He propped himself up on his elbow and looked down at me with concern in his deep blue eyes. Anger rose inside of me. Completely unjustified stupid anger.

"I'm fine," I said. But when he reached out to touch me,

I leapt out of the bed before he was able to make contact, not able to bear the idea of cuddling after what had just taken place. "Just, uh, gotta go shower. I'll see you in a minute."

I practically ran to the bathroom, a cowardly retreat. I could feel his eyes on me, questioning, but I shut the door on them and locked it. Then I walked over to the shower and turned it on. Made it really hot and steamy before stepping inside. Letting the water wash over me, almost burning me with its heat. Scrubbing every inch of my body, every inch of my skin.

But try as I might, I couldn't wash away the memory of what I'd just done. Had I just made a horrible, horrible mistake? By trying to get this whole thing over with, had I only succeeded in starting it up—all over again?

twenty-three

TROY

I knew girls liked to take their time in the shower. But Sarah was taking so long I started to worry something was wrong. The room service had arrived since she'd been in there and it was starting to get cold. I was also getting famished and wondered if it would be rude to start eating without her.

Finally, after what seemed like an eternity, she emerged from the bathroom, clad in a hotel bathrobe, her skin rosy-red and her cheeks flushed. Her wet blond hair dripped onto her shoulders and droplets settled in the valley between her breasts. Suddenly I was hungry for something else entirely, even though I knew I should have already had my fill.

God that had been amazing. Exactly what I needed. And something I thought, while trapped in that hole, that I'd never experience again. Especially not with Sarah of all people. I still could barely believe she'd been willing to go through with it.

Though now, judging from the way her eyes were darting

around the room, looking at everything except me, I began to worry that she was already regretting the decision.

I drew in a breath, trying to look casual. "Hey!" I said brightly. "The food's here."

She glanced at the trays. At first I thought she was going to say something. But then she forced a smile to her face. "Great! I'm starving."

I dropped my shoulders in relief. Okay. Back to safe territory. We could both act like cowards and pretend nothing had happened. Fine by me.

We dug into our food. I was ravenous from our romp in the sack, never mind the full day of work I'd just put in. My stamina had unfortunately shrunk big-time since I was back, and I was still having a hard time making it through an entire day. But God bless my little vegetarian ex-girlfriend— she had ordered me a burger. A big, huge, juicy steak burger with extra bacon and cheese—just the way I liked it. I wolfed it down, trying and failing to be mannerly about it. Thankfully, Sarah didn't seem to notice. She was too busy chowing down on her own vegetable panini and french fries.

"So," I said, after swallowing a bite of food. "You never did tell me why you decided to play hooky. Clearly you don't seem on your death bed."

She gave a small snort, then nodded slowly. I waited for her to reply, but at first she said nothing. I was almost convinced she wasn't going to speak at all when at last she opened her mouth.

"After you left my place, I found . . . a new threat," she said, a shadow crossing over her face. I listened as she explained Stephanie finding the red spray-painted warning on her garden wall. When she had finished I realized my hands had clenched into fists.

I abandoned my dinner, rising to my feet. I paced the

small room, rubbing the back of my neck with my hand. "What the hell," I muttered, not sure who I was angrier with. The asshole who'd scared her—or myself for not having stayed until she'd woken to make sure she was safe. I'd been so worried about getting to work on time and making a good impression. But if I had known she was in actual danger . . .

"What the hell, indeed," she said with a sad sigh. The large fluffy robe she was wearing now, along with her freshly scrubbed face, made her look younger and smaller than she had been before, when she was all dressed up. Like a little lost kid in her mother's clothes. My heart squeezed in empathy.

"My dad's looking into it, of course," she added. "Hell, he was almost gleeful about the whole thing. Supports the crime bill he's trying to get passed. You know him. Can't miss out on an opportunity."

"But who would want to hurt you?" I demanded. "I mean, do you have any enemies?" It seemed crazy that anyone might want to hurt her. She was so sweet. So innocent.

She shook her head. "Not since I used to hang out with you," she joked bitterly. "Trust me, after the whole Water World thing blew up in our faces I've seen the health benefits of laying low."

I winced as the big-ass elephant came trampling back into the room again. Of course it had always been there, lurking in the corner. But up until now we'd both done a bang-up job of not looking it in the eye.

"We haven't talked about Water World since I've been back, have we?" I said in a low voice. From across the room I could see her shoulders stiffen.

"There's no need," she replied.

"I don't mind," I added. "I mean, if you wanted to talk about it. If you wanted me to apologize again."

"No." She shook her head, her wet blond hair casting droplets of water as it swung from side to side. "It's in the past. It doesn't matter."

But it did matter. I could see that clearly on her face. It would always matter. She would never completely be able to forgive me for what I had done. To trust me again. And anything that happened between us now would always be poisoned by the past.

Something I totally deserved.

I still remembered the look on her face when it all came out in the end—Ryan's master plan revealed. My betrayal up on display for all to see. The hurt in her eyes had nearly killed me as I watched her learn the truth about our relationship. That she'd been used. Lied to. Deceived. By the group she'd worked so hard for—by the man she'd given her heart to.

I remembered wanting so badly to get her alone—to tell her that I would have asked her out anyway. That our relationship was not a lie, even if it had started out that way, part of Ryan's nefarious scheme. That even I didn't understand the true reasons behind what I'd done. That my heart had always been in the right place.

But it was too late at that point. Everything had already been poisoned. Everything had already been ruined. And the last thing her father would allow was for her to be alone with me.

"Sarah," I said now, my heart rushing with emotion. The apologies up against my mouth, ready to burst like an old dam.

But she was already on her feet, grabbing her clothes, most of her dinner uneaten. "I need to go actually," she said. "You're welcome to stay here as long as you like. The room's paid for until tomorrow." She stepped into the bathroom to change. Because of course now she didn't want me to see her naked.

"Where are you going?" I called through the door.

"Um, I need to grab a few things at home. And then I think I'll head to my dad's for the night."

"You don't have to do that. If you want, I can go." I rose to my feet. "I didn't mean to make you feel—"

She stepped out of the bathroom, waving me off. She wore a T-shirt now, with some kind of brown stain on the front, paired with old beaten-up jeans. I swallowed hard: In a weird way she looked even more alluring now than she had in that sexy dress.

Sarah. My Sarah.

No. Not my Sarah. I'd lost that right forever.

"It's fine," she said, her voice quavering. "You didn't do anything wrong. It's just . . . I just . . ." She shook her head. "It's fine."

I sighed, my shoulders slumping. This was exactly why I shouldn't have been there in the first place. I was taking advantage of her all over again. Demanding things from her that she wasn't ready to give. I'd been so desperate, so hungry, so pathetically needy, I hadn't stopped to think that maybe this was only going to end up hurting her more than I already had.

"Text me when you get to your dad's, okay?" I said, trying to keep the desperation out of my voice. "Just to let me know you're okay?"

"I'll be okay," she replied automatically.

"I know. I know . . . but . . . just text anyway, okay?"

She sighed. "I'll see you at work tomorrow," she said. And, with that, she walked out the door.

twenty-four

SARAH

You're back? Feeling any better?" Ben met me at the entrance of the entertainment office as I stepped into the newsroom the next day. I had come into work early, hoping to get a little catch-up work done alone before everyone came in, but evidently I was not early enough. I swore the guy slept here at night—there was never a time when he wasn't here, unless he was on assignment.

"Much better," I replied automatically, heading to my desk. Which wasn't exactly true, but the last thing I needed was Ben up in my business. He already had the tendency to get too personal as it was. No need to give him any more ammunition when it came to my private life.

In truth, I wasn't doing so well. Not after the disaster that was yesterday. For which I could only blame myself, of course. I mean, what had I been thinking? How had I thought jumping into bed with my ex-boyfriend could possibly be a good idea? Especially an ex-boyfriend I had to work with on a daily basis. We were taping our first He Said, She Said segment this week, too, so it wouldn't be like I could just avoid him, either.

It could have worked out. If only he could have managed to keep things physical between us. Chalked it up to good sex and moved on. But no, he had to get that look in his eye. He had to go and try to apologize for the past. Didn't he know how much I didn't want to remember what he had done? That I wanted to just move forward and forget it had ever happened?

But no. He couldn't forget. And evidently he couldn't move forward until I had forgiven him. Which was never going to happen. Which meant it was best if we stayed out of each other's way from this point onward.

I realized Ben had followed me to my desk. Awesome.

"I gotta say, that new guy they hired? He isn't very qualified," he was whining, while shuffling from foot to foot. "He didn't even know who J. Law was."

I sighed. "He's been overseas for a while," I reminded him.

"Um, last I checked even third-world countries have WiFi. And I'm pretty sure *The Hunger Games* was a worldwide thing."

"Yeah, well, maybe he let his *Us Weekly* subscription expire while he was occupied reporting on the refugee crisis." I couldn't believe I was having to defend Troy to Ben while at the same time being pissed off at him myself.

"I got no problem with that. What I do have a problem with is him having this job. We all know Richard gave it to him out of pity. But we're a major newsroom here—in Southern California, of all places, just a stone's throw from Hollywood. The entertainment beat is the reason many of our viewers tune in. And they just gave the head job to someone who doesn't know the difference between Chris Pine and Chris Pratt."

I bit my lower lip. I so did not have time for this today. "I know, I know," I told Ben. "Just . . . try to cut him some slack, okay? Or better yet, maybe give him a hand? I mean, you weren't exactly born knowing all the Chrises in Hollywood, either, right? Why don't you help him out? Give him a few of your favorite blogs to read. Maybe a few good Buzzfeed articles. It's not like it's rocket science. He can catch up."

"Why bother? He's just going to ditch us as soon as he gets a better offer."

I cringed, Ben unknowingly hitting way too close for comfort. Then I sighed. "Well, then, maybe you can apply for his job and stop bugging me."

Ben snorted. "Yeah, right. Only if I suddenly develop a cleft chin or a six-pack of abs overnight, right?"

He looked really upset now and I felt sympathy wash over me, despite my best efforts. "Look, Ben," I said. "If you ever want to . . . I don't know . . . I could look at your résumé tape—give you some pointers? Or maybe take you shopping or something? I can't help you get a six-pack. But maybe we could make you better look the part? I mean, believe me, I know that shouldn't matter, but . . ."

He stared at me, surprised. "You'd do that for me?" he asked. "You'd really take me shopping?"

"Yes. I would," I said. "After all, I may not know as much about movies as you do, but shopping? That's pretty much my superpower."

He laughed at this. "Well, thank you," he said. "I appreciate that actually."

"You just let me know when you're ready and we'll make the time."

"Thank you. Now if you'll excuse me, I've got some calls to make."

I watched him go. His steps already looking lighter, his

expression almost happy. I sighed. Poor guy. It had to be rough on him. If there was any way I could make this whole thing easier—or give him a chance—well, I'd do it. Problem was, I didn't know if it would be enough. If my efforts could make anything better for him in the end.

Sometimes I hated working in TV news.

And . . . speaking of things not getting better, Troy picked that moment to saunter into the office. He stopped at the entrance, his eyes locking on me.

"You didn't text me," he said quietly. Not exactly accusingly. More like I'd disappointed him. Which was kind of worse.

I felt my face heat. "I told you I'd be fine. I can take care of myself."

"I never said you couldn't."

I twitched at the thread of sadness winding through his voice, my heart betraying me with a low ache. I opened my mouth to say something—though I wasn't sure what I was going to say. But he had already crossed the room to his desk. Sat down at his computer and stuffed the earbuds in his ears. Evidently the time for conversation was over.

Giving up, I turned back to my own computer, pulling up my notes for this afternoon's review. No matter what was going on with Troy and me, we couldn't let it affect our work. We had to stay professional, no matter what.

Professional. I snorted a little. If only I had had this brainstorm yesterday. But when it came to Troy my brain only stormed with fire and passion. Leaving very little room, I realized, for common sense.

I don't know. I guess I'm just not a fan of heroines who are too stupid to live," Troy declared two days later, in the studio, as the cameras rolled on our first segment together.

"I mean, don't go into the basement, girl!" He shook his head. "This is also why I can't stand horror movies."

"Hold on a second," I interjected. "Yes, we've all seen the lazy scriptwriting of the Too Stupid to Live Girl," I argued. "But a girl taking a risk—that's not stupid. That's brave. I mean, what did you want her to do? Sit around, painting her nails, while the serial killer closes in on her and her friends?"

"If it kept her out of the path of murder and mayhem? Yes. That seems a very logical option, actually."

I rolled my eyes. "Okay, fine. Let's say our brave but stupid heroine were a guy instead. Do you want him to hide out in the house while the killer stalks his friends? Or would that make him a total wimp?"

Troy opened his mouth to speak, but I cut him off, on a roll now. "Look, everyone expects the guy to be the big hero. To take the risk, to put his life in danger. But when the girl does it? She's suddenly seen as stupid for taking on unnecessary risks. Or let's say she does it and succeeds by using her God-given talents—like that awesome move in this movie where she strikes him in the throat with her forearm? Well, then she's just a Mary Sue, right? All powerful and unrealistic?

"No one ever questions when Jason Bourne jumps out of an airplane. But when Rey in Star Wars flies a spaceship and kicks some bad guy butt—something she's supposedly grown up doing—suddenly the fan boys flip out."

"Hey. No one's knocking Rey here," Troy protested. "I know Rey. I like Rey. This girl? She is no Rey. And I stand by my original statement. She is too stupid to live. And that whole forearm-to-the-throat thing? That would never work in real life."

My eyes sparkled in challenge. "Want to bet?" I rose to

my feet. Troy looked at me, his eyes telling me I was crazy, but I just beckoned him forward. "Come on," I said. "Go ahead and grab me from behind."

Troy held up his hands. "Okay," he said. "But don't say I didn't warn you."

He rose to his feet, stalking over to me. My heart thumped wildly in my chest as he reached me, putting out his arms, grabbing me and pulling me backward until I was flush against him. I could feel his heart beating against my back, just as fast as mine probably was, and my whole body vibrated with his nearness.

"Sorry, babe. Don't think you're going to get out of this one," he whispered in my ear. His breath sent a tingle down to my toes, but I forced myself to ignore it.

Instead, I paused, taking a moment to mug for the camera. I had to make this good. Then, without warning, I slammed my foot down on Troy's as hard I could.

He cried out in shock, my surprise move making him lose his grip just a bit. Just enough for me to slam my arm backward, straight at his throat, as the girl in the film had done.

As he staggered backward, I pivoted 180 degrees until I was facing him again. Then I lifted my knee to his groin like a sword to the throat. Not making contact—I didn't actually want to hurt him—but proving I totally could.

He laughed, holding up his hands in surrender. "Okay, okay!" he cried. "You win! You Mary Sued the crap of me, okay? Mercy!"

I laughed, turning back to the cameras, giving them a salute. "To conclude, I give this film an A plus. For an awesome, kick-butt heroine who doesn't lose her head in a crisis."

"And I'm giving it a C minus," Troy added, rubbing his

foot as he sat back down onto his seat. "I may be able to get my money back from the theater, but those brain cells are gone for good." He paused, then added, "Along with the feeling in my left big toe, for that matter."

"And . . . cut!" the floor director said, clapping his hands together. A moment later the camera lights flicked off and the house lights came back on. I grinned from ear to ear, the adrenaline from the encounter still spiking through me. Troy rolled his eyes, but then laughed.

"Remind me never to piss you off," he said.

"So, what did you think?" I asked, turning to Mrs. Anderson. The station's owner had come down to watch the first taping. I knew she was a bit of a micromanager; no wonder she and my dad got along so well.

But I needn't have worried this time. She clapped her hands together, beaming from ear to ear. "That was brilliant!" she exclaimed. "I loved it. I knew I picked the right people for this franchise. You guys have the perfect chemistry to play off one another. And that fight scene? That was inspired!"

I felt my face heat at this commendation. Even more so once I felt Troy's eyes on me. Chemistry. That was one way to put it.

"Seriously, this is so great," Mrs. Anderson continued. "I don't want to change a thing." Her eyes locked on Troy. "You may be a good foreign correspondent," she told him, "but you make an excellent movie reviewer, too."

I could see Troy's jaw twitch at this. But thank you was all he said. Mrs. Anderson gave him another big smile and then followed the crew out of the studio.

"I expect more of this in the coming weeks!" she called out to us as she left. "This was great stuff."

The door closed behind her and suddenly Troy and I

found ourselves alone. I glanced over to him. He looked as
if he'd aged ten years in one minute.

"You okay?" I asked.

"I'm fine."

"You don't look fine."

"Sorry to disappoint."

I sighed. "You want to talk about it?"

"To you?"

I scrubbed my face with my hands. "Okay. I deserve
that."

"No." He shook his head, rising from his seat and taking
off his wireless label mic. "You don't. I'm sorry. Good segment. I'll catch you tomorrow."

"Troy . . ." My heart ached at the pain I could see in his
face—pain he was trying desperately to hide. I released a
long breath. "Look, I'm sorry about Monday, okay? I
shouldn't have left like I did. I was just . . . overwhelmed by
everything. You know. I went from not having seen you for
five years to . . ." I trailed off. "Well, you know."

He stiffened. "I'm sorry about that, too. That should never
have happened. I took advantage of you. And I'm sorry."

My lip curled. I couldn't help it. "I think I was the one
who took advantage of you," I said.

He shot me a surprised look.

"Look," I tried again. "There's no denying there are a lot
of unresolved feelings between the two of us. And not just
of the physical nature, either," I added quickly. "But Troy, I
do care about you. And I can see you're suffering."

He frowned. "I'm not suffering," he spit out, as if expel-
ling poison. "Suffering is being stuck in a dark hole, not
knowing if you're going to live or die. Suffering is having
your leg dislocated and not getting it set right. This"—he

waved his arm around the studio—"this is nothing," he barked out. "Absolutely nothing."

"No," I said quietly. "It's not nothing. This is your life now. And you have every right to have these feelings about it. Not everything from this point forward has to be weighed against your abduction." I gave him a small smile. "Little things are still allowed to suck."

He snorted, shaking his head as he paced the small stage. Then he turned to me. "Is this all I have left?" he asked suddenly. "Is this all I have to look forward to? This mindless bullshit?" He dropped to a sitting position, rubbing the back of his neck with his hand. "No offense," he muttered.

"None taken." I walked over to him, sitting down next to him, careful not to touch him. "Look, Troy," I said. "I know you don't want to be here. Doing this. This is never going to be your dream job—I get it. I really do. But I also get that this is just temporary. Just until you get back on your feet. You know Richard will put you back out into the field anytime. And the network would be overjoyed to have you back when you're ready. You can go overseas and continue where you left off."

He was silent for a moment. "What if I'm never ready?"

"Then you'll find something else. And whatever it is, I'm sure you'll be great at it. You told me you had been thinking of coming home anyway. Maybe in a really crazy way, this was a good thing. Not your abduction, of course. But the excuse to be back home. The chance to figure out what you really want to be when you grow up." I said the last part in a teasing voice and was rewarded by a small smile ghosting his lips.

"Have dinner with me," he said suddenly.

"What?" My heart pounded in my chest.

"Just dinner. At my place tomorrow night. I'll cook for you."

I bit my lower lip. "I don't know . . ." I said. "That might not be a good idea."

I wanted to, of course. In fact, every fiber in my body was screaming for me to say yes. But at the same time, I held back. Not wanting to make yet another mistake when it came to Troy. To dig myself even deeper into the hole I'd dug. After all, it was one thing to find him physically attractive and want to jump his bones. But this tenderness I was feeling when I looked at him now—when I saw how lost he looked. That was truly dangerous ground.

"Come on, Sarah," he begged, clearly not willing to take no for an answer. Typical Troy. "It's just dinner. No strings attached. I won't make a move on you. I won't bring up the past. We'll just eat." He paused, then added, "You said we could be friends. And, well, the way I'm feeling right now . . . I could use a friend."

I could hear the cost in his voice as he said the words. How hard it was to move them past his lips. He was asking for help. Even though it was the hardest thing for him to do. Especially asking it of me.

I found myself nodding slowly. What else could I do? What else could I say? He'd been through so much. And he was asking for so little now. Surely I could put my own feelings aside for one night to keep him company. To be his friend.

"Sure," I said. "You can cook for me. But I insist on doing the dishes after."

twenty-five

TROY

When I had volunteered to cook for Sarah, I hadn't really considered the fact that most of my go-to recipes were basically of the barbequed meat variety, which weren't going to work for my little vegetarian friend. In a panic, I'd called Griffin, who told me girls dug a man who could make a spaghetti sauce from scratch. Which seemed odd to me, since the stuff came premade in a jar, but what the hell. I found a recipe online, hit the store on the way home, and started sauce making. I did cheat and buy the pasta in a box. Hopefully that wouldn't take away from the magic.

I frowned, dipping my finger into the sauce now as it simmered on the stove. Did it taste all right? Did it need more salt?

Was this a totally crazy idea?

I glanced at the clock on the wall. Where was Sarah? Should I call her and make sure everything was okay? After work she'd gone back to her place to shower and grab some new clothes—which I'd tried and failed to talk her out of. After all, we still didn't know who'd been making threats against her. But we did know whomever it was knew where she lived. What if he was there, lying in wait? What if he was ready to do more than make idle threats this time? She promised me she'd call Stephanie and have her meet her over there—safety in numbers and all that. But what could two girls do against a full-grown male?

Then my mind flashed back to her little demonstration in the studio yesterday. Okay fine. Maybe she could hold her own.

I'd almost made the suggestion that she just shower here—but then decided she might take it the wrong way. After all, I had promised her that tonight would be platonic. Just two people, keeping each other company. And I was determined to stick to that promise if it killed me.

Which it very possibly would. Hell, she wasn't even here yet and I was boiling hotter than the pasta sauce.

As I stirred, my mind decided to stir its own memory sauce, treating me to a vivid flashback of a shower scene from the past. Sarah and I had just finished making love for the first time—a little awkwardly: We were just dumb kids after all and barely had any idea what we were doing. She had risen from the bed, all naked and sweaty and beautiful and I had tried (and failed) to be a decent guy who didn't stare at her ass.

I remembered her walking to the bathroom door. (Thank God I had a single dorm room with a private bath.) She'd turned around, batting her pretty eyes at me, a shy smile on her face as she asked if I'd like to join her in the shower. I was lucky I didn't break my neck in my haste to get out of bed. As it was I got completely tripped up in my blankets and banged my knee against the floorboards, scoring a killer souvenir bruise that would end up lasting for weeks. (I was seriously so cool back then!)

But God bless Sarah, she didn't seem to mind my dorky fall. In fact, if anything she looked a little relieved. And when I finally managed to limp myself over to the bathroom, she dropped down and kissed my knee, as if I were a child with a boo-boo that she wanted to make feel better. And then, after I followed her into the shower, she proceeded to make the rest of me feel better as well.

I glanced at the clock again. Where was she? She should be here by now. She said eight, right? It was half past eight— she was a half hour late. My heart stuttered in my chest. Oh God, what if something had happened to her? Maybe I needed to call her. If she didn't answer I could call 911. Send them over to her house. Or maybe I should go myself. Of course I needed to call first—where was my phone? Had I left it in the bedroom? What if she had already tried to call? I should check the messages.

I ran to the bedroom, my heart in my throat as I searched for my phone. But try as I might I couldn't find it. Not in the bedroom, not in the bathroom. The living room. My pulse kicked up in alarm. The kitchen—wait, was that smoke coming from the kitchen?

Oh crap, the sauce must be burning.

I ran to the kitchen. The entire room was filled with smoke. I blinked my eyes, trying to make my way to the stove. It was then that I realized I must have left the recipe too close to the flame—and the paper had caught fire, then spread to a newspaper I had laid on the counter. Flames danced on the granite now, greedily licking the cabinets above while smoke plumed, thick and black.

Shit. Shit, shit, shit!

Reaching out, I tried to knock the paper off the counter

onto the floor to better stamp out the flame. But my swing was too wide and I yelped as I accidentally brushed my hand against the hot pan. Icy pain shot up my arm like a bullet and I staggered backward clutching my palm.

My mind flashed back again. Not to Sarah this time. Not to a simple knee bruise, easily kissed away. But to one of the "interviews" I'd been subjected to when I'd first been captured.

What is your government's plan for Aleppo?

I'm just a journalist! I don't know!

You lie. There are consequences for lying.

The consequences—the hot poker dragging down my arm. The scorching heat, searing into my skin, leaving a blackened scar behind. The phantom pain echoed through me now, mirroring my current agony. I tried to remember what I told them after that—how many lies spilled from my lips, just to get them to stop. But all I remembered for sure was how I cried like a baby back in my cell, clutching my charred, throbbing arm. Helpless and alone.

Just like now.

A sudden wailing sound rang through my ears, mimicking the air raids we'd heard so often back then. I dropped to the floor, covering my head with my hands, my heart slamming against my ribcage as my mind fought and failed to regain control over my senses. My sight. My breathing. Squeezing my eyes shut, I prayed it would stop. That this would all somehow go away. Somehow. Someway.

Hands grabbing me. Nails digging into my flesh. Screeching sounds assaulting my ears.

You are going to die. You'd better get right with your God. The best you can hope for is that your death will come quick.

"Troy!"

Rough hands grabbed me now, jerking me away from the

flames. Startled, I looked up, my vision so blurry from smoke I couldn't see what was happening, who was here—and I fought wildly against them, struggling to keep control. It wasn't until she repeated my name, louder and more insistently this time—that I realized it wasn't my captors, come to do me harm.

It was only Sarah. My Sarah.

I watched, helplessly, as she grabbed a blanket off the couch, running back to the kitchen to smother the flames. Once they were out, she turned her attention to the stove, grabbing the pan and throwing it in the sink. Steam shot through the air as she raced over to my apartment's balcony door, flinging it open wide. Then she turned on the ceiling fans in each room. A moment later the wailing, which I now realized had simply been my smoke alarm, faded into obscurity. The air began to clear. Slowly, everything went back to normal.

Except me, that was. I remained a quivering mess in the corner. My breath coming in short gasps. My mind still racing. Oh God. If she hadn't come when she had I could have burned down the apartment. I could have inhaled too much smoke. I could have—

"Troy!" Sarah looked down at me, her eyes filled with concern. I tried to turn away, not wanting to look at her. Not wanting her to look at me. To see me like this. This total fucking mess of a man. I felt ridiculous—both incredibly relieved that she'd shown up when she had and also incredibly humiliated. God, what must she think of me? Falling apart over burned pasta sauce.

"Can you take my hand?" she asked.

It was a simple question, and I shouldn't have felt as grateful as I did for her to ask it. But still—the fact that she'd asked. That she didn't just grab me and drag me—like I'd been grabbed so many times in that hole. Even after I was rescued, my space had been constantly invaded. Well-meaning doctors and nurses, poking and prodding me with needles and tests without asking permission—as if my body were not my own.

But Sarah. Sarah had asked. And she was waiting for me to say it was okay.

I nodded wordlessly and reached out to take her hand. Her skin was soft, cool, smooth. But solid, real at the same time. I forced my brain to cling on to that fact as my hand clung on to hers. Trying to focus on the sensation of her silky skin against my rough palm.

I let her pull me to my feet and walk me over to the couch. She helped me sit down. My chest was still heaving up and down and I felt a little like I was hyperventilating. I think I was shaking, too.

To my surprise, Sarah ran to the kitchen. She grabbed something off the counter and ran back to me, pushing it into my hand. It took me a moment to realize it was a jar of peanut butter, of all things.

"Read me the ingredient list," she said.

I frowned. "What?"

"Just do it." Her voice left no room for argument.

It was the oddest request, but I did as I was told, slowly reading the tiny words on the jar, one by one, trying to pronounce the difficult ones. It seemed ridiculous, pointless, but I did it anyway, because she had asked me to and at that moment I would have done anything for her, I was so grateful she had come in time.

As I read the words, she stroked my back with slow, even fingers. And lo and behold, by the time I reached the end of the list, my heart had slowed down. My vision had cleared. I could breathe again.

I drew in a breath, a slow, steady one this time. It was funny: I'd never fully appreciated the effort it took to simply breathe before. But it really was a miracle, wasn't it? The fact that our bodies took regular breaths, even when we weren't thinking about them?

"I burned the sauce," I said after a moment.

"Yes," she agreed. "You did."

I felt a weird appreciation at her words. I'd expected her to say something like that it was no big deal. That she didn't like homemade sauce anyway. That this would just give us an excuse to order pizza instead. Something—anything—pitying like that. But she didn't. She just rose to her feet and walked back to the kitchen. She took the pan out of the sink and grabbed a sponge, working to wash it out. It was probably burned to the point of no return, but she scrubbed it hard anyway, as if she believed in it still. As if she believed it had some life left in it yet.

Now there was a metaphor if I ever heard one.

"I was going to cook for you," I said wearily.

She turned to look at me. Her eyebrows cocked. "You still are," she said. "I'm just doing the cleanup. As promised."

I sighed. When she'd made that promise, I'd assumed she'd meant a few dishes, not my entire world. But beggars couldn't be choosers, and I was grateful she was here. The attack had been a bad one. If I had been alone . . .

I rose to my feet, squaring my shoulders, determination surging through me. I'd been given a second chance. I wasn't about to squander it now. The shrinks had insisted the best thing to do was get right back on that horse. To face what scared you. Otherwise you might start avoiding it altogether, the fear building inside of you until it became insurmountable.

Reaching into the cupboard, I pulled out a jar of Ragu.

I held it in her direction. "It's not the gourmet sauce I imagined, but . . ."

She smiled, her lips stretching across perfect white teeth. "Meh," she said with a wave of her hand. "I always thought homemade sauce was vastly overrated anyway. I mean, why bother with all that simmering when you can simply grab a perfect jar from the store?"

I sighed. "You're just saying that to make me feel better."

"Is it working?"

"God yes."

I set the jar down and crossed the kitchen. Took the pot out of her hand and set it on the counter. Then I pulled her into a warm hug. At first she felt a little stiff—as if wary of my intentions. But then she relaxed, her soft body melting into mine. I buried my face in her hair and breathed her in. She smelled like burned tomato sauce . . .

And a little like my salvation.

twenty-six

SARAH

would have been totally cool with hugging Troy all night
long, skipping dinner entirely in exchange for the nourish-
ment I was getting from being in his arms. But, of course,
that would have been counterproductive. He needed to make
this meal, to get through it without panicking. To see that
he didn't have to be afraid.

So I broke from the hug and went back to the dishwash-
ing as he went to get the pasta on the stove. We worked side
by side, hardly speaking unless we needed something passed
across the kitchen. Separate but together all the same. By
the end, Troy had created a halfway decent feast and the
dishes were in the dish rack sparkling clean. The air still
smelled a lot like smoke, but I kept the windows open, hoping it would eventually air out.

I set the table and he brought over the food. Then we sat
down together and starting passing the dishes around, filling
our plates.

"Delicious," I pronounced as I took a big bite of spaghetti.

He rolled his eyes. "It's pasta from a box and sauce from a jar."

"And it's absolutely delicious," I reaffirmed, slurping up a large noodle. The sauce splashed onto my cheeks. I laughed. "So classy, right?" I asked, grabbing for a napkin.

Troy beat me to it, reaching over and dabbing my cheek carefully with his own napkin. I sucked in a breath, my stomach twisting as his gentle fingers moved across my face. Seriously, how could something so sweet and innocent feel so damned sexy? I mean, it wasn't like he was licking it off with his tongue.

Okay, Sarah, calm your hormones. The guy just went through a major PTSD episode and almost burned down his kitchen. The last thing he needs is you to be sexualizing him when he's just trying to be polite.

"So," he said, dropping the napkin and returning to his meal, "how did you know to tell me to read the peanut butter jar?"

"Oh." I felt my face flush. "Just something I . . . read about. Tricks to get someone out of a panic attack."

He frowned. "You read about it? Were you researching me or something?" He suddenly looked annoyed. As if I had gone behind his back. Had him investigated or something.

Fortunately I could answer truthfully. "Actually I've had a few panic attacks of my own over the years," I confessed. "I saw a therapist. She gave me a few coping strategies."

"And they worked?" he asked, looking curious despite himself.

I shrugged. "They worked . . . somewhat. It wasn't until I got on meds that they really started going away."

He scowled at this. I sighed. Here we went. I could have predicted Troy was anti-medication when it came to stuff like this. He was so manly. He would see it as a weakness, of course.

"There's nothing wrong with taking medication if you have a problem," I said. "I mean, if you had diabetes, wouldn't you take insulin? If you had cancer, wouldn't you do chemo?"

He stared down at his plate and I could practically see his thoughts warring through his head. "Sure," he said at last. "But in this case there's nothing physically wrong with me. I don't have some chemical imbalance. I just went through something tough. And my brain needs time to get a grip. That's what Griffin says anyway."

"Griffin? Is that your therapist?"

"My mentor, actually. Griffin Walker—you remember him, right? The reporter who got his leg blown off overseas a couple years ago? He lives right here in San Diego. I feed him beer, he gives me good advice."

I pursed my lips. "In addition to your therapist, right?"

Troy shrugged, not meeting my eyes.

"You are going to a therapist, aren't you?" I asked, concern welling up inside of me. When he didn't answer, I pressed on. "Troy, you went through something terrible. Something no person should ever have to go through. And while I'm sure Griffin is great at giving advice it's not the same as—"

He slammed his fist against the table. "Sarah, don't fucking start, okay?"

I shut my mouth, suddenly frightened at the look I saw in his eyes. This was not the look of the Troy I knew. It was as if a monster lay deep in its depths, warning me away.

"Sorry," I said. "I didn't mean . . ." I trailed off, not sure what it was, actually, that I didn't mean. I didn't mean to help? No, that was crazy. I wanted to help him—that was why I was here. I didn't mean to pry into his personal busi-

ness? Maybe. But he was obviously hurting. And if he'd
already shut everyone else out . . .

"No," he shot back. "No one ever means it. They just
want to help." His voice took on a mocking tone that sent a
shiver to my bones.

Oh my poor Troy.

He jerked to his feet. His body stiff and angry. As angry
as it was frightened just twenty minutes before. I wanted to
grab him and hug him again and tell him everything would
be okay. That it was all right to admit that you were scared.
That you were feeling your life spiraling out of control. That
you needed help. That you weren't coping well on your own.

But at that moment I wasn't sure what he would do to me
if I tried. The anger flashing through him was both bold and
frightening. As if he were possessed by some raging demon
he could barely keep under wraps.

"I need to get out of here," he muttered under his breath.

"Wait, what?" I rose to my feet. "Troy, we're eating dinner. Just sit down."

"No."

"I'm sorry. We don't have to talk about this anymore if
it makes you feel uncomfortable. We can just pop popcorn
and finish our movie marathon. I brought *Sunset Boulevard*
over—we can watch the rest." I could feel tears of desperation prick at my eyes. I did not want him to walk out that
door. Get behind a wheel. Not with the way his body was
shaking with fury and frustration.

But he was already putting on his jacket and heading to
the door. I watched, helplessly, as he grabbed it with jerky
hands and yanked it open. I waited for him to say
something—anything—but he just stepped through, slamming the door behind him. Leaving me alone in his
apartment.

I slumped back into my seat, staring at the unfinished plates of pasta. I felt as if I'd been punched in the stomach, and the tears fell down my cheeks like rain. Why I had pushed him? Everything had been going all right until I'd stupidly brought up the medication thing. But what was I supposed to say? He was the one who had asked. He'd asked and I'd given him an honest answer. I wasn't ashamed to have taken antidepressants when I needed them. In fact, if anything, antidepressants were the reason I could be here today.

And Troy—Troy who had suffered a thousand times worse than me—he wasn't even going to a professional? It made my heart sick to imagine him trying to deal with this all on his own, without any help. Well, besides his old war buddy who was probably just as messed up as he was. My mind flashed back to the scene I'd walked in on in the kitchen earlier that evening. Him on his knees, hands over his ears as the smoke alarm wailed. As the flames rose. What if I hadn't been there to switch off the burner? To throw the pan in the sink? To smother the fire?

He needed help, whether he wanted to admit it or not. And I was clearly the only one around willing to tell him that. And I would have to continue to tell him that—whether he liked it or not, I realized suddenly. Whether it ruined any chance of friendship we had—whether it caused him to hate me or think I was some horrible bitch. I didn't care. It didn't matter in the end. I cared about Troy. And I would get him help—even if it destroyed us in the process.

Because his life was more important in the end.

Firming my resolve, I rose to my feet and collected the dishes, no longer hungry. I would clean up, then I would wait for him to come home. And then we would talk—really talk and I wouldn't let him tune me out this time. I wouldn't let him turn me away. He could be as grumpy and mean and dismissive as he wanted to be. Those emotions were only symptoms of a deeper issue anyway. His way of coping with his fear, by driving everyone who loved him away.

Sighing, I set about washing the dishes, one by one—by hand, instead of the dishwasher. There was something soothing, I'd found, about washing dishes. Your mind focused on a simple task. The rest of the world's stresses fading at the edges. And I needed that right now. To wrangle control over my own emotions so I could be ready to help him when he returned. So I could be his rock—even if he was determined to cling on to quicksand.

I had just finished the dishes and was settling in to flip through some Netflix, still waiting for Troy to return, when my cell phone rang. A quick glance at the caller ID told me it was my father. I groaned. Seriously, could this day possibly get any crappier? I considered letting the call go to voice mail, but eventually gave in and answered. Otherwise he'd just keep calling back.

"Hey, Dad," I greeted into the phone.

"Hey, baby girl," he boomed back. "Where are you?"

"I'm safe, Dad."

"That's not an answer."

"I didn't mean it to be."

I heard his long sigh. "You love making things difficult for me, don't you? I'm only trying to look out for you, you know."

"I know, Dad. I'm sorry," I acquiesced. I paused, then added, "So were you able to find anything more about the threats against me? Who might be making them?"

"Yes. That's actually why I'm calling."

He paused, and the silence seemed to stretch out between us, long and sharp. I frowned, feeling a small bit of anxiety rise inside of me.

"Well?" I asked, when I couldn't stand it anymore.

"Look, sweetie, I don't want you to be alarmed. But I was just informed that Ryan Robinson was released a week and a half ago."

I froze, my heart suddenly in my throat. "Ryan? Ryan's out on parole? Already?"

"It's been five years, sweetheart. And you know how overcrowded the prisons are. Time off for good behavior is almost guaranteed these days."

Right. I sank back onto the couch, staring up at the ceiling, my pulse beating rapidly against my wrists. This was not good. This was so not good. Ryan walking the streets of San Diego. Me getting threats. The rock at the movie theater—only days after he got out of prison. It could be a coincidence, of course. But where I came from two plus two usually equaled four.

If Ryan was out of prison, I could be in big trouble.

My mind flashed back to the courtroom scene five years ago. The judge sentencing Ryan to prison as I watched from the back of the room. I still remembered the look on Ryan's face as he turned to me. The fury flashing in his eyes.

"You'll pay for this!" he had raged, as the guards attempted to drag him away. "You think you're untouchable. But you're not. Someday, somehow—when you least expect it—I will make you pay."

I shuddered, fear slicing through me like a sharp knife. I glanced at the front door, wishing Troy would hurry up and come back. I didn't want to be here alone. I didn't want to be anywhere alone, actually. Not with Ryan out there, somewhere, ready to begin his tour of revenge.

"Sweetie? Are you still there?"

I shook myself. "Yes. Sorry. I'm just . . . a little taken aback. I had no idea they'd let him out so soon. He was supposed to have ten years."

"I know." My father's voice was tight. "You see? This is exactly why the crime bill needs to go through. To prevent this kind of thing. We have to instill tougher penalties and give prisons enough money to carry them out. Otherwise we're just going to have more and more criminals roaming our streets."

I raked my hand through my hair, my thoughts torn. While I didn't necessarily agree with my dad's crime bill— I did agree on one thing. Ryan being out on the streets was bad news all around.

"Look, sweetie. Tomorrow morning I want you to go down to the police station. I need you to file an official restraining order against Ryan. At least then if he does try something we can get him. We can lock that bastard back up and this time we'll throw away the key."

I nodded absently, staring down at my hands. "I can do that," I said.

"Great. Where are you now? I can send Carl to pick you up. Bring you back to the house."

I bit my lower lip, wondering if I should answer truthfully. "I'm at Troy's apartment," I said at last. "But I'm fine. Really."

"Troy's apartment?" my father barked over the phone. "Sarah! What the hell are you thinking? You do realize, don't you, that getting mixed up with Troy was how this whole thing got started in the first place?"

When I didn't answer right away, he gave an exasperated sigh. "Sweetie, you've spent years trying to get your life

back together after what that man did to you. Don't go back-
sliding on me now."

I closed my eyes and opened them again, trying to reset
my sanity. "I'm not, Dad. I swear to God. Everything's fine,"
I said, trying to sound reassuring. "There's nothing going
on between me and Troy. I'm just helping him. He's going
through a rough time. He needs me."

"Like he needed you five years ago? To rob your own
family blind?" my dad demanded. I winced. Of course he
would go there.

"Dad . . ." I tried, then stopped. Because what good would
it do? My father would always think the worst of Troy. And
I couldn't really blame him, either.

"You know I could just track your phone," he said quietly.
"Find out where you are and pick you up?"

"I know," I said. "But you're not going to."

"Give me one reason I shouldn't."

"I'll give you three. Because you trust me. Because I'm
a grown-up now. Because I don't need you to save me." I
paused, then added, "This princess can save herself."

He sighed. "Okay," he said. "But I want you to fill out that
restraining order. First thing—even before you go to work."

"I can do that."

"And if anything else happens, you let me know first,
okay? Don't rely on Troy or anyone else. I'm your father. I
can help you. But only if you let me."

"Okay," I agreed. I paused, then added, "I love you, Dad."

"I love you, too, princess. More than anything ever."

I hung up the phone, setting it down beside me. I
squirmed in my seat, suddenly feeling very uncomfortable.
My eyes darted to the windows, then to the door. Then back
to the TV. Of course now I was way too nervous to watch

anything anymore. Instead, I found myself glancing back over to the door again, wondering when Troy would come back. If he would come back.

Then I thought about Ryan.

Ryan being out there, somewhere.

Ryan, ready to seek his revenge.

A revenge, in a weird way, he kind of deserved.

I sighed, thinking back to the first day I had met Ryan. At the Environmental Club meeting I'd attended at Troy's request. Even from the beginning he'd seemed a bit— smarmy to me. Like he was secretly laughing at the rest of us behind our backs. Troy, on the other hand, clearly worshipped the ground he walked on. Everything Ryan said was law. And when Ryan said, "Jump!" Troy only wanted to know how high.

Turned out? Pretty damn high. Or low, if you wanted to be technical. Criminally low.

In the end, it was my testimony that sent Ryan away. That exposed him for being the fraud he really was. I still remembered how disillusioned his other little followers had been when they learned the truth about their fearless leader. That he wasn't actually some hero, out to save the world, just a high-tech bank robber with a great spin. Sure, he tried to play it off like he was Robin Hood. Taking from the rich to help the poor. But I wasn't so sure his motives were as altruistic as he wanted them to appear.

I probably should have gone to jail, too. After all, I was the one who'd tricked my dad's IT guy into giving me the passwords to the accounts. The ones that allowed Ryan to hack the servers and hold them hostage until they met his demands. But my dad couldn't allow my indiscretions to ruin his political future. And so everything with my name attached had been swept under the rug.

Ryan had gone to prison. The IT guy had lost his job. And I had gotten off scot-free.

At least up until now.

But it'll be fine, I tried to assure myself. *I'll do the restraining order thing tomorrow. He'll know I'm onto him then. And at that point if he even tries to come near me, he'll go straight back to prison. No passing go. No collecting two hundred dollars.*

I turned back to the TV, squaring my shoulders and firming my resolve. It would be fine. Everything would turn out totally fine in the end. I was here, I was safe. Troy would be back any minute now and we could talk things through.

But all the assurances in the world flew out of my head when suddenly I heard a knock on the front door.

twenty-seven

TROY

I was a bastard. I was such a bastard.

After leaving my house, I drove around for nearly an hour not being able to will myself to pull over. To turn the car around and go home. To apologize to the one girl who, for some crazy reason, still gave a damn about me. Who wanted to save me from myself.

What was I thinking? What had I done? She'd gotten me through that panic attack like some goddamned superhero. She hadn't pitied me when I'd fallen apart on the kitchen floor. Instead, she'd respected my space. She'd talked me down. She'd given me the support I needed to get a freaking grip. Everything a stupid, pathetic bastard like me needed her to do, she'd done it—without complaint.

And then, when she'd dared to go one step further—to suggest I needed professional help (cause, like, *duh*), I blew up at her. I ran away like a fucking child.

She was right, of course. I did need help. This just proved

how much I needed it. I'd tried to be strong. Wanting so desperately to prove to those assholes who took me that they weren't able to break me. That I could come back doubly strong—doubly fierce. Like they'd never thrown me in that hole.

But I was just fooling myself. Refusing to admit what everyone else could clearly see. Because I was broken. Deeply and maybe permanently broken. And if I didn't find a way to get my shit together soon, the last few people in the world who still believed in me would be forced to give up and walk away.

Like Sarah. If she hadn't already.

I wouldn't have blamed her if she wasn't at my apartment when I finally crawled back. What reason did she have to stay? I'd done nothing but bring misery to her life over and over again. She could find a lot of better things to do with her time than waste it worrying about me.

A screeching horn startled me back to the present. Heart in my throat, I swerved, slamming my car into a stop sign, snapping the sign in two. My car jumped off the road, almost flipping over as it hit the dirt and I screamed. Somehow, by the grace of some higher power I didn't deserve, I managed to keep it upright. And stop before I hit a huge old tree.

I sucked in a breath, my vision spinning. The tree loomed before me, tall and strong. As if daring me to take it on. Thank God I'd managed to stop in time. There was no way my car would have had any chance against its solid trunk.

I slammed the steering wheel with my fist, fury raging through me again. Of all the stupid things. The stupid, stupid things. I mean, here I'd survived bombings, military coups, being imprisoned. Only to almost die in suburban San Diego at the hands of a fucking tree? What was wrong with me? I knew I'd been too upset to be behind the wheel.

But I'd done it anyway. Because the anger raging inside of me had burned away all common sense.

Was I slowly going crazy? Would this only get worse with time? Griffin had promised me it would get better—but at the moment that seemed like an impossible dream. There was no way I could ever go back to being the person I had been. So innocent and naïve. The idiot guy who believed he could single-handedly make a difference in this screwed-up world.

Now I knew better.

I raked a hand through my hair. I couldn't go back to being that guy. But I couldn't very well live like this, either. Tonight alone, I'd almost burned down my place and slammed headfirst into a tree. Who knew what adventures I'd have tomorrow and if I'd manage to survive them?

My thoughts turned to Sarah's suggestion of medication. Could something like that actually help? Or would it turn me into some mindless zombie, wandering through life, completely numb? Not that, at the moment, that idea didn't sound somewhat tempting. Something, anything, to dull the sharp pain that was stabbing me in the back on a daily basis.

I realized my car hood was steaming. Shit. I opened the door, practically falling out of the seat. Walking around to the front I inspected the grill. Great. I groaned. There was no way I was driving away from this. And so I rummaged in my pocket for my phone, finding the number of a tow truck company and placing the call. They told me to hang tight—they'd be there within a half hour.

I settled down on the side of the road to wait. I thought about calling Sarah, asking her to come pick me up, but I was too ashamed of my earlier behavior. What would she say if she saw me now? Sitting here, as broken as my new car. The thought made the anger roll through me once again like a heavy fog on approach and I fought to stanch the emotions raging through me. Push down the anger, the frustration, the fear.

My mind spun along with my vision and for a moment I indulged in the fantasy that she was approaching. My dream Sarah, the one who had visited me so often when I was down in that dark hole. Putting her arms around me, holding me close, whispering sweet nothings in my ear. Soothing my fears.

But no. I shook my head, forcing the vision to vacate my brain. After all, how could I allow dream Sarah to comfort me, when I'd pushed the real Sarah away? She'd been trying to comfort me, too. Give me tough love. And I had yelled at her. Run away like a scolded child. I didn't deserve her comfort—dream or otherwise.

Finally, the tow truck came. They put my car on the back of the truck and then offered to give me a ride back to my house, since it was on the way. I took it: What else could I do? Soon we were heading back to my place. As the driver chatted amicably, I found myself wondering if Sarah would still be there. Waiting for me to return. I knew I didn't deserve her to be. If she were smart, she would have taken off right away. But something deep inside of me prayed she would be there anyway. So I could apologize to her. Promise to do better.

To man up, once and for all.

When we pulled into the apartment complex, I was surprised to see red-and-blue lights flashing outside. Police lights. My heart leapt to my throat and a chill shivered down my back. I tried to tell myself that they were probably there for another apartment—there were dozens in my building, after all. No reason to suspect this had anything to do with me.

But when I got out of the tow truck, my eyes fell upon the line of reporters, just beyond the police tape. A sinking feeling dropped to my stomach.

"Troy! Troy Young!" they called. "What happened? Why are the police here? Is it true, the mayor's daughter is inside?"

I ignored them, picking up the pace until I reached my front door. A policeman stopped me before I could go in.

"This is an official investigation," he stated. "You'll have to get back behind the yellow line."

"I live here," I protested, my heart pounding in my chest now. Oh God. What had happened? Why were they here? Was Sarah okay? I craned my neck to try to see beyond the officer. "I'm Troy Young," I tried again. "This is my place."

The man squinted at me. "Oh. Right. Of course. Sorry. Come in."

I barely gave him enough time to step aside, pushing past him to burst into my apartment, my throat dry and my stomach churning. My eyes darted around the living room until they located Sarah, sitting on the couch, looking unharmed. Relief flooded through me so hard and fast I almost gagged on it.

"Sarah!" I cried, running to her. I dropped to my knees in front of her, looking her over, trying to figure out what the hell could have happened. "Are you okay? Why are the police here? Did something happen?"

Oh God. I had left her all alone. I had left her alone, knowing she'd been threatened. If anything had happened to her. If anyone had hurt her . . .

"I'm . . . fine," she said, but her shaky voice betrayed her words. "I heard a knock at the door and I went to see who it was. I thought it was you at first—like, maybe you'd left in a hurry and forgotten your keys. But then I looked through the peephole."

My heart thudded uneasily in my chest as I caught the flash of terror across her face. "And . . . ?" I asked, not sure I really wanted to know.

"It was Ryan."

"Wait, what?" I stared at her, horrified. "Ryan? Ryan Robinson? But he's—"

"—Out of prison," she finished for me in a dull voice. "My father just called and told me. Out early for good behavior."

"And he came here? To my apartment?"

She nodded. Her face was pale. Her expression grave. "I don't know if he somehow found out I was going to be here—or if he was just looking for you. I ran to the phone and called the police. He knocked three times, but then finally took off. They've been looking around the area—to make sure he isn't hiding out anywhere. But they think he left." She shrugged helplessly.

I closed my eyes for a moment, trying to quell the panic rising inside of me. I couldn't fall apart now. Not when Sarah needed me to stay strong. I forced myself to take a deep breath. To try to calm my nerves. My eyes darted to the peanut butter jar still on the coffee table. I tried to remember the ingredients, one by one.

Rising to my feet, I paced the room, my steps eating up the distance between the walls. Oh God. This was the last thing we needed now. Ryan out of prison. Ryan ready to seek revenge. Ryan showing up at my front door.

My fault. My fault. My fault.

I turned back to her. "I'm so sorry," I said, then cringed at how lame the words sounded coming from my mouth.

She shook her head. "It's fine. I mean—it's not fine. But it is what it is. In any case, my father is on his way to get me. Or . . . one of his people is . . . I don't know." Her voice cracked a little on the last part and my heart panged in my chest. I knew how much she didn't want to get her father involved in any of this.

But she'd had no choice. Because I'd left her alone.

I dropped to my knees in front of her, grabbing her hands in mine. They were cold—ice-cold—and stiff under my grip. "I'm going to fix this," I promised. "Someway, somehow. I will make this go away."

But she only shook her head again. "No. You have enough going on as it is," she told me. "Don't worry about it." But what I heard in her voice was more like *don't worry about me.*

I swallowed hard, feeling my heart shatter into a thousand pieces. I wanted to tell her I would always worry about her. That there was no possible way to get me to stop worrying about her. Because I cared about her. Hell, I probably still loved her. I probably never stopped loving her these past five years.

But I knew all the sentiments in the world wouldn't make a bit of difference in the end. After all, I couldn't even fix myself.

How could I possibly think I could fix things for her?

twenty-eight

SARAH

I walked into my dad's kitchen Saturday morning, raising my eyebrows as I found him and Mrs. Anderson having coffee while poring over the newspapers. I didn't know why I was surprised; the two of them had been thick as thieves for years—she was always wining and dining him in an effort to keep him as News 9's biggest advertiser. And he was never reluctant to eat up the attentions of a beautiful, powerful woman. Of course, up until recently she had been a beautiful, powerful, married woman and so any rumors of them being more than business partners were quickly put to rest.

But last year her husband, legendary weatherman Stormy Anderson—Asher's father—had brought her to divorce court around the same time my dad had announced he was running for mayor. And suddenly their meetings had become more frequent. Especially the "early morning" ones I wasn't entirely convinced hadn't started the night before.

"There she is!" Mrs. Anderson exclaimed, setting down the paper. She raised her coffee (likely Irish) in my direction. "The woman of the hour."

"What?" I squinted at her, puzzled as I wandered over to the coffeemaker. "What are you talking about?"

I hadn't slept much the night before and was still exhausted. I kept tossing and turning, thinking about Ryan showing up at the door, looking for some kind of revenge. What would he have done if I had opened the door without looking? Would he have gone through with his threats? Would I still be here this morning? Was he only trying to scare me? Or did he have something much worse in mind?

It was strange. He had never been violent back in the day. In fact, if anything he always came off as a peace-loving hippie. Of course he never came off as a white-collar thief, either. So clearly he had been hiding some of his less desirable qualities back then. And then, of course, he had made those threats in the courtroom as they dragged him off to prison. Promising to make me pay . . .

Evidently accounts had finally come due.

I shuddered again as I remembered peeking through that peephole. Seeing his face. He looked older than I remembered him being. I guess that was inevitable: We all had aged, after all. A little paunchier around the waist. Lines around his eyes. But what had really struck me last night was how tired he looked. As if the magnetic spark that had always shone in his eyes—the spark that had made everyone want to do exactly what he suggested—had been extinguished. Guess prison could do that to a guy.

Too bad it couldn't also quench his thirst for revenge . . .

And then there was Troy—poor, damaged Troy. The horror in his eyes when he'd walked through that front door after the police had arrived. I could tell he felt terribly guilty for walking out on me, for leaving me alone when the psycho showed up at his front door. Even though he could have had no way of knowing Ryan was lurking when he left.

It had been so awkward—I wanted to say a million things to comfort him. To tell him I didn't blame him for taking off like he did. But, of course, I couldn't say much with the police standing around.

But then he told me about his wrecked car. How he'd almost hit a tree. And suddenly all my sympathy went out the window and it was all I could do not to slap him upside the head. To scream at him for being so stupid. For taking off and driving when he was clearly not in control of his emotions. *You're sick!* I wanted to scream. *You need help! You cannot do this on your own!*

But I knew, in my heart, my words would only fall on deaf ears. With all that was happening, he had been way too upset to hear them. I'd have to try again later. When he was calm. When we were alone. Maybe, just maybe, I could convince him to seek help.

I realized Mrs. Anderson was talking.

"Why, my dear, haven't you heard?" she was saying, her eyes sparkling beneath her heavy makeup. "The ratings for your first He Said, She Said segment are through the roof! In fact, the most searched term on our website this morning was 'Are Troy Young and Sarah Martin a couple in real life?'"

I stared at her, my eyes wide. "What? You're kidding, right?"

"I never kid about ratings, darling," she huffed. Then she pushed the newspaper in my direction, opened to the Inside Track gossip page. I cringed as my eyes fell upon an article about "a certain mayor's daughter" caught leaving the apartment of a certain "American hero" late last night.

"A match made in TV news heaven!" exclaimed Mrs. Anderson, taking the paper back from me. "I couldn't have planned it better myself!"

I glanced nervously at my dad; what was his take on this? But he only shrugged. I sighed.

"Look, I'm glad the segment got good ratings. But Troy and I are not a couple anymore. And we have no plans on becoming one, either. We're just coworkers."

"Of course you are, sweetheart," Mrs. Anderson agreed, practically winking at me as she said it. I rolled my eyes. Whatever.

"In any case," my father interjected, "let me know when you're ready to go down to city hall this morning. We need to file that restraining order against Ryan. And I've scheduled a press conference for noon."

Wait, what? "A press conference? For what?"

He turned to me, his eyes grave. "You are being stalked. By someone who should still be in prison. We need to let people know. They have to understand what these bleeding-heart liberals are doing to the safety of our citizens."

I cringed. "Are you even kidding me right now?" I demanded. "You're going to politicize my stalking? To get your crime bill pushed through? That's low, Dad. Even for you, that's low."

"Come on, Sarah. This kind of thing is exactly why the bill needs to go through in the first place," my father shot back. "Here we have a dangerous criminal. Out on the streets. Threatening my own daughter. We need to make people aware that this kind of thing can happen."

I frowned, my skin suddenly feeling itchy. I set my coffee down on the counter, no longer thirsty. "Look, I'll get the restraining order," I said. "But I draw the line at doing a press conference about this. My personal life is already out on display too much as it is," I added, gesturing to the newspaper in Mrs. Anderson's hands. "I don't need to air any more dirty laundry than is already out to dry, thank you very much."

My dad looked disappointed, but to his credit didn't argue any further. Instead, he turned back to his own newspaper, as if dismissing me outright. I frowned, watching him for a moment. I knew him too well to think he'd just give up on the idea altogether.

I just hoped whatever it was he still had cooking, it wouldn't have anything to do with me.

twenty-nine

TROY

"A re you okay, man? You look like hell."
My body stiffened as I walked into the entertainment office on Monday, only to be greeted by my favorite person in the world—the sniveling Ben. He gave me a derisive once-over, shaking his head.

"I saw the news," he continued. "Some stalker showed up to your house? Pretty lame, man. Especially since you're 'America's hero' and all." He made air quotes with his hands, just to drive the point home.

"Yeah," I grunted, heading to my desk, trying to get away. I hadn't slept most of the night before after Sarah left and the police finished their investigation. The apartment had felt too big, too empty. Every sound jerked me back awake. Not that I was afraid Ryan would return; I was pretty sure I could take him in a fight if I had to. No, I was more stressed about the handful of reporters still gathered outside my front door. Earlier, I had tried to step out of my apartment—to meet the guy delivering my rental car until mine could be fixed—and they'd pounced on me, driving me back into the house with questions about government policies when dealing with terrorists. About whether I should have been rescued or left in that hole. The car rental guy had been so freaked out, I was lucky he left the car.

I didn't blame Sarah for calling the police when Ryan showed up—I would have done the same. But the fallout for that call had come regardless. And now everyone knew where I lived. Any semblance of privacy I once had was gone for good.

And so for the past two nights I tossed and turned and failed in chasing sleep. Last night I'd given up and started drinking around two AM, hoping to knock myself out. Instead, I only got drunk and paranoid and found myself securing every door with a chair and blocking every window. Just in case one of those bastards tried to sneak up and film me unaware.

I finally passed out around four, only to be woken by one of my makeshift barriers crashing to the floor. Which sent my pulse skyrocketing, of course, and my heart to my throat. I grabbed a baseball bat and ran to the living room, ready to protect myself at any cost—before I realized it was just a toaster that I'd piled on top of a box, which was on top of a chair.

Which was so stupid. And so pointless. As if any of this could keep me safe. As if anything could keep anyone safe anymore. In a rage, I tore it all down, managing to smash half of it in the process. Trashing my own house without apology. Hey, maybe some of those reporters were still out there, capturing this all on film. That should make a damn good top story. #AmericasHero #LosingItAtLast.

I realized Ben had followed me to my desk. He was looking down at me with concern. "You don't look so good," he said, frowning. "Maybe you need to take a day off. Go home, relax. I got things covered here."

I glared at him, anger coursing inside of me again. "You would love that, wouldn't you?" I growled. "Me going home so you could do my job yourself."

Ben raised his eyebrows, looking surprised. "No man," he said, holding up his hands. "I just meant—"

"You want to do my job? Fine. Do my damn job. I didn't want it anymore anyway," I added, rising to my feet, feeling the fury gushing through me now. "You do this ridiculous, pathetic, mindless job and I'll go to Richard and get my real job back."

I shoved a stack of papers in his face. Printouts of possible story ideas I'd found the day before. Stupid, ridiculous, pandering story ideas that meant absolutely nothing, but which our viewers were sure to love.

"Here," I said. "They say Khloe Kardashian wore two pairs of Spanx to Fashion Week," I told him. "Top story material if I ever heard it."

And with that, I turned on my heel and stormed out of the entertainment center. My skin was flushed with anger, and my steps burned up the distance across the newsroom floor. I could feel my coworkers staring at me from their little desk pods, but I ignored them all. They had been staring since day one. What the hell did I care about them? They were nothing. Nobody. Living their tiny lives. Working their stupid jobs. They'd never understand the hell it was to be me. No one could.

I reached Richard's office. His assistant stopped me at the door. "He's on a call," she said, stepping in my path. "You'll have to—"

I pushed by her. Grabbed the door handle and yanked it

open. Inside, Richard was indeed on the phone. He looked up when he saw me and frowned.

"Is something wrong?" he mouthed.

"I need to talk to you."

"I'm on a call. Can you come back in a—"

"No. Now."

He sighed, saying something in the phone I couldn't hear, mostly because the blood was rushing past my ears so loud at the moment it was hard to hear anything else. I forced myself to take a seat across from him, sucking in a shaky breath, trying to calm the fire raging inside of me. So I could make my case without sounding angry.

Yeah. Good luck with that.

Richard set the phone on its cradle. He looked at me, concern in his eyes. "What seems to be the problem?" he asked.

"I want my old job back."

He frowned. "What do you mean? Your network job? I don't think I can—"

"No. The reporter job. The general assignment reporter. I want to be back out on the streets."

Richard gave me a long hard look and I struggled not to squirm under his gaze. At last he sighed. "I don't think that would be a good idea right now," he said.

"Why not?" I demanded, feeling the anger raging through me again. "Why won't you give me another chance? That day? It was just a bad day. It won't happen again. I've done plenty of live shots now in the studio. I'm ready to get back out there. Go back to reporting real news."

"No, I get it," Richard assured me. "I really do. But I need you to understand that's not going to be possible. At least for the foreseeable future."

"Why not?"

He sighed. "Your He Said, She Said segment is too good."

"Excuse me?" I stared at him, my eyes bulging from my head. He had to be kidding me, right?

"Look, I was just on the phone with Cathy Anderson. You met her, right? News 9's owner. She was positively gushing about your performance. And evidently the ratings were through the roof."

"So I'm popular. Good. Then I'll be popular on general news as well."

He shrugged. "Maybe. But she wants you on this segment. And what Cathy wants?" He snorted. "She always gets. Sorry, man, you're a victim of your own success. In fact, she's even talking about creating an entire half-hour program with the two of you. Kind of a Siskel and Ebert thing, you know?"

Horror coursed through me. I could hear his words, but I could barely make sense of them. They wanted me to continue the entertainment segment? Forever?

"No." I shook my head. "I won't do it. She can't make me."

Richard pursed his lips. "No. She can't make you. But she can make sure you don't do anything else. At this station or at any of the others in San Diego. Don't underestimate her, Troy. She's a very powerful woman. She can make you . . . or she can break you. And trust me, you don't want her to break you."

"Yeah, well, I'm already pretty broken," I wanted to shoot back. But I didn't. Cause why bother? It wouldn't change anything in the end.

"Are you okay?" Richard asked, peering at me again. "You don't look good. Is it because of that thing that happened Friday night? With the stalker at your apartment?"

Great. Everyone knew about that. And, of course they did. This was a TV news station after all. Everyone knew everyone else's business.

"I'm fine," I shot back with a little more venom than I meant to. I wondered suddenly if Richard had sent a team to my house like everyone else had. Were my coworkers even now stalking my front door, waiting for a scoop? "I just want the job I deserve. The job I applied for and got. You told me this entertainment thing was only temporary—until I got back on my feet. Well, I'm back. And I want my job back, too."

Richard sighed. "Even if Cathy gave the go-ahead, I wouldn't put you back right now. I'm sorry. I'm looking at you now and you don't seem okay. You're yelling and you're pacing my office. You look a little crazy to tell the truth." He frowned. "Have you been taking care of yourself? Have you been sleeping at night? Have you been talking to a professional about what you went through?"

Rage exploded inside of me. "That's none of your god-damned business!"

I watched as Richard rose from his seat. He set his hands on his desk, staring me straight in the eye. "You need to go home," he said in an ultra calm voice that only served to make me angrier than I already was. "You need to go home and calm down. Take the rest of the day off. Hell, take the week off if you need to. But I do not want you here, in my newsroom, acting like this. Like you're some bomb that's ready to go off."

I staggered backward, his words hitting me with the force of a ten-ton truck. What was I doing? What was I saying? How did I look to my boss right now? The only boss who would even give me a chance, and I was proving to him I didn't deserve one in the first place. Oh God. This was bad. This was really bad. "Look, I'm sorry. I don't need to—"

"Stop right there, Troy. I don't want to hear it. And I'm not kidding around. You either walk out that door now on your own accord or I will call security and they will escort you out. And everyone will see you go." Richard leveled his eyes on me. "Is that how you want to play it?"

"No." I shook my head, my stomach twisting and turning. "No, of course not. I'll . . . leave. I'll leave now. I'm sorry. I'm so sorry."

I staggered to the door, trying to regulate my posture as I stepped back out into the newsroom. Trying to pretend nothing was wrong. But I saw the stares immediately and could hear the buzzing of whispers around the room. Of course. Everyone had probably heard the whole thing—the walls weren't exactly thick and I'd been yelling pretty loud. Great. Just effing great.

I sucked in a breath and held my head up high. Squared my shoulders and walked across the newsroom toward the door. Somehow I made it out of the building without causing any more of a scene than I already had.

But once out in the parking lot? I started running.

thirty

SARAH

I walked into the newsroom, feeling a little on edge. I'd spent the weekend at my father's but when I'd gone back to my own house to grab some more clothes this morning, I'd found two broken front windows—and the inside of my house trashed. Ryan striking again. I'd called the police and gone through filing yet another report. The officer on duty swore up and down that they'd find him for me. That they'd lock him up and throw away the key. But their promises did little to ease the dread I felt at the pit of my stomach. As long as Ryan was still out there, I would never be completely safe.

My fathers' press conference and the new crime bill seemed to be the story of the day at News 9. And the second I stepped through the door I was bombarded by questions and interview requests. Even though my dad had promised to keep my name out of the headlines, no one was stupid—they all knew he was talking about me and I was suddenly the top story on every station. I told them I'd think about it when it came to the interview requests, but that was just my way of stalling them. The last thing I needed was to piss Ryan off further by talking about him on TV. I needed to lay low and stay out of sight and hope he would take the hint and move on.

I stepped into the entertainment office, realizing it was empty. Ben was probably off working with one of the editors to put together tonight's piece. But where was Troy? I glanced at my watch: He should be here by now.

Worry threaded through me as I headed to my desk. I saw my phone blinking a message and wondered if it could be him. Though wouldn't he call my cell phone? Sitting at my desk, I dialed in to check my messages. There was one new one to listen to.

But it wasn't from Troy.

"Yeah, hi. This is uh, well, you can call me Don? I guess? Sorry, I'm a little nervous. I've never done something like this before. So yeah. I work at Water World, you see. And I saw on the news this morning that you once tried to shut them down? And that now you work at News 9? I just thought . . . if you wanted to continue your investigation, I could get you in. I could show you what's really going on here—what's been going on. It's pretty bad—but maybe you can still help them? I don't know." He gave a nervous laugh. "I sound like a crazy person, don't I?" he continued. "Anyway, you can call me at this number, but please don't share this with anyone else. I don't want to lose my job."

The message ended. I stared down at my phone for a moment, shock reeling through me. Then I replayed the message again, listening more carefully this time and taking down the guy's number. As my heart thudded madly in my chest, I found myself playing it a third time, still hardly able to believe what I was hearing.

Finally, I set the phone back on its cradle, leaning back in my chair. Troubled thoughts raced through my head. When my dad had suggested the press conference, I'd thought only about the effect it would have on Ryan. I had no idea the ripples would go further than that. That some whistleblower would take notice and suddenly want to talk.

I frowned, indecisiveness prickling at my skin. Was he legit? Should I call him back? Did I really want to get involved in all of this all over again? I mean, I wasn't that same girl anymore. The one eager to expose wrongs and save the world. I had a job now. A life. If I dove back in, I could risk those things. I could get caught and arrested and maybe this time my dad wouldn't be able to bail me out.

And what if it was all some kind of trick? It didn't sound like Ryan's voice on the phone, but he could have gotten someone else to call. What if this was simply more stalking? Trying to reel me in with an offer I couldn't refuse?

But what if it wasn't? What if it really was an employee wanting to help me accomplish what I'd failed to do five years before? What if it was my one chance to finally make good? I had no doubt those whales and dolphins and other sea creatures were still suffering. Still being neglected and maybe abused. I'd turned my back on them five years ago after everything had blown up in my face. But Ryan's crime and Troy's betrayal had nothing to do with them. They were innocent. They needed help. What if this was my chance to make that happen? If I threw away the guy's number, pretended he never called, could I live with myself? Knowing I'd turned my back on those poor animals, all over again?

I rose from my seat. I needed to find Troy. Needed to tell him about the phone call and see what he thought I should do. Maybe he'd even want to help me. Maybe we could go meet this guy together and see for ourselves whether he was the real deal. My heart thudded in my chest at the possibility.

"Hey! There you are!" Ben walked into the entertainment center, a stack of papers and tapes in his hand. "Did you hear about Troy?"

I frowned. "What about him? And where is he, anyway?"

"Home, I guess. He totally flipped out on me—and then at Richard. He sent him home for the day. Evidently the whole newsroom heard his little temper tantrum." He rolled his eyes. "Reporters."

Oh God. I bit my lower lip. *Troy, what did you do now?*

"What happened?" I asked. "I mean, what set him off?"

Ben shrugged. "Turns out he's evidently not a big fan of the entertainment beat, go figure. I think he tried to get Richard to give him his old general assignment job back. Which, actually, in my opinion would be a really good—"

"Right," I said, cutting him off. My heart pounded in my chest as I pictured how it all must have gone down. "Look, I need to go try to find him, okay?" I told Ben. "Can you hold down the fort for me until I get back?"

"Duh," Ben said, looking thrilled at the opportunity to get rid of both of us in one afternoon. Two birds, one stone, and all that. He glanced down at his notes. "You already taped today's segment Friday so there's no live shot to worry about. There's a screening later you're scheduled for, but I think there's another showing tomorrow." He gave me a surprisingly thoughtful smile. "Don't worry. I've got things under control."

Relief flooded through me. "Thank you," I said. "I appreciate that more than you know."

"Of course. Though I'm still holding you to that shopping spree offer," he reminded me. "To get me looking the part of a reporter. If they do give Troy his old job back eventually, I want to be ready to step in."

"Anytime," I promised. "Just name the date."

I raced out of the newsroom to my car, then jumped in, heading to Troy's house. I tried calling, but he didn't answer the phone. Hopefully he'd gone straight home. He'd already wrecked one car and if he was as angry today as he had been that night, he'd definitely be a danger on the road.

My heart ached in my chest as I tried to imagine how things had all gone down. Troy storming into Richard's office, demanding to get his old reporting job back. Of course Richard would turn him down flat—it was only this past weekend that Mrs. Anderson had been gushing about his work and how popular the segment was with viewers. No way was she just going to let her new star go back to general reporting now. After all, anyone could do general news. But it took a special talent to rock the He Said, She Said segment.

Which was, in a way, kind of a big compliment. But Troy wouldn't see it like that. He was too much of a hard news guy. To him, this job was a demotion. And while I knew he'd been doing his best to treat it seriously, for my sake if nothing else, his heart was clearly not in it. And if he was already feeling riled up by all the chaos that had happened this weekend, I could see how things could come to a head.

A red light stopped me in my tracks and I slammed my fist against the steering wheel in frustration. As I waited for the light to turn, my mind raced, trying to decide how to best approach Troy when I got there. What to do, what to say. Short, of course, of dragging him by his collar to a psychiatrist's office and forcing him to seek the treatment he so desperately needed. I mean, how rock-bottom did we have to go before he'd finally admit he needed help?

Of course, somewhere, deep down inside of him, he had to have already known that. He wasn't stupid, after all. Just stubborn. Pigheaded. Proud. He'd always been so proud. Even now, when he was so broken, he couldn't admit that he needed help being put back together. Because in his mind help equaled weakness. And Troy Young, of all people, could never let himself be seen as weak.

Finally, I reached the apartment complex and pulled into the parking lot. To my dismay I realized a group of reporters were still camped out there, outside of Troy's front door. I scowled at them as I passed.

"Don't you have anything better to do?" I demanded.

One of them laughed. "Come on, sweetheart. This guy's international news. We get him to talk, we get paid. I got nothing better to do than get paid."

"Well, he's not going to talk."

"You don't know that. Trust me, I've been doing this a long time. They eventually talk, if only to make us go away."

Rage exploded inside of me. "You guys are sick. This is a man's life we're talking about here!"

The reporter shrugged. "It's nothing personal, darling. We gotta feed our families, too." He paused, then added, "Wait, you're Mayor Martin's daughter, aren't you?" He raised his camera.

I held my hand over my face. "No, thank you," I said.

"Come on, baby. Give us a smile. You're at least worth a small payday—if only for the gossip columns." He paused, then added with a bit of a feral grin, "Are you guys hooking up? Is that why you're here? I heard you were here the other night, too. So is he your new boyfriend?"

"No comment."

"Wait a second," interjected the second reporter, walking up to the conversation. "You're the one being stalked, right? I saw your daddy on TV yesterday, talking about some crime bill he's trying to push through." The reporter stepped closer, invading my space. "Who's stalking you, huh? Are you scared for your life? What do you think he's going to do to you if he catches you?"

The questions came like bullets, one after another. I staggered backward, as they all loomed toward me, cameras raised and ready. It was then that I glanced back at Troy's apartment, noting that while the window shades were all pulled, a corner of one was slightly lifted—just a couple of inches. As if he were watching the scene from inside.

With newfound strength, I turned back to the vipers in front of me, invading Troy's nest. I needed to get rid of these guys. At least for a short time. So I could extract Troy and get him somewhere safe. Where no one could bother him.

Sucking in a breath, I pasted on my biggest, brightest smile. "Fine. You want a story? I'll give you a story. But you need to promise to get the hell out of here once I do."

"Sure, baby. You give us something to sell, we'll take off."

I nodded. I knew they would come right back. But that would at least give me enough time to extricate Troy without them watching. Of course I didn't really have much of a story to tell. The last thing I wanted was to talk about my stalking. There had to be something else they'd be interested in.

Suddenly, I remembered the phone call back at work. The one from the employee of Water World.

"Okay, here's the deal," I said. "I'm going to be staging a new protest against Water World. Remember how I did that back in the day? Well, now I'm going to shut those bastards down, once and for all. And when I do? I will give you guys the exclusive story behind my investigation. But only if you leave now."

They looked at one another and I could see the greed and excitement in their eyes. They knew that this could be a big story. But they still weren't sure they could trust me to tell it. One of them turned back to me. "How do we know you're going to call us?" he demanded.

"If I don't, well, you can always feel free to come and stalk me yourselves," I told them. "You know where I work. You probably know where I live, too. I don't think it would be too hard for you to make my life miserable."

They laughed at this. "Okay, fine," said the older guy. He turned to his friends. "This is old news anyway." He reached into his pocket and handed me his card. Then three others followed suit. I collected the cards and put them in my purse.

"Bye-bye boys," I said with a smile. "We'll talk soon."

They nodded and headed back to their cars. I stood in front of Troy's apartment, watching them go. When they had finally all pulled out of the parking lot, I turned and knocked on the door.

thirty-one

TROY

I heard Sarah's knock and stepped away from the window where I'd been watching the scene, trying to make sense of it all. How had she made those assholes just walk away? Seriously, she must have had some kind of crazy superpower against paparazzi. I was impressed to say the least.

But that didn't mean I wanted her to come into my apartment now. I didn't want her to see what a mess I'd made last night, when trying to build the barricades. The place looked like a crazy person had shacked up inside. And hey, maybe there was a reason for that.

But Sarah wasn't going to make it easy for me to turn her away.

"Come on, Troy," she called through the door. "I know you're in there. I saw you peek out the window. Just open up. The reporters are gone, I promise."

Sighing, I forced myself to walk over to the door. She wasn't the enemy, I tried to remind myself. She was only trying to help. Not that I deserved any help. Especially not from her.

I pulled open the door, my heart aching in my chest as I found her on the other side. Despite my reluctance for her to see how far I'd fallen, I was happy to see her. I was always happy to see her.

She gave me a bright smile and pushed a box of donuts into my hands. "Hungry?" she asked.

"Not really." But I took the donuts anyway, though I didn't move from the doorway. My heart beat nervously in my chest. *Please don't ask to come in. Please don't ask to come in.*

"Uh, can I come in?"

"The place is kind of a mess," I stammered. "I really don't think . . ."

She pushed past me, grabbing the donuts out of my hand and heading to the kitchen. I sighed and closed the door behind her. I should have known I couldn't keep her out. I glanced warily over to her, then to the mess I'd made, waiting for her to comment on it. But she just set about opening the box and grabbing a donut from inside.

"You may not be hungry," she said. "But I'm freaking famished. I'm pretty sure I could eat the whole box."

I watched as she put a donut to her mouth, her face morphing into pure joy as she bit into it. My stomach betrayed me with a growl. I bit my lower lip, watching her devour the donut, then gave in and joined her in the kitchen, taking one of my own. What the hell, right? It was just a donut. Everyone needed to eat.

"So," she said, after swallowing. "Want to talk about what happened at work?"

"Not really."

She sighed. "Then at least tell me you're okay."

"I'm fine."

"That's the worst answer ever."

"Sorry to disappoint." I frowned, the donut dropping like dead weight into my stomach. I wondered if it would be rude to ask her to leave. Or if she'd agree to do so, even if I asked. It was crazy how much I wanted her here—yet didn't want her here, all at the same time. Half of me wanted to kick her out the door and tell her to never come back. While the other half wanted to drag her into the bedroom and hold her all day long—like some kind of security blanket.

I really was going crazy, wasn't I?

She closed the box of donuts. "Look, do you want to get out of here?"

"Excuse me?"

She glanced at the front door. "My guess is we have about a half hour to vacate the premises before new reporters show up." Her eyes flashed with mischief. "Which gives us just enough time to run away from home."

I raised my eyebrows. I didn't want to be as curious as I was. "Don't you have to be at work?"

"Ben's got it covered."

Right. "And where would we run away to, exactly?"

A smile played at her lips. "I'll give you three guesses. And the first two don't count."

"Oh." My heart thudded in my chest, a little too hard for comfort as I suddenly realized exactly where she was suggesting. The place we used to retreat to back in the day when things got stressful at school or with her dad. We'd jump in the car and "run away from home" as she liked to call it. Heading south of the border to Rosarito, a charming little beach city just south of Tijuana.

I bit my lower lip. "I don't know," I hedged. The idea sounded heavenly, to get away from it all. To leave all the stresses behind. But the idea of being alone with her—in a place we used to find so romantic. Would I be able to handle that?

"Come on," she cajoled, clearly not willing to take no for an answer. "I mean, do you really want to be here when those guys come back?"

I shook my head, giving in. "I need five minutes to pack a bag."

She glanced at her watch. "I'll give you three. And don't forget your bathing suit."

I nodded, though the idea of going swimming—doing something so normal and innocuous—seemed half like an impossible dream. But I threw my trunks in the bag just in case. Then I added a couple of shirts and a pair of shorts and some sandals. Out of the corner of my eye I could see her in the kitchen, her eyes straying to the pile of stuff I'd used in the barricade. I felt my face heat.

"Sorry," I said as I emerged. "Maid's day off."

She waved a hand dismissively. "You should see my place."

I'd seen her place; it was immaculate. But I appreciated the sentiment anyway. She had to know this wasn't a normal mess. But she'd made me feel a little bit more normal by accepting it as one.

"You ready?" she asked, raising her eyebrows at me.

I sighed. "As I'll ever be."

"Then let's get the hell out of here."

We jumped into her convertible and she opened up the top, allowing the warm San Diego air to ruffle my hair and tickle my neck. Soon we were driving down I-5 toward Mexico—officially on the lam, once more with feeling.

Rosarito was a bustling beach community, about ten miles south of the border. Home to restaurants, nightclubs, shops and waterfront hotels, it was a popular Southern

California tourist destination. Random trivia? It was also the source for the rocks in the collectible Pet Rocks craze of the 1970s.

We had discovered the place back in college. Sarah had been complaining about her father micromanaging her life and how it made her want to run away from home. The idea that she could just leave the country, at the drop of a hat, with no plans and no destination, gave her the sense of power she needed to take back her life.

Something I wouldn't mind doing right about now, if we were being honest.

She turned to me, the wind whipping through her hair, a big smile on her face. "Book us a room at the Rosarito Beach Hotel," she instructed. "I can pay cash when we get there." She winked at me as she said it and I remembered our old scheme. If she paid cash, her dad couldn't track her down through her credit cards.

It really was, suddenly, feeling like old times. Better times.

I nodded, reaching into my pocket for my phone. While there were many hotels in Rosarito, none compared to the Rosarito Beach Hotel, so it wasn't a surprise she wanted a room there. We'd spent many a night there, back in the day. Many of which we never ended up leaving the room. I swallowed hard as I remembered some of the adventures we'd had in those hotel rooms. And I couldn't help but cross my fingers for a redo, even though that was probably the last thing we needed at this point. I needed to get myself back together before I could hope to share anything new with her.

I made the reservation and we crossed the border, heading past Tijuana, down Route One toward the beach. We didn't talk a lot, but that was more of a relief than anything. I didn't have a lot I wanted to say and I appreciated the fact she wasn't pressing me. I had no idea if that would change once we reached our destination, but I decided not to borrow trouble for now.

Soon we had arrived at the hotel, driving through its magnificent archway entrance, welcoming guests to the beach. It was an old-style hotel, originally built in the 1920s, and still retained a sense of old-world glamour to this day. Over the years, it had played home to royalty and celebrity and more than its share of surf bums, looking to catch the perfect wave. In short, it was a perfect hideaway for two lovers trying to escape the world. Like we had been once upon a time.

She paid in cash, as promised, and I was surprised at first when the hostess didn't call her by name. She used to be such a regular they'd recognize her instantly. Envelop her in a big hug and welcome her back. Guess she didn't come around here very much anymore. Which made me both happy and sad. Sad that she'd abandoned her favorite place. Happy that she probably hadn't brought any new men around to share it with her.

We went up to the room and she immediately walked out onto the balcony, as I knew she would, to gaze out onto the sea. It was funny; the more time I spent with her, the more the memories flooded back. I'd started to remember her small tics, the way her mind worked. The way she moved. Which made me remember what she'd always do next after the balcony thing. Take off her clothes and walk around in the nude.

That probably wasn't going to happen this time.

I plopped down on the bed, suddenly feeling awkward. What were we doing here? What was on our agenda for the day? She had mentioned bathing suits . . . did she seriously want to go take a swim?

I cleared my throat as she walked back into the room. "Have you gotten any more threats from Ryan?" I asked.

She gave me a wry look. "Remember how I said you should see my place? I swung home this morning and found two broken windows. And the place was trashed on the inside."

"Oh my God. Did you call the police?"

"Of course. But I can't prove it was Ryan. I mean, it looked like your everyday break-in."

"They should at least pick him up for questioning."

"I'm sure they will." She sighed deeply. "I just wish he would go away. With everything else going on, I so don't have time to deal with this."

I nodded. "I'm sorry," I said simply.

"It's not your fault."

"Well, that's not entirely true," I reminded her. "In fact, in a way this is all my fault."

She shook her head. "It doesn't matter," she replied quickly. Too quickly. And I could tell from her tone that it did matter. It mattered a lot.

"Sarah . . ." I tried. But before I could get the words out—the apology I so desperately wanted to repeat—she had crossed the room. Invaded my space. Pressed her body against mine.

"I don't want to talk anymore," she said.

And then, she kissed me. Wrapping her arms around me, pulling me close to her. Soft curves melting into hard flesh. For a moment, I couldn't move. I was shocked into stasis by her unexpected advance. But that didn't last long, and soon my body woke up as I grabbed her and pushed her down on the bed. A low growl escaped my lips as I climbed on top of her, kissing her hard on the mouth. My knee between her thighs. My hand on her breast.

The memories of before were still flooding back, but suddenly paled in comparison to this reality unfolding before me. In that moment, I didn't want to think, I just wanted her. Just as I'd always wanted her. And so I pulled her shirt over her head, then unclasped her bra, tossing it to the side. Dropping down, I pulled one of her nipples into my mouth, rejoicing in the feel of her against my tongue. She writhed beneath me, her fingers grabbing fistfuls of the duvet, her body thrusting against my knee. I dropped my hand between her legs, finding the sweet spot and using my fingers to coax her to climax. The way she was moving under me now, I wasn't sure I'd even have to take off my jeans to fall over the edge.

Then, suddenly, she stopped short. Jerked away from me, retreating to the far side of the bed, her arms crossed over her chest. I looked up, confused and dazed and stupid, feeling as if half my soul had unexpectedly been ripped away.

"What's wrong?" I somehow managed to ask.

She winced, burying her face in her knees. "What are we doing?" she moaned.

My mouth dipped to a frown. "You tell me. You were the one who started this. Who brought me here to begin with." I paused, then added, "Why did you bring me here, Sarah?"

She shrugged her thin shoulders, at first seeming unwilling to answer. Then, at last, she let out a heavy sigh. "I heard what happened at work. And I saw those reporters camping outside your house. I thought it would be good for you to get away. To get your mind off things for a bit."

"So, what, this was supposed to be just a pity screw?" I demanded, anger rising through me now. I struggled to push it back down. I didn't want to lose control again.

"No!" she cried. "Of course not! I didn't even mean to—oh God." She let out a small cry, grabbing her shirt and yanking it over her head. "I just wanted to help you. That's all. But then we got here and all these memories started flooding back and . . . I just couldn't help myself."

I felt an unexpected tingle of pleasure at her reluctant confession. The realization that I wasn't alone in any of this. That she'd also been taken by the moment, the memories of this hotel. I crawled toward her, up the bed, slowly, so as not to scare her. "Then don't," I said. I reached out a hand to stroke her leg with gentle fingers. "Don't fight it."

"You don't understand," she whimpered, though she didn't, I noticed, pull her leg away. "I can't do this to myself all over again. I can't let myself care for you. I did that already and you broke my heart. I want to help you. But I have no wish to put myself in that situation ever again."

She drew in a shaky breath. "I'm sorry. I thought I could control it. To make this just a physical thing—no strings attached. But I just can't. Not with you."

I fell back on the bed, staring up at the ceiling. My heart shattered at the pain I could hear in her voice. Pain I had caused. Of course she didn't want to be with me. Not after what I had done to her back then. Not to mention how little I had to offer her now.

"I care about you, Troy. I really do," she continued. "But I have to protect myself, too. And you should be trying to do the same." She gave me a rueful look. "I'm worried about you, Troy. I know you don't want to hear this, but to be honest, at this point, I don't really care. I can't just sit back and watch you self-destruct. And I'm sorry if that makes you mad, but it's true. I can't help it. Like I said, I care about you. And I don't like what I see happening to you. I don't want to see you like this."

My body stiffened and my eyes turned to the door. Every fiber in my body begged me to get up and walk away. To salvage what pride I had left. To prove to her I didn't need her help or her pity. That I could fight this, I could get back what I'd lost. I could regain control.

But in my heart I knew that wasn't true. She was right. I was cracking around the edges. I was falling apart. If I kept going, if I let myself get worse, I'd probably end up losing my job. My apartment. Any friends I had left. I'd seen those veterans on the streets, homeless and alone. Before now, I'd never understood how that could happen to someone.

Now I understood all too well.

Everyone had tried to help me. And I had done nothing but push them away. Except for Sarah. Sarah, who kept coming back. Sarah, who had her own issues to deal with—a man stalking her, threatening her. And yet, she was still here. Still trying desperately to help me, even as I stubbornly refused that help.

I didn't deserve her—that I knew. But she was here. Now. Ready to listen. And God did I suddenly have a lot to say.

I drew in a shaky breath, turning to her now.

"You know how they say if you think you're going crazy you're probably not?" I asked with a brittle laugh. "That's been, like, my only reassuring thought since I've been back. But I don't know how true it is anymore. My mind is a mess. My emotions are out of control. I can't sleep at night—and when I do I have terrible dreams. Some days I feel so exhausted I can barely get out of bed. Walk out my front door and face reality.

"Like today? If you hadn't come to drag me here? I don't know when I would have been able to leave the house again. And not because of those reporters outside. Well, not just because of them anyway. But because I'm afraid of what I might do to them. When the anger rises I feel completely out of control. I'm afraid I'm going to hurt someone."

I shook my head, the emotions raging through, hard and fast. "That's why I had to leave Friday night. And I'm sorry—you didn't deserve me to walk out that door. I know you were only trying to help. But I was scared. Scared that I was going to lose it again. And that you would see me crumble to pieces."

I paused, daring to glance over at her, expecting to see horror, maybe disgust, and probably fear on her face. But instead of that, I saw only concern in her eyes. Not pity, either. Just . . . empathy. Kindness. Maybe even a little affection. Which was insane, of course. How could anyone feel affection for me after what I'd just admitted?

"Troy," she said, after a pause. "I hope you don't mind, but I've been reading up on PTSD. And what you're describing? It's not crazy. It's a completely normal reaction to what you went through. You were pushed to the limits of your sanity. You were forced to face things no person should ever have to face. Of course it's not going to be easy to get back to where you were. Of course you're going to be stressed out, amped up, emotional. Of course there are going to be times when you want to withdraw from life because it's too hard. Or too scary or too stressful to deal with." She gave me a rueful smile. "But the good news is? You're not alone. There are literally millions of people out there going through what you're going through now. And the even better news? There's help available."

I opened my mouth to speak but she raised a hand to stop me. "I know you don't want to go on medication," she said. "And that's fine. That's your choice. But there are other resources out there—other professionals who will help you with other kinds of therapy. Cognitive therapies, exposure therapies. Sometimes just talking through what happened can make these symptoms lessen. I'm not saying you're going to be instantly cured. But you can start wrestling back control of your life." She gazed at me with her huge, beautiful blue eyes. "That's all I want for you, Troy. For you to find peace again. Maybe even happiness. Is that so wrong to want?"

I felt the tears prick at my eyes and angrily tried to swipe them away. "I don't deserve you," I whispered. "After what I did to you . . . Why are you still even here? I ruined your life. I ran away. You shouldn't be here now, trying to save me."

"Oh, Troy . . ." I heard the pain in her voice. "Don't you get it? I still care about you. And yes, maybe that makes me an idiot, but I'm okay with that. What happened back then, it wasn't good. And yes, it broke my heart. But it didn't break me. I'm still here. I survived. And you will, too. If you just give yourself half a chance."

I rolled over, peering down at her, at her beautiful face. At her deep, soulful blue eyes—eyes I could stare into forever. I drew in a breath, knowing suddenly what I had to do. What I had to say. What I should have said long ago.

"How can I move on?" I asked quietly. "Knowing you will never forgive me? That you won't even listen to me when I try to bring up the past? You talk about therapy, talking things through. Yet you refuse to talk about what happened with us." I swallowed hard. "If I'm really going to be able to work through this, I have to start at the beginning. I have to make things right with you."

I paused and I could see her shoulders stiffen, as I could have predicted they would. She didn't want this. Didn't want to deal with it anymore. She would rather push it all under a rug—try to forget it ever happened in the first place. Just like she'd probably been doing for the last five years. Like I had been doing, too. But I couldn't keep pretending. I couldn't keep staring at the elephant that followed us around to every room. If I had any chance of reclaiming my life, it had to start with her. With us.

"Talk to me, Sarah," I begged. "Tell me how angry you were with me. Tell me how betrayed you felt. I can take it—really."

She stood up abruptly, walking out onto the balcony, once again staring out at the sea. For a moment I thought she was going to refuse me altogether. And I wondered what I'd do if she did. But then she turned, stepped back into the room. Her face was a mess of mixed emotions. Her eyes were rimmed with tears.

"I loved you," she said. "I trusted you. I gave you my heart."

I forced a nod. "I know."

She paused, something flashing across her face. Something . . . angry. "No," she said, waving a frustrated hand across her body. "That's not exactly it. I mean, that's part of it, of course, But there was so much more as well. Because it wasn't just our relationship that you stole from me. It was my whole life. And I know that sounds completely over-dramatic, but in a way it's true." She raked a hand through her hair. "When I was with you, when we were protesting— it was the first time in my life I'd ever felt like more than just my father's daughter. This precious princess, heir to the throne." She scowled. "I always wanted to be more than that. And with you, I felt, for the first time, that I was." Her voice cracked. "And then . . . to find out it was just a lie all along?"

"It wasn't a lie!" I corrected fiercely. "You were that person. You worked tirelessly on that campaign. You protested. You went undercover. You were willing to risk your safety and your family's future—all to save those animals."

"But for what?" she demanded, giving me a look that pretty much killed me. "It was for nothing! No one gave a shit about those animals in the end. Ryan was just out to rob my dad blind. And you—you simply parlayed it all into your own personal dream job. You both used me. And then you left me behind. And none of us ever helped save any freaking whales."

I drew in a breath. "I know. And you're right. I should

have never left. I should have stayed by your side. But I was scared. Your dad told me if I didn't take this job and leave the country I would go to prison like Ryan. I was a dumb kid and I was petrified and I reacted before thinking things through." I shook my head. "But that doesn't mean I wanted to leave you."

"Then why did you? Why didn't you agree to run away with me when I asked?" She bit her lower lip. "Oh, right. I remember," she added, her voice thick with sarcasm. "You told me you didn't want to live a small life. Or, in other words, I wasn't enough for you."

I hung my head. I wanted to deny it. To tell her she'd misunderstood. But I respected her too much to do that. She deserved to know the whole truth—no matter how painful it might be.

"I did say that," I agreed. "And I was fool enough to believe it at the time. But, Sarah, I was wrong. I realize that now. I was so wrong. A life with you would have been huge and wonderful and as important as anything else in the world."

A sob escaped her throat. But she turned her face away.

"There's something you don't know," I added. "Something I've been wanting to tell you since that day."

She was silent for a moment. Then, "What?"

I drew in a breath. Here went nothing. The secret I'd been keeping for five long years, out at last. "The first day of the trial," I said slowly, "I saw you standing in the courtroom. And suddenly I changed my mind. I realized how much I wanted to be with you. How awful life would be without you at my side. I ran out of that courtroom and found the first jeweler I could find. I bought you a ring. A diamond ring." My voice broke. "I was going to propose to you. I was going to agree to run away."

She turned to me, her eyes welling with tears. "But you didn't," she said, her voice filled with accusation, mixed with grief. "Why didn't you?"

"Your father wouldn't let me see you that night. I tried and begged but he wouldn't allow you to come to the door. The next day I went to court again, determined to talk to you on the way out. But that was the day you learned the truth—through Ryan's testimony. That he had orchestrated our relationship from the start. After that, you refused to talk to me. Never mind run away with me."

She swallowed hard. "Do you blame me?" she demanded. "I mean, what was I supposed to think?"

I shook my head. "I don't blame you one bit. I was wrong. I had made a terrible mistake. But at the same time, you never let me give you my side of the story."

She looked at me warily now. As if I were some wild dog she wasn't sure was about to bite. "What side? Are you trying to say Ryan was lying?"

"No. Ryan was telling the truth. He did ask me to date you. And he pressured me into getting you to flirt with that IT guy to get access to your father's network passwords. All of that was his idea. And I went along with it, like an idiot." I shrugged. "It was wrong. It was stupid and shortsighted. And you have every reason to hate me for what I did." I straightened up, meeting her eyes with my own. "But for you to say our entire relationship was a lie? That's just bullshit."

She opened her mouth, but I waved her off. I needed to finish this, once and for all. Lay all the cards out on the table.

"I loved you. I loved you from that very first day when you were selling those disgusting, undercooked cookies out on the campus lawn. I suggested you sell them at the Environmental Club meeting because I was too chicken to ask you out on the spot. So, yeah, when Ryan suggested I hook up with you? I was all in. Absolutely. One hundred percent. To me it was like being granted the winning numbers of the lottery.

"What happened between you and me? That was real. That was true. Ryan wasn't in the bedroom with us. He didn't tag along on those long walks on the beach. I didn't report back to him our conversations or share with him what I hoped would be our future. And in the process, I fell in love with you. Not what you could do for the cause, but you. You were so much fun. So passionate. So beautiful. So perfect for me. My girlfriend in every sense of the word. And the stupid way we'd first gotten together? That didn't matter a bit."

"Oh, Troy . . ."

"I would have run away with you. I would have married you. I would have had babies with you. And it wouldn't have been a small life. It would have been the biggest, most wonderful life I could ever imagine. And I'm so fucking sorry it didn't turn out like that in the end. I wish there was a way I could make it happen now. That I could melt your heart and force you to see how much you meant to me. How much you still mean to me."

I groaned. "I'm not going to lie. I'm an absolute mess. My life is in shambles. Half the people in this country think it would be better if I'd had my head chopped from my shoulders. I'm damaged goods, baby. The last thing you probably need is to be with a guy like me," I said. "And I know that. And I can accept that. But I can't accept you thinking that I don't love you. That I don't wish to God every single day of my life that things had turned out differently."

I stopped, suddenly feeling completely spent. Unable to say another word. Let her digest what I'd told her—let her come to her own conclusions. No matter what she decided in the end, at least I had been able to say my piece. To get it all out at last.

I felt her looking at me, but I couldn't raise my eyes to meet her own, too frightened of what I might find in their depths. If I caught even a hint of disappointment, I think it would have done me in.

But then she stepped forward. Taking my chin in her hands. Tilting it up and forcing my eyes to gaze upon her face. And what I saw there? It wasn't disappointment. It wasn't anger. It wasn't an accusing glare. There was sadness, yes. But there was also something deeper. Something tender. Something that looked a lot like love.

"Oh, Troy,' she said, shaking her head. "Do you really think I could have ever stopped loving you?"

And then, before I could reply, she kissed me, to make the words true.

thirty-two

SARAH

Our lips came together. Hungry, eager, but also soft and sweet. Surprisingly gentle for all the heat that had built up between us. I pressed further into him, playfully nipping at his lower lip, unabashed joy washing over me as his words echoed in my ears.

He loved me. He'd always loved me. He'd wanted to marry me—he'd even bought a ring. Yes, he'd made mistakes, but I had made mistakes, too. He'd acted terribly, but he'd also been wonderful. He'd brought light to my life. He'd given a sad little rich girl a reason to live. And now, all he was asking for was a second chance. A chance for him to prove this wasn't about Ryan. But about him and me—about us.

His mouth parted, a guttural growl escaping as his warm, velvet tongue slipped into my mouth. I gasped as his hands skimmed my sides, lifting my skirt to trace my hipbones, then dragging his fingers across my belly, dipping low, my stomach pooling with heat.

His hands rose to my breasts, cupping them softly as he continued to kiss me with growing passion. As his fingers found the tips, he squeezed them gently, sending a jolt of electricity straight through me, igniting my senses. I let out a small, eager cry, feeling the tears well in my eyes as my body blossomed back to life under his hands.

Yes, we'd already had sex. But, I realized, it'd been forever since we'd made love. And as he lay me down on the bed, floodgates of emotion broke inside of me all at once, memories surging unchecked with every kiss, with every caress. At that very moment, I would have given anything in the world just to remain in this room forever with Troy. Living that simple life we never got a chance to live.

"Sarah. My sweet Sarah,'" he murmured as he crawled on top of me, his body heavy over my own. His hand dropped down between my legs, stroking me gently, while his mouth trailed a searing path from my lips to my breast. I gasped, sensations rocketing through me now as his lips closed over the nipple under my bra, the sweet pressure of his hand caressing me below stoking an ever-building fire. God, he was going to make me come before he'd even taken off my clothes.

But no. Instead, he pulled his hand away, naughty boy, shooting me a mischievous smile as he raised himself up on the bed to pull off his shirt. My eyes went immediately to the blackened brand on his arm and I found myself reaching for it, wanting to touch it. To absorb the pain he must have gone through. Pain no one in the world should have to suffer.

He grabbed my hand before I could reach him, jerking it over my head. Clearly he wasn't ready to go there, and the thought sent an ache straight through me. He was still holding back. Still keeping that part of his life under lock and key. It made me so sad. But I told myself that at least this was a start—he had opened up to me about the past. The rest could come later. We had a lifetime, after all.

I scooted up on the bed, reaching down to pull up my own shirt over my head, then unclasped my bra. He watched me as if mesmerized by my actions, a clear hunger flashing in his eyes. Then, as if he could bear to wait no longer, his hands came forward, cupping my breasts again, running his calloused thumbs over the sensitive tips as his mouth met mine in a feverish kiss.

And so we kissed. And we touched. But we didn't rush this time. I didn't demand he go hard or fast. This time, I wanted it to be sweet, I wanted him to take his time—even if that was painful in and of itself, in a different way. After all, we had the room to ourselves. No one knew we were even here. For all purposes, at this moment, we were the only people on earth. Living the simplest life of all.

Not to mention the most blissful.

thirty-three

TROY

We made love three times. And each time was better, sweeter, more wonderful than the one before. The last time we were both so exhausted we took it slow. Deliciously, lazily slow. We'd barely finished when we fell asleep, locked into each other's arms. I had never felt more comfortable in my life than lying there, my limbs entangled with hers. It felt like a dream and I never wanted to wake up.

But we did wake up eventually. And when we did, I caught the wariness back in her eyes. Even after all we'd said. After all we'd done. She still couldn't trust this. She couldn't completely trust me. And I got that, I really did. But I couldn't accept it. Not anymore. I had to do better. I had to prove myself to her, once and for all.

And so I took her into my arms again, kissing her softly, my hands caressing her lower back. How could I convince her I was here for her? How could I make her see that I would do anything to prove my devotion?

Then realization hit me over the head. A light bulb that felt more like lightning in its intensity. How had I not realized this before?

Sarah had never asked me for anything.

Except one thing.

One thing that was more for me than it was for her.

I could give that to her. I could make that promise I'd refused to make.

I sat in bed, clearing my throat. Trying to push down the sudden nervousness that rose to my chest. I could feel her watching me, curious, a little worried.

"What's wrong?" she asked, tracing a finger along the inside of my thigh. I swallowed heavily; it would be so easy for me to grab her and start everything up all over again. Hell, I could already feel my body responding to her touch, as if she was pressing an ignition button.

But no. That was playing the short game. And I didn't want to do that anymore. If this was truly going to work between us, it had to go further than physical desire. I had to give her my heart as well as my body.

So I lay a hand over hers, my fingers closing around her palm. I brought her hand to my mouth and kissed it thoroughly, before setting it down on the pillow, a safe distance from my thigh.

Her mouth quirked. "Had enough of me already?" she teased.

"God no. I will never get my fill of you," I said with a laugh. "But I wanted to talk about something. Without being distracted."

She gave me a puzzled look but sat up in bed, pulling the blanket up to cover her breasts. Which was probably for the best, though I found myself missing them the second they went back under wraps.

I drew in a breath. Here went nothing.

"I love you," I said simply. "And I know you love me. But this time—I know I need to be worthy of that love."

She opened her mouth to interject—but I held up a hand to stop her. I had to get this out before I lost my nerve.

"You asked me to get professional help. And I'm ready to do that now. For you, I will do that. I don't promise I'll get medication, necessarily, though I'll hear what they have to say. But I'll talk to someone, no matter what. That, I can definitely do." I paused, searching her eyes with my own. "I would do anything for you."

To my surprise, her mouth dipped to a frown. "No," she said, shaking her head. "I don't want you to do it for me. Don't you see? I want you to do it for yourself."

"Sure. I mean, obviously I'd do it for me, too," I said quickly, hating that all-too-familiar annoyance rising up inside of me again. Why couldn't she just accept this for what it was—the ends justifying the means—instead of questioning my intent? I sighed. "I was trying to make a gesture here, Sarah. To show you how much you mean to me. I want to become a man who's worthy of your affection. And that requires me getting help to become that man again."

She gazed at me, her expression softening. "And I love that," she assured me. 'It's just . . . I worry about you. I want you to get better—of course I do! But not because I want it. But because you want it, too."

"I do want it. I'm not a fool, Sarah. Of course I want my life back. And I promise you, I will make it happen. I will make that appointment."

"Okay. Then do it."

"Wait, what?"

She grabbed my phone off the nightstand. "Make the

appointment." She handed me the phone then reached over to her side of the bed for her handbag. "I actually did some research and found a list of good doctors who specialize in PTSD. They mostly deal with veterans, of course, but I figured your case is so similar . . ."

"I can find a therapist, Sarah," I said, cutting her off. "I know how to use Google, too, you know."

Her face fell, hurt welling in her eyes. I sucked in a breath, closed my eyes and tried to reset. When I opened them again, I gave her a rueful smile. "I'm sorry," I said. "I'd love to see your list. I'll go online right now and make an appointment. For first thing tomorrow morning if that works with our schedule at News 9."

"I'll make it work," she assured me, her face glowing with excitement. "No problem at all. Oh, Troy. Thank you. This is the right choice, I promise. You'll see."

I nodded slowly, pasting a smile on my face. She looked so happy. So relieved. And it caused something inside of me to squirm uncomfortably, though I wasn't exactly sure why. Of course I should get help. It would be stupid not to get help.

So why was my noble effort of good faith to prove myself to her becoming more and more terrifying by the second?

thirty-four

TROY

Dr. Remington's office looked like it had been beamed straight out of a Hollywood film set with its large, built-in bookcases, a cozy plaid armchair, and the requisite couch in the center of the room. As I entered, she motioned for me to take a seat on said couch, then settled into her armchair, grabbing a pen and paper. I obliged, praying she wasn't going to suggest I actually lie down. I didn't need to become cliché on top of everything else.

"So, Troy," she said, looking down at her notes. "I want to start out with full disclosure and let you know that I have heard of you and your situation. At least what they've said on the news. But there's no judgment here. No preconceived notions. I don't want to talk about other people's versions of your story. I want to hear it from you."

I nodded, wringing my hands together in front of me. My heart was pounding in my chest and my breaths were shallow.

I tried to focus on what she was saying, but the blood rushed past my ears, making it difficult to hear her.

Dr. Remington gave me a stern look. "Are you okay?" she asked. "Are you feeling anxious, sitting here, talking to me?"

"It's not exactly a day at Disney," I admitted, feeling my face heat. "But I'm fine."

"Hm," she said, taking down a note. I strained to look, but couldn't read what she'd written down. Then she looked up. "Why don't you start by telling me what's been going on in your life the past few months? Since you returned home."

And so I did, haltingly at first. The words seeming to stick in my throat. Dr. Remington listened without saying much, taking a few more notes down in her notebook. I tried not to let the idea that I didn't know what she was writing distract me, but of course it did. I also tried to remind myself that she heard stories like this all the time—many of them, I imagined, much worse cases than mine. She wasn't going to judge me or think poorly of me because of something I admitted here. That was her whole job, after all.

Still, I decided not to mention barricading my door against the reporters. That was still a little too embarrassing to admit out loud.

"Okay," she said, when I finished up. "Listening to what you've told me, I'd completely recommend medication as a start. We could put you on an antidepressant. There are many great ones out there. We could try one and see how it goes and then reassess if it's not doing any good or giving you too many unwanted side effects. A correct medication should stabilize your moods. Make the anger and anxiety you're experiencing go away. Help you regulate your sleeping and make you comfortable at work."

"No." I shook my head. "I don't want medication."

I waited for her to argue like the first guy I had seen had. Singing the praises of modern medicine and how it had the power to make everything painful in life magically disappear.

Instead, she surprised me by nodding her head.

"Okay," she said. "That's your choice. And if you change your mind, the option is always there. In the meantime, I would then suggest we look into cognitive behavioral therapy as an alternative. It'll help you become more aware of your thoughts and feelings and help wrestle them back under control. I'd also like to try some prolonged exposure therapy. That would mean putting yourself in situations that cause you anxiety and stress. The kind of situations you've probably been avoiding. Studies show the more you can confront these situations the more your distress will eventually decrease."

My heartbeat picked up in my chest. "Like what?" I asked warily. "It's not like I can just go back overseas and relive the whole cave thing."

"No. Of course not. But you can talk about it."

I stared at her. "What do you mean?"

"Have you told anyone what happened to you down in that cave?"

"Sure. The government. The military. I was debriefed pretty hardcore when they rescued me."

"I'm not talking some dry chronological account of the events," she clarified. "I want to talk about what actually happened to you. And, most importantly, how you felt while it was happening to you." She shrugged. "Talking through the trauma can work like virtual exposure. It can help you take control of your thoughts and feelings when it comes to the trauma. In other words, the more you can talk through it, the less power it will have over you."

I bit my lower lip. "Okay. I guess." My pulse thrummed

uncomfortably at my wrists. Really not liking the idea of having to air my dirty laundry to a complete stranger.

She's just trying to help you, I scolded myself. *Just like she's helped soldiers coming back from the war. That's her whole job. It's nothing personal.*

Besides, what else could I do? If I wasn't willing to take medication, this was the only other option, as far as I could see.

For Sarah, I told myself. *You man up for Sarah.*

"We can try right now, if you're up for it," she said, pulling out a tape recorder and setting it on the desk. I eyed it warily.

"What's that for?"

"I tape your stories," she said. "And I give you the tapes at the end. Then you'll go home and listen to them from start to finish. Not just once, but every day. While you listen, I want you to record your anxiety levels on a scale from one to ten. The idea is the more times you listen, the more control you get over the narrative. Your anxiety should start to lessen. In the end, if we are successful, you should be able to talk to your loved ones about what happened over there and feel very little distress by doing it."

"But . . ." I shook my head, now completely unnerved. "I don't want it to mean nothing. It changed my life. I can't just let it go and make it nothing."

"If you can't, then you'll never be able to move forward with your life," she said sternly. "Is that what you want?"

"No. Of course not." I raked a frustrated hand through my hair. What I wanted, at this point, was to get up and walk out that door and never come back. But I'd promised Sarah I'd do this. I couldn't bear the disappointed look I knew I'd see on her face when she learned that I'd failed.

"Okay then. Now, before we get started, how is your anxiety level right now?"

I squirmed in my seat. "On a scale of one to ten? About fifty." I snorted.

She gave me a sympathetic smile. "Understood. And that's fine. But let's try to bring it down a notch before we get into this. I want you to think of something, now, that makes you happy. That makes you feel peaceful and calm. It could be a beautiful sunny day. An adorable little pet. Even a pleasurable sexual experience might work. Whatever it takes to bring that level down. Not to zero, necessarily—you're going to feel anxious the first time you tell your story—that's pretty much a given. But if it starts to feel like too much, like your skin is crawling and your heart is pushing through your chest, you can stop. You can think about this good thing again, dial it back down. You have that power."

I swallowed hard. She made it sound so simple. And maybe it was. Maybe I'd been overthinking this whole thing all along. Maybe this could actually work.

A thin strand of hope seemed to wind its way through me and I breathed in deep, searching my mind for something that made me peaceful and happy.

Or, more precisely, someone.

"What are you thinking about?" Dr. Remington asked. "What's brought that smile to your face?"

I felt my cheeks redden. Had I been smiling? I let out a nervous laugh. "There's this girl. She's my ex, actually. But we've been talking a lot since I've been back. Well, sometimes more than talking . . ." Now my face was burning red.

"Do you want her back in your life?"

"God yes. I want her to be my life. But I'm not worthy of her. Not like this. I need to get better. To be the man she needs me to be."

"That's a great motivation, Troy. Okay, think of this girl for a moment. Think of her arms wrapping around you, holding you close. Maybe stroking your hair. She loves you. She will keep you safe. No matter what you say, no matter where your memories take you, she will be there. And you will be safe. Okay?" After I nodded, she pressed record on the tape recorder. "Okay. Now tell me about the day you were kidnapped."

"I was delivering a news broadcast," I said slowly, each word taking an effort to form in my mouth. "I was reporting live on this attack of Damascus. The network had told me not to go to the area—that it was too dangerous." I made a face. "But I laughed at them. I told them we'd be fine. I knew the area. I knew the people. I thought . . ." I let out a breath. "I was stupid and cocky and reckless."

Dr. Remington nodded. She didn't make a note this time, thank God. "Go on," she said instead.

"As I was doing my live shot, this guy came up behind me and grabbed me. He was wearing a mask. I tried to fight, but he put a gun to my head. Told the folks back home that I would be executed tomorrow if the government did not agree to their demands."

When I paused, for breath, Dr. Remington looked at me. "Okay," she said. "Those are the facts of what happened to you. Now, I want you to dig deeper. What was going through your mind? What emotions did you feel?"

I squirmed in my seat. "I was fucking scared, of course," I blurted out after a moment. "I mean who wouldn't be? I thought I was going to die!"

"You were scared," Dr. Remington repeated. "What else?"

I raked a hand through my hair. I could feel my heart pick up its beat. "I was . . . angry, I guess. And annoyed in a way. Like I kept thinking I had this dinner that night with the network brass. And I wasn't going to make it." I gave a brit-

tle laugh. "How stupid is that? I knew I was going to probably be killed and I was mad I was missing a dinner date."

"Good. What else?"

"What do you mean?"

"What else did you feel?"

"I don't know." Now my heart was pounding in my chest.
I tried to remember that moment as it happened. "I guess . . .
damn." I sucked in a breath. "I guess I felt lucky, okay?" I
stammered at last. "And guilty, too. They killed my producer. My cameraman. Right then and there. They weren't
valuable enough to take I guess. I don't know. I was the big
bad celebrity reporter and they weren't shit."

My voice cracked. "Except that they were. They were awesome. They were my friends. They were fathers. They had
children waiting for them to come home. And I was the one
who put them in danger." I could feel the tears stream down
my cheeks now but didn't bother to brush them away. "They
didn't want to come. They wanted to do what the network
said and play it safe. But I dragged them there anyway. I even
teased them that morning, calling them cowards." My voice
broke. "But they weren't cowards. They were brave. They
were so brave and they died because of my arrogance. And
I'll never be able to forgive myself for that."

"Okay. That's good. That's really good," Dr. Remington
said.

Rage exploded inside of me. "That's not good!" I cried. "I
might as well have pulled the trigger myself. They died and
I was able to walk away unscathed. How is that even fair?"

I lurched to my feet, knocking over a nearby potted plant.
It crashed to the floor, dirt and pottery flying everywhere.
Broken, destroyed, because of me. Just like Tom and Joe
had been. Because of me.

Because of me.

"I need to go," I said.

"No. You need to sit down. Get back to your safe place."

"My safe place?" I repeated incredulously. "Are you even kidding me right now? Why should I have a safe place? Tom and Joe didn't get a safe place. They got their heads blown off. Why should I even be here? No one even cares that I'm alive. They had kids, damn it. Kids and wives and families. They should have been the ones to survive, not me!"

My mind whirled, my stomach cramped. I leaned over, wondering if I was going to puke. I had to get out of here. Now.

"I'm sorry," I said. "I have to go."

And with that, I ran out the door.

thirty-five

SARAH

How'd it go?" I asked, rising from my seat as Troy walked into the entertainment office late that afternoon. I'd been on pins and needles the whole time, waiting for him to return. Wondering how it would go with the psychiatrist I'd helped him line up. I knew Rome wasn't built in a day, and that it would be a long time, likely, before we saw any solid results. But it was a step in the right direction. And I was so proud of him for taking it.

The rest of the day in Mexico had gone by in a delicious blur. We'd made love a few more times, then actually gone downstairs to check out the pool. We swam for a while, then walked the beach and had dinner at a little seaside restaurant that served the best fish tacos I'd ever eaten. After that, we headed back to the room, both exhausted. We tried to continue watching *Sunset Boulevard* off of my iPad, but we both fell asleep almost immediately. I had a feeling we were never going to finish that movie.

In short, it had been the perfect day. But when we woke up the next morning, things felt a little weird again. I guess it was the idea of going back to civilization. We'd successfully hidden out from our problems, in this little pod of paradise south of the border. But that didn't mean they had gone away. Ryan was still out there. My home was still unsafe. Troy probably still had reporters camped outside his front door. And he had to go back to work.

But he was going to get the help he needed. And that was a victory in and of itself. One major concern, taken away. And so we packed up our bags and headed back north, grabbing the rental car outside his apartment and promising to rendezvous at work after his appointment.

He flashed me a smile now. One that didn't quite reach his eyes. "The session was great," he said. "Well, I mean as great as it could go, being what it is."

My shoulders dropped in relief. A part of me—a very small part—had worried that he would chicken out at the last minute. Refuse to go. In fact, I'd almost volunteered to drive him and wait in the car for him to finish. But I didn't want him to think I thought he was some child who couldn't follow through with his promises. Plus, he had to do this on his own, for himself. Otherwise it wasn't going to work in the end.

I placed a hand on his shoulder. "I'm proud of you," I whispered. "This is a huge step. I know it couldn't have been easy."

"It wasn't that bad," he said, stepping backward, out of my reach. I frowned, a small thread of worry winding through me. But I pushed it back down. Again, it wasn't as if he'd just returned home from a morning at the beach. He was bound to be a little emotionally unstable, maybe a little stressed out, too, after being forced to bare his soul to a stranger.

I wanted to ask him everything. How it went, what she said, what her plan of treatment would be? Did she bring up medication? Did Troy refuse it once again? Did she offer an alternative plan? And was he more amenable to that?

But I kept my mouth shut. This was not my business. Therapy was a very personal thing—between him and his doctor. If he wanted to share it with me, he would. Otherwise I needed to just be grateful he was going in the first place.

I decided to change the subject. "So," I said, "we have a screening to go to this afternoon. One you might actually like. They say it's a reimagining of *Vertigo*. Initial reviews have been extremely positive. Charlize Theron is playing the Madeline character."

He smiled. "That sounds pretty cool, actually. Maybe we can even smuggle in some popcorn."

"Absolutely," I agreed, feeling my body relax. See? It was all going to be okay. We could go to the movie, eat our popcorn. Maybe even cuddle a little in the back row, just like old times. It sounded like heaven.

Almost a bit like a happy ending at last.

The week went by quickly, each day better than the last. Troy seemed to be a new man, coming into work on time, looking much more well rested than before, the haunted look almost disappearing from his eyes. I didn't know if it was due to the therapy he was participating in or the fact that the two of us had become closer than ever after our little Rosarito rendezvous.

Whatever it was—I'd take it.

Thanks to a short-term, furnished apartment rental I'd secured downtown, we'd been able to spend almost all our time together. Holed up in a cozy little nest, away from stalkers and reporters and fathers . . . and anyone else who dared tread on our new happiness. We'd walk to work, then walk home. Cuddle on the couch and watch TV. Or cuddle in the bed and watch each other. It was a little slice of paradise and I never wanted it to end.

But I did want to move forward with something else. Something I'd been researching myself all week, without mentioning it to him. I wanted to make sure he was stable before I brought it up. I didn't want to accidentally open up old wounds.

But I did want to set things right, once and for all.

So one afternoon I approached him as he worked on the day's scripts. Pulled up a chair and gave him a cautious smile.

"So," I said, a little hesitantly, not quite sure where to begin. Or what his reaction might be to this turn of events. "There's this story idea I've been looking into. I wanted to get your thoughts."

"Oh?" he turned to me, his eyebrows quirking. "Let me guess. Another celebrity hooked up with his nanny and is undergoing a conscious uncoupling with his former wife?"

I laughed. "No. Well, probably. But that's not what I was talking about."

"Hm." He tapped his finger to his chin. "Someone had a Twitter feud with someone else and they broke the Internet except not really?"

I rolled my eyes. "Cute. But no."

"Oh, oh, I know! Miley Cyrus took off her clothes and took a selfie." He shook his head. "Though, is that even news anymore? Or is that just Tuesday?"

I shoved him playfully. "Will you listen?" I begged, giggling. "This isn't even an entertainment story."

"Interesting." He cocked his head in question. "Okay. Shoot."

I felt my face flush as his eyes focused on me, almost losing my nerve. I thought about saying "forget it" or "actually it was a new nanny scandal, how did you guess?" But then I thought back to our conversation in Rosarito. Of all the memories that conversation had brought raging back. If the two of us really wanted to come full circle—to show Ryan he hadn't won, well, this might be our only chance.

"Come here," I said, not wanting to be overhead. I led him over to the He Said, She Said studio and shut the door behind us. When I was sure we were alone, I turned back to Troy.

"Water World," I said with a secretive grin.

He frowned. "Wait, what? What about Water World?"

"It's still open for business."

"Yes. . . . And?"

"And it's presumably still violating state and federal animal rights laws on a daily basis."

He nodded. "Seems likely."

I swallowed hard. My pulse buzzed at my wrists. Here went nothing. "Well, as you know we lost all our undercover video back when everything went down. Ryan may have it—but he's obviously not going to hand it over. Besides, it's five years old at this point—clearly they would just argue that they've cleaned up their act since then."

"Right. Of course." Troy's eyebrows furrowed. "What are you getting at, Sarah?"

I twisted my hands together, nervous excitement rioting through me now. "Last week, before we went to Mexico, I got a call from a whistleblower. He'd seen my dad's press conference and remembered how I used to protest back in the day. He says all the bad stuff we were trying to stop back

then is still going on. And he's willing to take us through
the park at night, undercover, so we can get new video."

Troy frowned. "And what would we do with this new
video exactly?"

"Come on, Troy! We're reporters. We work for the number one news station in San Diego. We can get the video,
then show it to experts and get their opinions. Then we can
air the segment on TV as a big exposé."

"That sounds good in theory," Troy replied. "But they're
never going to let us work on something other than entertainment. Remember what happened when I tried to get my
old job back? Richard refused—saying I wasn't ready."

"Right. And maybe this is your opportunity to prove him
wrong!" I exclaimed. "Show him you are ready for real news
again." I shrugged. "I mean, think about how big this could
be. Imagine if this story went national. If it led to Water
World being shut down. It could be Emmy worthy." I smiled.
"Besides, we don't have to tell them we're working on it.
We can still do our regular jobs. And have Ben fill in if
anything conflicts. It's just one story, after all. They'll never
even realize we're working on it until it's ready to air. And
then, once they see it, how could they refuse?"

Troy bit his lower lip. I could practically see the gears in
his head turning as he considered the idea. I held my breath,
waiting for his reply.

"And you're sure this guy is legit?" he asked. "This isn't
some kind of trick?"

"I called Water World," I told him. "He definitely works
there. Evidently as some kind of security guy. Which is
perfect, if you think about it. He'll have the access to get us
in without getting caught."

Troy didn't answer at first. And he didn't look at me. My

heart began to feel heavy in my chest. Did he really think it was a bad idea?

I sighed. "Look, Troy, if you don't want to do this, that's totally fine. I mean, I know what you're going through—and you've only just started getting help. It's going to take a while before you're back to your old self. Unfortunately this can't wait. I can't risk this guy changing his mind. If I'm going to do this, it has to be now."

I gave him a pleading look. "Five years ago, I ruined my chance to save these animals. And it's something I've lived with every day of my life since. The idea of getting a second chance—to make things right at last . . . Well, I can't in good conscience pass that up."

He nodded, giving me a small, sad smile. "You're truly beautiful when you get all passionate about something, you know that?" he teased. "I mean, not that you're not always beautiful," he added quickly. "But when you get that determined look in your eye . . ." He shook his head. "What mortal man could resist you?"

I rolled my eyes. "I can think of plenty," I told him. "But if that's your way of saying you'll help me with this story? I'll take it."

"I will help," he said. "And not only for the chance of getting back to reporting on the streets. You may not realize this, but once upon a time I cared for those animals as much as you did. And the idea of shutting down those bastards for good? Well, how could I possibly say no?"

He reached up, taking my face in his hands, tilting my head until his eyes met my own. Then he leaned down and kissed me hard on the mouth. Chills raked through me, all while heat rose in my belly. When we came up for air, I glanced over at the studio door.

"You know," I said. "I did lock it when we came in . . ."

He grinned. "And we're the only ones with the key . . ."

"And we do have a couple hours to kill before our taping."

"Well, Miss Martin," he declared. "I know exactly what 'He' would suggest we do about this situation."

My eyes danced. "For once I'm pretty sure 'She' is in completely agreement."

thirty-six

TROY

To be fair, I really did try to go back to my therapist to continue my treatment, as promised. But the next day I got stuck behind a massive traffic accident, which would have caused me to miss half the session anyway. And the next day I had to meet with a Realtor to try to find a new place to live—I just couldn't stand all those reporters knowing where to track me down. On Thursday, I accidentally slept through my alarm, which wasn't a bad thing, necessarily—these days I needed all the sleep I could get. But it did mean missing appointment number four.

It was at that point the therapist called me on the phone. And left a message on my voice mail letting me know that this may not be working out. She had some long rambling speech about me having to want to put in the work if I wanted to get better. Which was ridiculous, of course. Because I really did want to put in the work. It was just hard to find the time.

I was too embarrassed to call her and beg her to take me back. So I decided it would be better to just find a new therapist and start over. Of course I would need to do some research first—to find someone who was a good fit for my personal situation and wasn't a big pill pusher.

Which was fine. I knew it was all going to be fine. But in the meantime, I felt terrible about Sarah. I knew how much she wanted me to go to therapy. And I'd promised I'd do it for her. No, wait. She wanted me to do it for myself. And I was. I was totally on the therapy train, heading down to the station. I just had to pick the right person and we could go to town. Next stop, PTSD Cure City.

But Sarah wouldn't believe that. Not if she knew that I'd accidentally lost my first therapist—the one that she'd found for me. She'd be hurt and angry and it would ruin all the newfound happiness we were sharing. She would see it as a sign that I wasn't jumping into our relationship with both feet. She would get cagey again, maybe. Maybe even call it off altogether. Which would be crazy, of course. Because I was getting help. At least I would be soon.

I had it all under control.

In any case, everything else? It was going great, with Sarah and I spending almost all our time together—at work, after work, all night long—and it was helping me feel so much more like myself. More than any shrink ever could. She'd put her beach cottage on the market and rented an apartment downtown and half the time I ended up just staying there instead of going back to my place. And who could blame me? There was something so cozy about the place she had rented. Small, but warm. In a huge skyscraper building with a doorman that made me feel safe and protected inside. No one could get in. No reporters could peek through my window. It was almost as if we had truly succeeded in running away together and hiding out from the world.

And it seemed to be working on all accounts. My stress levels had gone way down and Ryan seemed to be suddenly MIA, too. I didn't know whether that was because he didn't know where she was now or if he had just gotten scared away by the restraining order and her calls to the police. In any case, for the last week there had been no calls, no broken windows, no scrawled threats. Life was good again.

But perhaps the best part? The fact that we were working on something important together. Something that would hopefully make a difference. Sure, we still had to work on the entertainment drivel, but Ben was always on hand to help out with the daily pieces, so we could concentrate more on the He Said, She Said segment alongside our special investigation.

Our special investigation. I still got a thrill of excitement every time I thought about it. A chance to finally free myself from the mistakes of the past. To make everything right once and for all. I imagined the joy I'd see on Sarah's face when we finally shut those bastards down for good. Got those poor whales and other sea creatures the justice they deserved.

"Okay," Sarah said, curling up on the couch that night, a glass of wine in one hand, a stack of papers in the other. "Let's walk through this. Make sure we're not missing anything."

Since we couldn't talk too much about the investigation while at the station, in fear we'd be overheard, we did much of the work at Sarah's apartment in the evenings. Going over our notes and talking through what we'd learned that day. Sure, technically it was unpaid overtime, but it felt more like we were part of some secret superhero organization, working undercover to save the world.

"Okay," I agreed. I looked down at my laptop. "I did find some very good news today. When digging through the financials I found that about four years ago, your father sold off all his shares of the auxiliary company that controlled interest in Water World. Right around the time he started his mayoral bid, I guess."

"Sure. Because he didn't want to have whale skeletons in his closet," Sarah concluded, making a face. "Not out of any compassion for the creatures themselves."

"Hey. Whatever works. The good news is now you're completely an impartial party when reporting on this. Which you need to be, for full credibility. From what I can determine the company is now owned by some kind of foreign investment group who probably bought it in bulk and has never even stepped through its front doors."

"Okay." Sarah took some notes. "Try to track down a spokesperson for them. If we can't interview them on camera we'll at least try to get a statement. But not until we have our undercover proof."

I nodded. "How's that end of things going, anyway?"

"Good, I think. I watched the preliminary on-camera interview you did with the guy yesterday. He's still working on the arrangements to get us in to film. Evidently the park closes early on Sundays, meaning the cleanup crew finishes earlier as well. So we'd only have to deal with a few night watchmen. My guy says if we pay them enough they'll be happy to look the other way."

I frowned a little at this. "That sounds sketchy."

"I know. But in this case I think the ends justify the means. Construction workers on the Death Star and all that!"

I snorted. "What about cameras?"

"That's the best part. Our whistleblower is their security guy. So he has all the passwords to get into the system and turn them off. So there will be nothing to alert anyone off-site that something's going on."

I nodded. 'You don't think he'll change his mind, do you? Chicken out at the last minute?"

"No. He seems really passionate. And he's got all these ideas—maybe almost too many," she added with a laugh. "I had to remind him that the simpler the better in this case."

"Absolutely," I agreed. "Get in, get the video, get out."

"Shut them down," she finished with a grin. She gave a happy sigh, setting down her papers and curling herself into my arms. She looked up at me with her beautiful blue eyes and smiled. My heart melted and I leaned down to kiss her forehead, feeling so happy and content I could barely believe it. I never in a billion years thought I could get back here. But now that I was here, I never wanted to leave.

Which was why tomorrow morning, I needed to make that therapist appointment. I needed to prove to her I was worthy of this perfection.

."It's funny," she said, reaching out and entwining her hand in my own. "I'm so tired. And yet, at the same time, I've never felt so alive. It's like for these last five years I've been living half a life. Flitting from party to party. Having a great time, but never finding meaning in any of it. But now . . ." She shook her head, her face practically glowing as she spoke. "I feel like I'm on the precipice. Of something so great. Not just with Water World—that feels like just the beginning. Only the start of what the two of us can do to better the world."

I smiled down at her, my heart feeling very full. I squeezed her hand and brushed my lips across her cheek. "I know what you mean," I said. "I feel like I've been given a new life. And it's all thanks to you."

"Me . . . and your therapist, of course," she said, looking up at me. She smiled. "Obviously I can't take all the credit. You're the one putting in all the work."

I felt a blush creep across my cheeks. "Right," I said quickly. "All that work." I untangled myself from her, my stomach churning as I rose to my feet. She watched me, the smile slipping from her face.

"Is something wrong?" she asked.

"No." I leaned down and kissed her on the forehead. "I just have to hit the bathroom. I'll be right back. So we can finish up and get to, uh, more important things." I winked at her.

She tossed the papers on the table, a devilish smile returning to her lips. "Well, if they're that important," she teased, "maybe they shouldn't wait." She paused, then added, "Meet you in the bedroom?"

"I think I can make that work."

thirty-seven

SARAH

O h, yeah, baby! Look at that sexy piece of meat!"
I laughed as Stephanie catcalled Ben as he walked
out of the men's dressing room, modeling the gray suit,
navy-blue tie combo we'd picked out for him. His face red-
dened, but he did a little twirl, showing off the goods. Stephanie clapped her hands.

"Oh, yeah. That's the one!" she cried, jumping to her
feet. "Viewers are going start licking their TVs if you wear
that on air."

Ben rolled his eyes and turned to me. I nodded. "She's
right," I assured him. "Maybe a little tacky in her delivery,
but her instincts aren't wrong. Go ahead and put that in the
keeper pile and we'll move on to shoes next."

We'd spent all morning at the Fashion Valley mall, working on Ben's new look. At first it had been like pulling teeth
trying to get him to try something on. Turned out he was
pretty shy and awkward once you got him away from the

TV station and his beloved movies. And so, in desperation, I was forced to call in reinforcements. After all, no one knew fashion like my girl Steph. And before we knew it, we had three awesome outfits picked out and Stephanie had made appointments at her favorite Hillcrest hairstylist and manicurist as well.

"You need the complete package," she scolded him. "A suit is only the beginning."

"You know, if this whole reporting thing doesn't work out, you'd make a great *Extreme Makeover* host," I teased.

She waved a dismissive hand. "Meh. I'm about through with working for a living, thank you very much. I'm aiming for trophy wife next time around."

I snorted. "Any particular man in mind with room on his shelf?"

Her eyes glittered. "Julian, of course!" she cried, referring to the new News 9 sportscaster. "He's got more money than God after his NFL career. Though I'm not entirely sure the guy has room on his shelf for any more trophies. Not with all the baggage he carries around." She made a face. "Which is ridiculous. It's not like it was his fault he got hurt on the field and had to retire early."

I shook my head. "Trust me. If at all possible, stay clear of men with baggage."

She pursed her lips, giving me a curious look. "I thought all was happy and shiny in Sarah-and-Troy land these days."

"It is. I mean, mostly." I sighed. "He's doing much better. He hasn't had any panic attacks, which is good. And I think working on the Water World story is really helping him keep up his spirits. So that's good, too."

"So what is it? Don't tell me the sex is bad!"

"God no." I laughed. "The best sex ever. That is definitely not the department in which we fall short."

"Well, that's a relief. So what is it then?"

I sighed. "Communication. Of course. That's always been our core issue—even back in the day. And now, well, he's always so worried about looking weak in front of me—like he's not handling things. And so he ends up shutting himself off and keeping things from me."

"Like what?"

"Like, I don't think he's going to therapy."

"But I thought—"

"Yeah. Me, too. Until I ran into the therapist I introduced him to at the grocery store the other night. She asked how he was. And I was so confused because I thought they had a session that morning. Well, it turns out he walked out of their first session—right in the middle—and never went back."

"Oh, Sarah . . ."

I shook my head. "I mean, he could be going to someone else. Maybe he just didn't feel like he and Dr. Remington clicked. But every time I try to bring it up he gets this weird look on his face and he changes the subject." I stared down at my hands. "So I'm guessing not so much."

"But you said he was good. He wasn't having panic attacks. He's been happy. Maybe it's not a big deal?"

I looked up sharply. "No. It is a big deal. His brain went through major trauma. You don't just walk away from that unscathed. He's like a powder keg. He looks fine on the outside, but any time he could just explode."

"Have you tried to talk to him about it?"

"Sort of. But . . . well, I just wanted him to be able to come to me." My voice broke a little on the words. "I want him to be able to trust me to talk about these things. He says he loves me. So why is he keeping this from me? And if he's keeping this from me, what else will he keep from me?"

"Oh, honey." Stephanie reached over and gave me a small

hug. "I'm so sorry. I know how much you wanted this to be a happily ever after."

"Yeah, well, I'm not giving up," I told her. "Not this time. I've started going to this group. It's for people who have loved ones with PTSD. It's actually really helpful to hear everyone's stories. Makes me feel less alone."

Stephanie shook her head. "And here I thought you were so happy."

"Oh! Don't get me wrong. I am happy. I'm so happy to have Troy back. And I love being with him. This is where I belong. It's just . . . I have to be willing to play the long game here. There's going to be ups and downs. He's not going to just get better overnight. I have to be patient. I have to let him take the lead on this and not pressure him. It's so hard for me, though. Sometimes I want to wring his neck and be like, 'Why won't you go get the help you need?' But even if I got him to go, he wouldn't be going for himself. He'd be going for me. And that's not good enough. If it's going to work, he's got to do it for himself."

Stephanie opened her mouth to speak but at that moment Ben emerged from the dressing room, back in his old geek T-shirt and faded jeans. He held up the suits in his hand.

"Am I ready for my close-up?" he asked.

Stephanie shot a look at me. I shook my head. We both laughed and jumped off the bench. "Not even close," Stephanie declared. "But don't worry. We'll get you there. By the time I'm done with my magic, Ryan Seacrest himself will have nothing on you."

We made our purchases and headed out of the store. As we passed a burger/pizza joint on the way out, my stomach growled and I suggested we take a break for lunch. Everyone agreed and we piled into a booth to place our orders.

As Stephanie started describing reporter-appropriate hairstyles in great detail to Ben, my eyes wandered to one of the TVs at the bar. It was on CNN. And there seemed to be some kind of breaking international news. I squinted for a moment, trying to read the scroll on the bottom of the screen to determine what was going on. Then I gasped, leaping from my seat and running to the bar.

"Turn it up!" I begged the bartender.

He gave me a strange look, but obliged, clicking the remote. A moment later the volume of the news report was blasting through the restaurant. I sank back down in my seat, my heart pounding as I listened to what the anchors were saying.

"Good evening," said the anchor. "We have breaking news to share with you tonight. Two freelance journalists have been reported captured just outside of Raqqa in northwest Syria late this morning."

The second anchor continued. "Details are still coming in, but it's believed these journalists were taken by the same group that abducted network news reporter Troy Young early last year. Back then, the government did eventually meet the group's demands and Young was sent home unharmed. No word from the president now about what will be done for this new case . . . or what the group is asking for, this time around."

"We're here now with Senator Baker from North Carolina. Senator, you were one of the most outspoken voices back during the Troy Young incident. What are your thoughts on this new situation?"

"Well, Kelly, I think it was just a matter of time. You negotiate with a terrorist, they're going to see you as weak. They're going to come back for more. I'm sorry for Mr. Young, but if we had acted decisively back then, I don't think we'd see this case come now."

I glanced over at Stephanie. Pretty sure my face was as white as hers was. My heart pounded in my chest. I turned to Ben, giving him an apologetic look.

"Sorry," I said. "We'll have to take a rain check on the rest of the shopping spree."

I had to find Troy. Now.

thirty-eight

TROY

"TROY!"

I jerked up from my seat, startled, as Sarah burst into the apartment. She looked at the TV accusingly and then back at me.

"What are you doing?" she asked. "Don't watch that." She ran over and grabbed the remote. I watched as the news broadcast faded to black.

I closed my eyes, sinking back onto the couch, sucking in a shaky breath. Then I opened my eyes again, staring at the TV. It was now blank. Black. But somehow I could still see the faces of those two journalists, embedded on the screen. Still hear the words of that senator, echoing through my head.

"You know, just because I can't see it, doesn't mean it's not happening," I remarked, picking at a piece of lint on my jeans as I tried to steady my heart rate. What had the therapist said about rating your anxiety from one to ten? Cause right now I was clocking in at about fifteen. Hell, maybe fifteen hundred.

Sarah gave me a worried look, then came over to sit beside me. She put an arm around my shoulder, rubbing my back with a gentle hand. I knew she meant the gesture to be comforting, to make me feel safe. But the way my skin was crawling now it wasn't much help.

"I know," she said softly. "But it's the last thing you need to see right now. You are going through enough on your own. And this could be really triggering for you."

"Yeah, well, maybe I should be triggered," I retorted angrily. God, I hated that word. "I mean, did you hear the senator? This is only happening because of me. The government agreed to their demands to set me free. Now they think they can do it again to get the next thing they want on their little list." I winced, the thought hitting me like a punch in the gut. I wondered if the men kidnapped were down the same hole I had been kept in. All alone, in the dark, the rodents scratching on the rocks. With that awful feeling of not knowing whether they were going to live or die. They were probably, even now, cursing my name.

"Don't listen to that idiot. He doesn't know what he's talking about. And besides, you've told me a billion times, you didn't ask to be saved. That wasn't your choice. You didn't make that deal."

"But that deal was made because of me," I said quietly. "So essentially the same thing."

Bile swam in my stomach, as if burning me from within. I wondered if I should go to the bathroom, try to throw up. Try to expel the poison churning inside of me. The guilt threatening to choke me.

God, I had been doing so well. Trying to forget. Trying to move forward. Trying to enjoy what life was now. And then something like this happens, throwing me back all over again. Making me realize I hadn't come as far as I thought had. That I hadn't made any progress at all.

That try as I might, this was never going to go away. I was never going to be the person I used to be again.

Sarah rose to her feet. She paced the room, wringing her hands together. "You can't just sit here like this, dwelling on things. You need to go talk to someone before you spiral into panic again." She turned to me, giving me a pointed look. "Do you have a therapist I can drive you to?" she asked.

I flinched at the question. "I . . . I'm fine. I don't need a ride," I muttered.

Her eyes zeroed in on me. "You don't need a ride because you can take your own car?" she asked. "Or you don't need a ride because you don't have a therapist to go to in the first place?"

I swallowed hard. Everything inside of me wanted to lie. To tell her I had been seeing someone—of course I had!— since that day I promised I would. But how could I lie to her, straight on? She deserved better than that. She'd been so supportive of me. So patient and loving and kind. I'd lied to her once and it had destroyed us. I couldn't do that again now.

I stared down at my hands. "Because I don't have a therapist," I admitted, the words scraping through my throat with great effort.

She let out a breath of relief. "Okay," she said. "Then let's find you someone."

I looked up, surprised. "Wait, what?" I stammered. "You're not mad? Or did you . . . already know?"

She gave me a heartbreaking look. "I . . . suspected," she admitted. "But it's okay. Really. We can start now. It's not too late."

Anger and frustration mixed with embarrassment swirled around in my head. Oh God. She'd known. She'd known all along and she hadn't even said anything. She'd waited for me to admit it. And now, once again, I'd let her down.

"But I've been fine," I added, unable to keep the desperate sound out of my voice. "I haven't had any panic attacks. I've been happy. I've been exercising even. And working. And everything's been fine."

I sounded pathetic. I sounded like a crazy person.

"Yes, Troy, You've been fine. At least on the surface. But that doesn't mean you're suddenly better. You can't pretend this didn't happen. You can't push your trauma down inside of you and expect it to stay buried. It'll always come back up. Things like this happen—and they're going to happen— and you'll find all that stuff you buried erupting out of you like a volcano. Bringing you back to ground zero time and time again."

I stared at her, speechless, a sudden realization smacking me upside the head. I hadn't made any progress at all. All of this happiness—it was nothing more than a smoke screen. A lie. And Sarah? She was no better than my dream Sarah had been for me down in that hole. A tiny Band-Aid placed over a mortal wound. A fantasy to hold on to, to ignore the ugly reality surrounding me.

She took a step forward now, her eyes radiating a mix of love and desperation and hurt and hope. It was crazy. So crazy to think she still retained hope for me. After all I'd done to her, all the times I betrayed her, lied to her, disappointed her and let her down. And yet she was still here. Still coming back for more like a wounded dog. And I kept letting her back in, knowing I was going to hurt her again. And again and again and again.

"I can't do this anymore," I ground out. "I'm sorry, but I can't."

She reached out to put a hand on my shoulder. "Troy . . ."

I shook her hand away, stepping out of her reach. "I'm sorry, Sarah. But we both need to stop pretending. Stop living in this fantasy world. This thing between us? It was over five years ago. And there's no going back. I'm not that guy anymore. And you're not that girl. And I can't keep going around in circles, knowing every time I fail, I'm hurting you. I'm letting you down." I hung my head. "You need to walk away while you still can. Find someone who deserves a girl like you."

"No. Troy. I don't want to walk away. I want to be with you." Her voice broke. "I love you."

I shook my head, my heart as heavy as my steps as I walked toward the apartment door, knowing full well once I stepped over that threshold I could never allow myself to go back again.

"Please, Troy," I could hear Sarah beg from behind me. "Don't do this to me!"

"Don't you understand?" I asked, pausing for a moment before taking that final step. "I'm doing this for you, Sarah. I'm finally setting you free."

thirty-nine

SARAH

Troy didn't show up to work the next day. Nor did he show his face the day after. My calls to him went straight to voice mail. When I went to his house, he didn't answer the door. If Richard hadn't told me he'd gotten a call from him, asking for a couple days' unpaid leave, I would have been freaking out worried.

Instead, I was just incredibly sad.

I tried to throw myself into work. But I found my mind wandering every time I sat down for a screening, and I could scarcely focus on the film. Instead, my mind chose to replay footage of Troy's exit from my life, over and over on endless loop. The way he had looked at me. With eyes filled with terror and guilt and desperation. The words that had come from his mouth.

I'm doing this for you.

But if that were true, then why was I the one who felt so broken now? Who felt like a total failure? I'd tried everything in my power to support him, to love him, to not set high expectations and not get angry when he didn't meet them. I'd been patient. I'd been kind. I'd loved him with everything I had. And it still wasn't enough. Because he was sick. And all the love in the world wasn't enough to cure this kind of sickness. He needed help.

More importantly, he needed to believe he needed help. And he needed to go get it. And keep getting it. Otherwise he would only get worse.

I still went to my group meetings. It felt kind of silly now, to be learning how to support someone with PTSD when I no longer had anyone to support. But listening to the other women talk about their experiences made me feel a little less alone. These women knew what I was going through. And they urged me to not give up on Troy. But what was I supposed to do—when he'd given up on me?

Stephanie tried to cheer me up. Forcing me to dress up, dragging me to night clubs, trying her best to show me a good time. Once upon a time her strategy would have worked. But now, it just seemed so vapid. So pointless. Watching the revelers weaving drunkenly down the street, dressed in their bar-hopping best. High heels, shiny faces, complete ignorance to what was going on in the world around them. How people were suffering. Hurting. Barely getting by.

It was hard to believe, watching them now, that I had once been one of them—and not that long ago either. Flitting from party to party, never thinking past the next club, the next cocktail, the next potential hookup.

In a way, it sounded kind of blissful. A total blackout from the pain I was suffering each and every day. But I knew, in the end, it wouldn't make me happy. And if given a choice, I would always choose this life instead. This brutal, exhausting, painful life. Because it was real. And I had the opportunity to make a real difference.

Because Troy or no Troy, I was still determined to save those whales. To shut Water World down for good. I'd finally gotten my whistleblower, Donny, to set the date for our undercover shoot. Sunday night, at midnight, I would meet him at the back gate, undercover camera locked and loaded and ready to film.

The plan was this: He'd take me around to get the footage of these animals and then I'd go back and show this footage to the marine biologists I'd lined up, so I could get their opinions on the conditions the animals were living in.

Once I had everything together, I'd package it up in editing and show it to Richard and ask him to air it as part of a special News 9 investigation. I didn't even care if I was the reporter on the piece—if he wanted the I-Team to treat it as if they'd done the work, that was fine by me. I didn't need the credit. I just needed it to air. For people to see, once and for all, what was going on there. And prompt them to take action at last.

I might never get my own fairy-tale ending. But I was determined to give those poor sea creatures their happily ever after, no matter what I had to do.

And as for Troy? Well, I wasn't giving up on him either. If he wouldn't talk to me, well, then maybe it was time to call in reinforcements.

forty

TROY

I'd been in the house for five days straight when Griffin rang my bell.

I considered not answering the door, but the ring was followed by a knock. Then he started calling my name. I realized the guy wasn't going to give up. And so I reluctantly headed to the door.

It wasn't that I didn't want to see him. Truth be told, I'd been going a little stir-crazy sitting in my house for so many days in a row. Each day I'd wake up and tell myself I should get out of bed. Go shopping for groceries. Maybe even go for a run. But each day that seemed harder and harder to do. And more and more pointless. Instead, I ate. I drank. And I watched the twenty-four-hour news station, waiting for updates of the kidnapped journalists. Wondering if they were still alive. If they had any hope of rescue.

It was as if I couldn't move forward with my life until I

knew for sure whether they would have lives to move forward with as well.

I opened the door. Griffin held up a six-pack. "You didn't want to meet me at the bar," he said, referring to his unanswered text, I assumed. "So I brought the bar to you."

"Um," I said, "this really isn't a good time."

"There's no bad time for beer," he insisted, pushing past me and heading to the kitchen. I watched him go with a sigh, resigning myself to my fate. Closing the door, I headed over to the breakfast bar, where he was busily opening two bottles. He pushed one in my direction. I took it, obediently taking a swig.

"So," he said, "I'd ask you how you are, but I'd be a fool to not know, just looking at your face." He took a long pull from his beer and sighed contentedly. "Nothing like a cold beer on a warm day." His eyes locked on me. "When's the last time you were outside?"

I shifted uncomfortably. "Um, yesterday I think?"

"Mmhm." He didn't sound like he believed me. Which was fine, since my statement was a complete lie.

I sighed. "What are you doing here, Griffin?"

"Checking up on you, of course," he said, looking surprised at the question. "From what I hear, you haven't been to work all week."

"Who told you that?"

His eyes locked on mine. "I think you probably know the answer to that."

I raked a hand through my hair, frustrated. Sarah. Of course. Why couldn't she just leave well enough alone? It was bad enough I missed her like fucking crazy. That every thought I had led directly back to her. The past few days had been torture, not being able to call her and talk to her. Not being able to kiss her and hold her close. I hadn't realized how much I'd gotten used to cuddling up with her at night, falling asleep in her arms. Until I had to fall asleep alone.

Or try to fall asleep at all, as the case might be.

But that was my problem to deal with. For her, I had done the right thing. I had set her free. I wasn't ready for a relationship. And she shouldn't have to wait for me. She might not see it that way now, but in truth I had done her a favor. And someday, when she met a guy who was normal and boring and safe and fell in love and popped out a few kids, she would realize what a bullet she'd dodged with me.

"She never gives up, does she?" I muttered now, staring down into my beer. My stomach churned, and I was no longer sure I wanted to drink it.

Griffin was silent for a minute. "Do you really want her to?" he asked in a low voice.

"Yes. I mean, not really. I mean . . ." I screwed up my face. "You don't understand."

"Then explain it to me."

I bit my lower lip, trying to figure out how to phrase it. In a way that didn't make Sarah seem like an idiot. Or me like an ass.

"She knew I wasn't going to my therapist," I blurted out at last. "She knew all along. And yet she didn't say anything about it. She just watched me stumble around trying to prove everything was fine. That I had been miraculously cured or whatever." I looked up at Griffin. "Why would she do that?" I demanded, my voice cracking on the words. "Why wouldn't she confront me about it? Yell at me for lying to her all over again? Tell me I was being a moron."

Griffin shrugged. "Probably because she wanted you to come to that conclusion yourself," he replied. "Loved ones can only tell you so much," he added. "You have to be willing to admit some things to yourself, too." He patted me on the arm. "Sounds like you've got yourself a smart girl there, kid. If I were you, I'd try to hold on to her with both hands."

I groaned, looking down at the hands in question. "No. I can't do that to her. I can't hold her back. She's amazing. I'm a fucking mess. She could do so much better with someone else. Someone with his shit together."

"Is that what she needs? Someone with his shit together?"

"Yes. Of course. She deserves that at the very least."

"Then why don't you go get your shit together, boy?"

I stared at him, shocked at the sudden roughness I heard in his voice. "Excuse me?"

He shrugged, finishing off his beer. I watched, incredulous, as he slowly, deliberately opened the next without answering. My heart pounded in my chest and my stomach churned.

"The way I see it," he said at last, "is that she's going to love who she's going to love. And she clearly loves your sorry ass. And there ain't nothing you can do about that. Except put in the work to make your sorry ass worthy of that love."

I shook my head, anger and frustration building up inside of me all over again. He didn't understand. I was doing this for Sarah, not myself. I was never going to get back to where I'd been. It wasn't fair to make her wait.

I turned away, my eyes catching the television in the other room as I did. They were finally giving an update on the two kidnapped reporters. Abandoning my beer, I ran to stand in front of the TV.

"The jihad group has released a video of the two hostages," the anchor was saying, "to show they're still alive. However the group's leader does insist they will execute them within the next week if the US does not respond to their demands."

I sunk down on the couch, scrubbing my face with my

hands, then squeezing them into fists by my side. A moment later I could feel Griffin sit down next to me, placing a hand over my fist. For a moment, he said nothing. Then . . .

"You think it's your fault, don't you?" he asked quietly.

"Of course."

"That's funny," he said.

I looked up, surprised. He gave me a sorry look.

"Well, not funny ha-ha, of course. But, you know, go figure, I thought the exact same thing when you were abducted."

I stared at him, confused. My heart beat wildly in my chest. "What the hell are you talking about?" I demanded.

He rolled his eyes. "Come on, kid. You only started reporting in that sector after I got my leg blown off, right? You wouldn't have even been near there if it wasn't for me being out of commission."

"Yeah, but that wasn't your fault," I protested. "It's not like you asked to be hurt!"

"Like you asked to be kidnapped?" Griffin replied, raising his eyebrows.

I groaned, sinking back onto the couch as his words hit me like a ton of bricks. For a moment I couldn't think of anything to say.

"Look," Griffin interjected. "Maybe you could have changed things. Or maybe things were meant to go this way all along. Doesn't matter. We can't go back in time. We can't erase our pasts. The only thing we can do is admit we need help and then try to follow through with getting that help." He gave me a stern look. "I know you think seeking help is admitting weakness. But I swear to you on God and everything, it's the biggest show of strength you'll ever make in your life."

He paused, then added. "You got out of that hole, Troy. And now you've stuck yourself in another one just as deep. But you don't have to stay there. That's the best part. You have the key. You just have to get off your ass and walk out that door." He smiled. "And you know what? I bet that girl of yours will be out there, on the other side, standing in the sunshine waiting for you when you do."

I nodded slowly. My mind was racing. My stomach churning. Part of me wanted to argue. To dig myself deeper into the hole. But in the end, I knew Griffin was right. At least I wanted him to be right. If there was any chance at all to escape this pit of despair I'd put myself in—to find a new lease on life, to get Sarah back—I would be an idiot not to at least try.

After all, I had very little left to lose.

I swallowed hard, turning to Griffin. Meeting his eyes straight on. "I want to get help," I whispered.

He grinned widely. Then he slapped me on the back. "Get me another beer," he said. "And then we'll get you some help."

forty-one

TROY

If life were a movie, at this point we'd probably be at the start of our first musical montage—with the next three months of therapy fast-forwarded in an upbeat series of clips set to a lively tune. I'd alternate between sitting and lying on the couch, maybe even dance around the room as I underwent some breakthrough or another. There'd be moments of laughing and crying, of course, and maybe a tear-jerking scene of me hugging my therapist as the music swelled. At the end of the song, you'd see me walking out of my shrink's front door, raising my fist in the air in triumph. Who knows, maybe there'd even be a freeze-frame.

But life was so not a movie. In fact, in my first session the therapist didn't even attempt to start the whole immersion therapy thing like the other one had. Instead, he suggested we get to know each other a little better first, before we dove headfirst into the healing. To help me to relax in the present before bringing in the added anxiety of reliving the past. I appreciated this in a sense, though I was also in a hurry to get to the good stuff, so I could start my road to recovery.

So I could get Sarah back.

That said, I did exit the building feeling a little better. Not fist-raising, movie freeze-frame better, but enough to go to the store by myself and buy much-needed groceries. As I wandered through the aisles, picking out fresh produce and whole grains (the shrink suggested a healthy diet could cut down on my stress levels, too), my eyes flickered to the people around me. Trying to imagine me someday being just like them again. Shopping for groceries, not a care in the world.

It seemed an impossible dream at the moment. But maybe, just maybe I could make it a reality. After all, Griffin had gone through much the same thing, and while he was quick to admit he still had bad days, mostly, he claimed, life was pretty good.

When I returned to my apartment, I realized the reporters had gathered again, shouting more questions about the kidnapped journalists and my thoughts on their plight. But this time I forced myself to walk by them instead of run, holding my head up high. They weren't the enemy, I told myself. Just guys doing their jobs. Trying to make ends meet. Just like I had been doing at News 9.

Speaking of News 9, I wouldn't be going back there anytime soon. After I explained what had been going on at work, my therapist suggested I apply for short-term disability until I could get back on my feet. So I could concentrate fully on my recovery and not lose my job in the process. I wasn't looking forward to sending in the paperwork—basically an admission that I couldn't hack things anymore. But the therapist insisted it was actually the opposite. It was a show of strength. A commitment to my recovery.

I hoped Sarah would see it that way.

Sarah. My heart ached as I stepped through my front door, closing it securely behind me. God, I missed Sarah. It had only been two weeks now and yet every time I had a down moment I thought of her. Of what she was doing. Of what she was thinking. Was she still working on the Water World project? Had she gotten the undercover video yet?

Actually, I could probably find that out. I grabbed my phone and scrolled to today's date on the calendar app. We'd set up a shared calendar back when we were working together, and I'd never bothered to unsubscribe once we split. Somehow I found it comforting to look at it from time to time. To see the films she was screening, what segments would be on TV. Even her manicure appointments interested me, imagining her going into the salon to get pampered as she deserved.

But there was no manicure tonight. Just a special little smiley face, scheduled for midnight. The emoticon code that meant undercover shoot.

I drew in a breath. So tonight was the night. When everything would come full circle. Was she going by herself? Or had she solicited Stephanie or Ben to come with her perhaps? For a moment I actually contemplated calling her and seeing if she still wanted me to come around to help her out. But in the shape I was in, I knew I'd be nothing more than a liability. And I didn't want our emotional strain to distract her from the shoot. I had screwed this whole thing up for her once upon a time; I wouldn't do it again.

I had wanted to call her after Griffin had come to see me, too. Though I wasn't sure exactly what I wanted to say. To thank her, I guess. For not giving up on me. Even when I had given up on myself. For not taking no for an answer. For sending Griffin to my door. For forcing me to see the truth. I wanted to tell her that she'd been right all along. And that because of her, I might have a chance now to reclaim my life.

I'd almost finished dinner when there was a knock at my door. I groaned, then reassessed. Maybe it was Griffin, come to make sure I'd gotten through my therapy session okay. Or just to grab that last beer he'd accidentally left in my fridge. No soldier left behind and all that.

And so I set down my plate and walked over to the door, peeking through the peephole before pulling it open, just in case it was one of the paparazzi getting brave again. Seriously, these guys really needed to get lives.

But when I looked through the peephole, I realized it wasn't a reporter. It wasn't Griffin, either.

It was Ryan.

forty-two

TROY

My first thought as I stared at Ryan through the peephole was how terrible he looked. A totally random, ridiculous thought, and yet, at the same time definitely true. His once round, cheerful face was almost gaunt. His skin was pale and pockmarked. And his eyes looked sunken into his skull. It was weird—he'd once been such a good-looking, charismatic man. Now he appeared a shell of his former self.

A shell that should definitely not be standing at my front door.

"What do you want, Ryan?" I demanded, not opening the door. Seriously, this was the last thing I needed right now.

"Can I come in? I need to talk to you."

"Sorry, I'm really not in the mood."

"You might be once you hear what I have to say." He paused, then added, "It's about Water World."

I pursed my lips, indecision racing through me. The last

thing I wanted to do was let him back in my life by opening the door. But then, wasn't he still in my life already? In a sense he'd been haunting me for the last five years. Maybe this was my opportunity to exorcise him for good. From my life . . . and more importantly, from Sarah's.

"Fine," I muttered, turning the handle and opening the door, allowing him entrance. He stepped inside and looked around, nodding his head.

"Nice place," he remarked.

"Yeah, it's the freaking Taj Mahal. Now what do you want?"

Ryan ignored me, instead wandering over to the living room and sitting down on the couch. I followed him over, my heart beating wildly in my chest. Why was he here? What did he want? Did this have anything to do with Sarah?

I crossed my arms over my chest. "I'll hear you out," I said. "If you promise me one thing."

He looked over, raising an eyebrow.

"Once you're finished, I want you to go away. For good this time. Do not bother me anymore. And especially stay clear of Sarah."

He made a face. "Oh God, not you, too."

"What?" I frowned.

"Sarah." He groaned. "Everyone in this town seems to be under the impression that I'm stalking her or whatever. The bitch even took out a restraining order on me—even though I never went near her. And her dad's all over the TV talking about some crime bill he wants to introduce, using me as his prime example. Me—who hasn't even freaking jaywalked since getting out of the joint." He scowled. "It's getting kind of old, to be honest."

I stared at him, incredulous. "You're really going to deny it? She saw you. You came to my front door."

"Yeah. I did. I was looking for you."

"Okay, fine. Then what about the graffiti? The vandalism at her apartment? The rock at the movie theater? Was that all for me, too?"

"Dude, I have no idea what you're talking about. But if Sarah thinks I'd really risk my newfound freedom to mess with her? Well, she's even more delusional than I remember her being. I wasted five goddamn years of my life in that godforsaken prison. The last thing I need is to give her dear old dad an excuse to throw me back in."

I swallowed hard, truly at a loss now. He sounded so convincing. And while he could be lying, of course, something in his face told me he wasn't.

"You told her in the courtroom you were going to make her pay," I reminded him, feeling as if I were grasping at straws.

"I said a lot of things back then. You did, too, if I remember right."

I sighed. "Okay, fine." I held up my hands in defeat. "You aren't stalking Sarah. Whatever. But you did show up to my front door. So what is it you want to say to me?"

I watched as Ryan reached into his bag, drawing out a thick stack of papers and setting them on the coffee table. Then, he pulled out a DVD and placed it on top before turning back to me.

"This is all the stuff we'd put together for our Water World protest," he explained. "I thought you might be able to do something with it. If you were still interested, I mean."

I stared at the stack, then at Ryan. "You're giving it to me? But why?"

He shrugged. "Isn't it obvious? You still have a chance to do something with it. To shut those bastards down for good. No one's going to listen to what I say anymore—I'm a convicted felon. I lost all credibility for what I did." He paused, staring down at the papers, his face filled with a regret that surprised me. "But those animals—they don't need to pay for my mistakes."

I drew in a slow breath. "Why did you do it, Ryan?" I asked quietly. It was a question I'd wanted answered for five years now. But had never had a chance to ask. Despite what Sarah thought about Ryan, I knew for a fact he actually cared about saving the world—or at least had cared back then. So why had he risked everything he'd worked so hard for his entire life—over something as petty as a cash grab?

He looked up at me, looking so much older than his thirty years. "I was desperate," he said after a pause. "My mother had been diagnosed with cancer. And her insurance wasn't properly covering her treatments." He closed his eyes for a moment. "And then I saw this guy—this guy who was so rich, he'd never even miss the money. Money that would save my mother's life. And even if he did, well, his insurance would have compensated him, I'm sure." He sighed. "And so I went for it. I would have done anything to save my mother."

My heart gave an unexpected tug as I caught the look on his face. I wanted to ask if his mother was still around, but I had a feeling I knew the answer already. All this time I'd been so angry at him for tricking me. For playing me like a fool. But now—well, now I felt more foolish than ever. Because I had never once bothered to ask why he had done what he'd done. I'd never given him a chance to explain.

"Thanks for bringing these over," I said instead, gathering up the documents and paging through them. My voice sounded a little rough, but I pushed on anyway. "And you'll be pleased to know Sarah's actually reopened the investigation. She's even doing an undercover shoot with this whistle-blower we found who works there."

Ryan nodded slowly. "That's great," he said. Then he rose to his feet. "Well, hopefully some of this will be of use to her then. All the transcripts from our interviews are in there. All our e-mails back and forth. I had hidden everything in a storage locker after it all went south; I didn't want it confiscated as evidence." He shrugged. "Some of it's old and outdated, of course. But there's probably still some useful stuff. At the very least, it's an opportunity prove just how long these abuses have been going on."

"Right." I stood up, putting out my hand. "Thank you for bringing it over. I'll start combing through it tonight and send everything relevant over to Sarah."

"Great. And . . . when you do?" Ryan gave me a hesitant look. "Tell her I'm sorry about everything, will you? That I regret everything that went down back then." He sighed. "Trust me, I don't expect her to forgive me or give me a second chance. But I would like her to know that I'm sorry all the same."

I gave him a rueful smile. "I will tell her," I promised. "And I'm sure she'll appreciate that."

Ryan's face shone with relief. "Okay," he said. "Well, then, I guess I'll see you around. And I'll be watching for that report. It'll really be great to see that place shut down for good. Justice served at last."

And with that, he headed out the door, closing it behind him. I watched from the window as he got into his car and started the engine, feeling contemplative, relieved, and, at the same time, a little sad. Once Ryan had been a great guy. He had really wanted to change the world. Hopefully, somehow, someday he would get another chance to do that. A chance to make that difference he'd always wanted to make.

It wasn't until he had pulled away, driving out of the apartment complex and into the night. that another question suddenly struck me.

If Ryan wasn't Sarah's stalker . . . then who was? And if he hadn't done those things . . . who had?

And most importantly, what would he do next?

forty-three

SARAH

The place was dark when I pulled into the parking lot—Donny, my whistleblower, had explained that the park closed at six PM on Sundays and therefore most of the custodial staff finished by nine. They usually turned off most of the lights, too, he added, to save on electricity. In fact, even the heaters were turned down at night—way too low for some of the poor animals. Just another abuse, seen as cost savings. To keep this atrocity performing like a cash sea cow.

I parked in the back, as he had instructed. Then got out of my car. It felt a little creepy here in the dark. Creepier than I had imagined it would be. Originally, of course, I had planned to have Troy by my side, acting as partner in crime. Which would have made me feel a whole lot better about the whole thing.

But Troy had not called me. And he'd not returned my calls.

I'd tried to recruit Ben as well. But his grandmother got sick again and he couldn't leave her bedside. I'd tried Asher, too, but he was off on his honeymoon with Piper. After that I'd gone through almost my entire Rolodex looking for backup, but everyone was either too busy or didn't bother to text back. Clearly I was on my own with this. I had considered trying to reschedule, but Donny had worked so hard getting everything in place for tonight. We might never have this perfect opportunity again.

The wind whipped through my hair and I gave an involuntary shiver. It was cold tonight and slightly foggy, adding to the creep factor. Reminding me, oddly, of that first film Troy and I had reviewed for our He Said, She Said segment. The one with the girl wandering around the abandoned house, looking for her friends, while the axe-wielding serial killer closed in on her.

Don't go into the basement, girl, Troy had quipped. It no longer seemed like bad advice.

I snorted, squaring my shoulders. "Please," I muttered under my breath. "This princess saves herself, bitches."

But the adage was not as comforting as it should have been.

My phone rang, the sound causing me to almost jump out of my skin. I looked down at the caller ID. Dad.

"Hello?" I said into the receiver.

"Sarah!" he boomed from the other end of the line. "Great news!"

"What is it?"

"I just got a call from the police. They've picked up Ryan. He was spotted leaving Troy's house earlier this evening."

"Troy's house?" I repeated, a little alarmed. "What was he doing there?"

"I don't know. I don't care, either. Point is, they got him.

They're going to charge him with the break-in at your place. Stalking. Whatever they can throw at him." I could hear my father's smile in his voice. "We got him, sweetheart. You're safe again."

I let out a breath of relief. "Thank you, Dad," I said. "That's great news. I really appreciate you letting me know."

"No problem, baby. I told you I'd keep you safe."

We said our good-byes and I slipped the phone back in my pocket, all my earlier fears fading into oblivion. Ryan was back where he belonged, behind bars. Hopefully this time he'd stay there for a long time.

With a new spring to my step, I headed over to the back gate. When I got there, I texted Donny, letting him know I had arrived. Thankfully, he texted back immediately, informing me he would be there in a minute, and I contented myself by checking my Facebook wall while I waited, trying to concentrate on the shiny happy pictures of puppies and kittens and babies posted by my friends and acquaintances.

Finally, the gate creaked open. I stepped inside, squinting to make out the silhouette that stood tall and silent in front of a large spotlight.

"Donny?" I asked, squinting into the light. "Is that you?"

"Hey, Sarah Martin," he replied, stepping forward. "It's great to finally meet you in person at last."

"Same here!" I greeted, taking a step forward. I put out my hand. I couldn't see him too well in the dark, but it didn't matter much. Once I flipped my camera to night vision it should be fine for interviews. Troy had already interviewed him once anyway, just as a preliminary background type thing. So we did have him on tape already, if we needed it.

"Thanks for coming and getting me," I added. "I was beginning to feel kind of creeped out out there."

He laughed, taking my hand and shaking it with a firm grip. "Come on," he said when he had finished. "We all know the real monsters are the ones who own this place. And, trust me, they're all safe and snug in their beds, as rich people always are at times like these."

I gave a half laugh, feeling a little unnerved by that statement, though I wasn't exactly sure why. Maybe because my dad had originally been one of those rich people. Thankfully Donny wouldn't know that. He'd just started working at Water World recently. And most people had no idea that my dad was ever involved in the first place.

I stepped in line beside him, following him deeper into the park. But the farther we went in, the more my nerves prickled. It was weird being here at night. With everything so quiet and dark. The little concession stands were boarded up and the rides were silent and still.

Come on, Sarah. Get a grip, I scolded myself. *It's just a closed amusement park. There's nothing that can hurt you here.*

"So," I said, looking around, trying to get my bearings, "where do we begin?"

Donny stopped walking. He turned to look at me. Stared at me for a moment. Then, to my surprise, he started laughing.

"What's so funny?" I demanded, my pulse kicking up in alarm. There was something so strange about his laugh. As if he were laughing at some private joke. A joke that was totally on me.

"Oh," he said, his shoulders shrugging. "It's just . . . this isn't a beginning."

"What?" I stared at him, my heart now thudding madly in my chest. I involuntarily glanced behind me toward the back gate I'd originally walked through, realizing it had already slid shut at some point. And that the top was rimmed by electric wire. My nerves skittered. "What are you talking about?"

A weird smile stretched across his face. "This isn't a *beginning*," he repeated, stressing the word. "This is the end, Sarah Martin." He paused, then added. "Your end."

forty-four

TROY

After Ryan left, I finished dinner and then debated whether or not to watch some TV before going to bed. But as I walked into the living room, my eyes caught the documents still on the coffee table, and I knew what I had to do. If Sarah completed her undercover shoot tonight and got the video she needed, she was going to want to start putting the piece together as soon as possible. If I could find her some relevant information from the old files, it might help.

And I really wanted to help. In some small way, anyway. Maybe it could make up, in some way, for how much I'd messed everything up the first time around.

I slipped the DVD into the player and watched our undercover video from five years before. I had to admit, it was good stuff, and it would be great to use in comparison to whatever she shot tonight, to show how long these poor conditions had gone on. This way Water World couldn't blame the dirty water or the animals' skin conditions on something temporary. We could establish a pattern to convict them.

After writing down the time codes of the best video and recording them on my laptop, I then turned to the huge stack of paper on the coffee table. Ryan had always been a bit OCD about things—and had kept meticulous records on everything—even what we'd eaten for lunch the day we discussed the hack. Most of the e-mails were useless now. Back and forth arguing about how we'd put together the story and whom we would send it to when it was done. Ryan wanted to post it on YouTube, I'd wanted to send it to a network news station. Sarah had just wanted to play it on the jumbotron at Qualcomm Stadium for everyone to see.

I kept flipping until I came to a grainy photo that had been printed out off the Internet in black and white. A photo of a man with long hair dressed in a white button-down shirt and wearing a bow tie.

I stared down at it for a moment, frowning as a weird shiver of recognition seemed to trip down my spine.

Wait a second. Was that . . . Donny? Our whistleblower? The one Sarah was out with at Water World tonight? But what would he be doing in these files?

Confused, I grabbed my laptop, logged into the News 9 shared server, and opened up the video clips of my recent interview with Donny. The one I'd done for background information on what we would likely see during the undercover shoot. My heart beat uncomfortably in my chest as the video popped up on the screen and I clicked play. I watched for a moment, then grabbed the photo from Ryan's files, looking from one to another.

He looked different. His hair had been long back then. And he'd had a mustache, too. He was also about fifty pounds lighter. But it was definitely the same guy.

But why on earth would Donny be in Ryan's old files? Donny had told us he'd only worked at Water World for a few months now; he wouldn't have been around five years ago when we originally started this campaign. In fact, he'd told me he'd only moved to San Diego recently. This didn't make any sense.

Anxiety rose inside of me as I abandoned the computer, turning back to the stack of files, flipping through them more quickly now, trying to figure out how Donny fit into this puzzle. Why he'd be part of this research. But as I scanned each document I saw nothing about anyone named Donny. No explanation as to why that photo had ended up in this pile.

Something was very weird here.

I reached the last sheet of paper. A printout of an e-mail from Sarah, addressed to both Ryan and me. I scanned it, biting my lower lip.

Hey all!

Good news! Your plan totally worked. I went in and sweet-talked dear old Johnny Westwood into giving me the master passwords to my dad's account! What an idiot, right? In any case, we are SO IN like Flynn! Okay, just let me know how you want to proceed. I'm ready to go when you guys are!!

Love and kisses and saving the whales,
Sarah

I stared at the e-mail, my mind whirring madly. Something felt as if it were pricking at the back of my brain— some kind of memory, just out of reach.

Johnny . . .

Donny . . .

My jaw dropped. I turned back to the computer again. With shaking fingers I typed *John Westwood* into the search engine. A moment later a LinkedIn entry appeared on the screen. I clicked on it, holding my breath, my nerves taut as piano wire. Really, really not wanting to be right about this.

But, of course, I was.

A moment later the profile popped up onto the monitor. A profile containing a picture of the very same man in both the photo and the video. John Westwood. Age forty-one. Former Internet security officer at Martin Enterprises. Left his job five years ago. And unless he just didn't update his profile, he hadn't had a job since.

I sank back into my chair, my stomach churning with nausea. John Westwood. Johnny Westwood. The IT guy Sarah had tricked to put this whole thing into motion. Who got fired from his job after everything went south.

Who had probably been stalking Sarah from the start.

Who was at Water World with her . . . alone . . . now.

forty-five

SARAH

This is the end, Sarah Martin. Your end.

I stared at him, his odd words buzzing through my ears. Panic rioting through my brain. For a moment, I was frozen, trying to figure out what he meant. Then, instincts took over and I tried to turn—I tried to flee. But he was too quick, grabbing me before I could get away. Hands clamping down on my arms, nails digging into my flesh—so hard I was sure he'd leave a bruise. I struggled to get free but to no avail.

"Let me go!" I cried. "You're hurting me!"

But he only tightened his grip. My mind raced with panic, my heart banging so hard against my ribs I was half-sure it would burst from my chest altogether. I turned my head, trying to face him. To figure out why he was doing this. What he could possibly want from me.

"Please. Let me go," I begged, wondering what I could say at this point to get him to set me free. To let me walk away unharmed. "Whatever it is you want, I can make it happen. We can make this all go away. My father has money and—"

"Oh. I know all about your father, princess," he growled, his eyes flashing angry fire. "You and your precious father— you ruined my life."

"What?" I shook my head, completely confused. "What are you talking about?" Was this man the victim of some law my father had introduced? Like the guy Troy had done the story on who lost his job and robbed a store? My father had a lot of enemies, of course. But this guy had specifically mentioned me.

Had this whole thing been a trap? Had Ryan not been my stalker after all? Was this guy the one who had been tormenting me all along? My pulse kicked up, alarm rioting through me. But why? What had set him off?

And now that he had me—whoever he was—what did he plan to do to me? All alone, in this park, with no one to help me get away.

He shoved me up against the wall and I winced as my back slammed against concrete. He glared at me with such hatred in his eyes it succeeded in chilling me to the bone.

"Why are you doing this?" I whispered, tears springing to my eyes. "What do you want from me?"

His lip curled into a sneer. "You don't even remember me, do you? You used me. You tore my entire life apart. And yet you don't even have the decency to fucking remember my face?"

I sucked in a shaky breath, trying desperately to quell my nerves. My stomach twisted, and I was this close to puking on the spot. Who was this guy? What was he talking about? What did I do to him? And why couldn't I remember it? I stared at him through tear-blurred eyes, trying to identify his face.

"Please," I whimpered. "Just tell me what I did."

I could feel my cell phone vibrating in my purse. But he had my arms pinned so I couldn't reach for it. I should have never agreed to have come here alone. I'd been so determined to get this story—to get justice for these whales and closure for me—once and for all. I'd knowingly put myself at risk.

Don't go into the basement, girl . . .

This princess saves herself.

But how could I save myself when I was pinned against a wall? The man outweighed me by at least a hundred pounds. And he looked plenty eager to have an excuse to bring on the hurt.

No. I wasn't going to be able to fight my way out of this. But maybe—if I kept my head—I might have a chance to argue my case. But what case was I arguing? Why was he doing this? I needed to know that, at least, if I was going to have a chance.

My captor stepped forward, invading my space. He pulled off his baseball cap. "Come on," he cajoled. "You don't recognize this face? And here you told me it was so handsome, too, once upon a time. So handsome you could barely keep your hands off me. Or . . ." He sneered. "Was it those passwords you really wanted your hands on?"

I stared at him. Oh my God.

Suddenly everything clicked into horrifying place. And I realized exactly who this man was. Who he must be. And, all at once, it all came full circle.

"You're that IT guy," I whispered. "The one that gave me the passwords."

My mind raced as I connected the dots. He looked totally different than he had back then. Which I guess is why I didn't recognize him when I scanned Troy's interview. His hair was shorter. He'd lost his gut. And he no longer had a mustache.

But it was him. It couldn't be anyone but him. My mind flashed back to that fateful day when I'd gone into his office five years before and given him a pretty smile. Batted my eyes and thrown some compliments around as Troy and Ryan had instructed me to do. A simple flirtation, but enough to flatter him into doing something very stupid. Handing over the keys to the kingdom to the usurper. So Ryan could work his magic.

Or his crimes, as it turned out to be.

"The name's Johnny," he reminded me, spit flying at my face as he talked. "Not that you would bother to remember that. And why would you? I was just a fucking pawn to you and your little rich friends. Just some poor slob you walked over to get what you wanted."

The cold, hard hatred in his eyes chilled me to the bone. I didn't even know what to say. Mostly because he wasn't wrong. That was exactly what we had done. And after that, when trying to deal with the fallout, I'd pretty much forgotten he even existed. At the time I'd been too worried about Troy to think of anyone else.

"I was fired," he informed me. "In case you were wondering. Fired by your dear old dad. No severance. No COBRA. Just a big black mark on my record and the threat of jail time if I didn't walk away without making a fuss." He scowled. "Do you know any corporations who would hire someone like me after that? An IT guy who allowed his entire network to be hacked by thieves?" He shook his head.

"I tried for years to get a new job. My wife left me. She took the kids. The bank foreclosed on my house. For a while I was homeless—my credit was shot, my debts were through the roof. I tried doing menial jobs—construction, fast food. When that didn't work, I turned to petty theft. Ended up in prison." He scowled. "Where I spent the last three years thinking all about you."

I swallowed heavily, emotions swirling through me, too hard and fast to catalog. While I knew I should be very frightened—and I was—I couldn't also help but feel this weird sense of guilt at the same time. What had we done to this man? We'd destroyed his life without a second thought. Even if Ryan had been nobler in his intentions—the fallout for Johnny would have been the same.

All these years I'd put blame on Ryan and Troy for tricking me and using me for their own personal gain. But hadn't I, in the end, done the very same thing to Johnny? Yes, I'd had a noble purpose: I'd clearly wanted to save the animals. But at what cost to my fellow human being?

Construction workers on the Death Star.

Because Jedis don't have 401(k)s.

This man standing before me hadn't abused any animals. He probably hadn't even known Water World was part of the corporate conglomerate at the time. He just wanted to do his job. Make a living. Feed his family—get by. And then I walked in with a low-cut dress and a smile and tore it all away.

"I'm so sorry," I blurted out, though I was pretty sure the statute of limitations for apologies had long run out. "I was wrong. I was totally wrong. And I'm so sorry you were hurt by my stupid mistakes. I will make it up to you now—I promise. No matter what I have to do. We'll get you a new job. Or I'll get you money. Whatever you need—or want—I promise I will—"

"No. It's too late for that now," he snapped back. "I don't want your apology or your pity. I just want to see justice served. You and your father destroyed my life. Now it's my turn to destroy yours."

He laughed at this, as if it were some crazy joke, his cockeyed glare sending fear spinning down my spine. Once he might have been sane, but that had clearly ended long ago. And now he was hell-bent on revenge. And no smooth talking was going to get him to change his mind.

"What are you going to do?" I asked, trying to keep my voice steady. But it cracked on the last words, betraying my fear.

He smiled, evidently enjoying the terrified look on my face. "Isn't it obvious?" he asked. "I'm going to give you exactly what you asked for. An up-close and personal look at those goddamned whales."

Oh God. Realization hit me with the force of a ten-ton truck. He was going to throw me in the tank. And those whales—the ones I was working so hard to save—would tear me apart.

"You won't get away with this!" I cried. Mostly because that was what people always said when stuck in situations like this in the movies. Problem was, I wasn't so sure that was true in real life. The park was empty. He'd turned off all the cameras. Bribed the security guards to stay away. Everything that had been supposedly set up for me to get my undercover video was now turned into a perfect way to end my life.

"Come on, princess," he sneered. "Everyone knows your history with Water World. How much you love those sweet killer whales. No one's going to be all that shocked when they find you floating in the tank, your undercover camera in your cold, dead hand. They'll assume you were out doing an exposé. It's just so tragic you got too close. That you fell in." He gave a chilling laugh. "And who knows? Maybe your death will prompt others to start looking into the case? Maybe your death will end up bringing these animals a second chance.

"That's all you wanted, right? To save the whales? It's just too bad you can't save yourself at the same time."

He grabbed me, ripping off my purse with my cell phone inside and throwing it to the ground before dragging me over to the tank. I screamed, trying to kick myself free, but to no avail. He was just too strong. We reached the tank and I looked down, watching the killer whales swimming beneath the surface of the water. From first appearance they looked like gentle giants. But I knew all too well they could also be killers.

"Any last words?" Donny—Johnny—asked, wagging his eyebrows at me. "Do you want to beg for your life again, perhaps? I'll be honest; I get a kick out of listening to you grovel. Sweet music to my ears after all this time."

I shook my head, sucking in a breath, closing my eyes and forcing myself to not panic. I couldn't lose my head—or I would quite literally lose my head. There had to be a way out of this, somehow. There had to be.

Don't go into the basement, girl.

This princess can save herself.

I stopped short.

Oh my God.

She struck him in the throat with her forearm.

That was it.

That was totally it.

I swallowed hard, firming my resolve. Waiting for the right moment. The moment he made himself vulnerable, just as the girl had done in the film. Just as I had demonstrated with Troy during our segment. My heart thudded in my chest and I could barely breathe. But at the same time, determination welled up inside of me. I could do this. I could totally do this.

I could Mary Sue the shit out of this guy.

"What are you waiting for?" I demanded. "Just throw me in!"

I made a move, as if I was trying to struggle. He grabbed me harder, trying to boost me over the wall to push me in. As he shifted position, I made my move, stamping hard on his foot, then slamming my elbow backward and upward, straight into his throat. This time with all the force I could muster.

He let out a cry of bloody murder, loosening his grip. I whirled around, kneeing him in the balls as hard as I could. He doubled over.

I took off running.

"You bitch!" I could hear him scream behind me. "I'm going to gut you, you stupid bitch!"

Not that stupid, I thought, adrenaline rushing through me. In fact, that was pretty goddamned smart.

That said, I was far from out of the woods—or out of the park, as the case might be. I had no idea where I was or where the nearest exit could be. Not to mention whether I could even get out at any of the exits if I found them—or if they'd all be shut and locked like the one I'd come in through. I could try to hide, but he would have all night to find me. And now he was really pissed off.

What to do? What to do? I could hear his footsteps behind me, chasing me, getting closer. Would he catch up to me? Would all my efforts to escape only make it worse in the end?

Suddenly my ears caught the sounds of sirens. Wailing in the distance, then coming closer. I kept running, my lungs burning in my chest, trying to follow the sounds. Were they really coming here? Oh, please let them be coming here. Because he was gaining on me. Because I was running out of breath. Out of options. If those sirens weren't for me . . .

"Freeze! Put your hands on your head! This is the police!"

Oh thank God. I stopped short, obeying the command. My legs buckled out from under me and I could barely stand, but I held my hands up high, showing them I wasn't the threat.

"He's chasing me!" I called out to the officers. "He's trying to kill me."

A moment later three officers rushed past me, giving chase. A fourth stayed behind, approaching me. I sank to my knees, no longer able to keep standing. I was shaking so hard I was almost convulsing. Now that I was out of danger, the tears ran from my eyes like rain.

"Are you okay?" the officer, a woman with dark hair, asked me. "Did he hurt you? Do you need medical attention?"

"No. I don't . . . think so." My heart was pounding so hard in my chest I felt as if I was going to pass out. The officer studied me for a moment, then helped me to my feet, putting her arm around me to lead me to the exit.

"How about we just make sure of that?" she asked gently. I nodded and she led me out of the gates toward the waiting ambulance.

"How did you know?" I asked, turning to her, puzzlement breaking through my fear. "How did you know to come? That I was here and in danger?"

"I told them."

I whirled around, my knees buckling again as my eyes fell on the lone figure behind me. Standing tall, strong, without a trace of fear in his eyes.

"Troy . . ." I whispered, my heart exploding.

He gave me a sheepish smile. "Sarah," he said.

And then we were in each other's arms. I wasn't even sure how it happened. I didn't see him move toward me or feel myself move toward him. It was as if we'd just fast-forwarded to the spot where we were hugging. Kissing. Crying. The part where we were together.

"I'm so sorry, Sarah," he murmured, his mouth moving against my ear, sending shivers to my toes. "I should have been here. I should have always been there for you."

I closed my eyes, snuggling against him, feeling warm and safe. "You're here now," I told him. "That's all that matters in the end."

forty-six

TROY

I led Sarah over to the EMTs, insisting she get a full workup, even though she promised me she was fine. I told her I wasn't taking any more chances. They did a quick once-over and pronounced her physically sound, though they offered to call her in a prescription for some Xanax to calm her nerves. She declined, saying she just needed to go home and get some sleep. I told them to call in the script anyway. Just in case.

I drove her home and helped her back to her apartment. The cozy little space the two of us had been sharing before I'd taken off like a child. I wondered if she'd go back to her beach house now, once things had shaken out. Her actual stalker behind bars.

The police had caught Johnny at the back of the park where he had angrily confessed to everything—including the prior attacks—and allowed himself to be arrested. If Sarah's father's crime bill went through, he would probably be put away for a very long time.

"I still feel a little bad for him," Sarah said as she settled down on the couch, pulling the afghan over her knees. "All this time, I've been thinking about how Ryan ruined my life. And I never stopped to realize I wasn't completely innocent in the whole matter, either."

"Your heart was always in the right place," I reminded her, sitting down on the couch at her side. "You wanted to help those animals."

"And yet now, once again, we're back to square one," she said with a heavy sigh. "No video. No story. No happy ending for anyone."

My heart ached at the pain I heard in her voice. I turned to her, taking her face in my hands, forcing her to meet my eyes with her own. "That's not true," I told her. "The way I see it? This is just a minor setback. I promise you, one way or another, we're going to save those animals. We're going to get Water World shut down."

She gave me a half smile. "We?" she repeated.

"If you'll have me," I said simply. Then I sighed, giving her a rueful look. "Look, Sarah, I know I haven't made things easy for you. Hell, for myself, either, for that matter. And I'm still a long way from ever getting back to being the man I used to be. But I have taken that first step. I have a therapist I like and I'm taking a leave from work so I can concentrate full-time on my recovery. I've even, well . . ." I could feel my face flush. "I've even filled a prescription for an antidepressant. Just to see how it goes."

Her face lit up. Joy radiating from her eyes. It made me want to both laugh and cry, all at the same time.

"Oh, Troy, I'm so glad," she whispered. "I know it couldn't have been an easy thing to do."

"Yeah, well, it should have been," I said with a grimace. "But as you know, I can be a bit pigheaded at times."

She gave me a shy smile. "I know. That's one of the things I've always loved about you actually."

I groaned, rolling my eyes. "You always were a glutton for punishment," I teased. Then I grew serious. "Look, I'm not asking for a second chance," I told her. "Well, at least not right away. I don't want to rush into anything until we're ready. I have a lot to work on, obviously. But I thought, maybe, there might be a way for us to do some of that work together? On us? I mean, I know they have marriage counseling. Maybe there's something for non-married people as well?"

She laughed, the sound ringing through my ears like Christmas bells. "That's called couples counseling," she assured me. "You don't need a marriage license to apply."

I met her eyes with my own. "Would you be willing to do that with me? I want to set things right with you. And I don't want to screw it up again."

She nodded, tears welling in her eyes. "I would love to do that," she said. "Trust me, you're not the only one who needs a little guidance at this point."

I smiled at her, feeling tears prick at the corners of my own eyes. "You know I love you, right?" I asked her, squeezing her hands in my own.

She nodded, but didn't reply. And for a moment I panicked that maybe she no longer felt the same love for me. But then I realized it was because she just couldn't speak. Not without bursting into tears. And so I reached up, tracing her cheek with my hand.

"It's okay," I said, gazing into her beautiful eyes. Eyes that once upon a time I thought I'd never see again. "You don't have to say it. I know. I've always known."

She smiled at this, and I leaned down and kissed her softly on the mouth. And then I kissed her again. Slowly, unhurriedly. Because, I realized, with Sarah there was no need to rush. If all went well—and I was determined that it would this time—we would have the rest of our lives to kiss each other. Because this time, no matter what, I was never, ever letting her go.

And even if I never got back to where I had been, even if I had to work the entertainment beat for the rest of life. Even if we quit the news business altogether and finally ran away to Mexico as we'd once dreamed about, living a simple life on the beach, our children playing in the waves. It wouldn't be a small life. It wouldn't be a disappointing life.

It would be the best life ever. Because I would be sharing it with her.

forty-seven

SARAH

six months later

"Thank you, Ben, for that illuminating Where Are They Now of all the old Bachelorette contestants. It's amazing how far some of them have fallen since their appearance on the show." Beth turned the camera. "And now, stay tuned. After the break we have a very special report from our honorary I-Team members, Sarah Martin and Troy Young. An undercover investigation you won't want to miss."

I glanced at Troy, giving him a nervously excited look. He reached over and grabbed my hand, squeezing it tightly in his own. It had been six months since we started dating again, and I still couldn't get used to the sparks that flew from even the simplest touch. I squeezed his hand back and then got into position in front of the camera.

"Are you ready for this?" he whispered.

"So ready."

It had taken a lot of convincing to get Mrs. Anderson to let us work on an investigative story together. She preferred we concentrate on our continued success with the He Said, She Said franchise, which was getting its own half-hour slot in a couple weeks. But once we showed her the footage we'd gotten she couldn't very well say no. After all, this was about to be the biggest story in San Diego. Maybe even the US. She wasn't about to let us take it to the competition.

The floor director held up his hand. "One minute," he said. My heart picked up its pace. This was it. The moment I'd been waiting for for five and a half years. The moment I thought was never going to come.

The floor director pointed at us. "Thirty seconds." I shot Troy a nervous smile.

"Here goes nothing."

He grinned back. "Here goes everything."

The camera light came on. Ready for my close-up, Mr. DeMille.

"Thank you, Beth," I said. "I'm Sarah Martin. You probably know Troy and me from our He Said, She Said film review segment. And, actually, we've got some film for you tonight, too."

"But this isn't some Hollywood blockbuster this time," Troy added. "Though you may find it a bit of a horror show. An undercover look at some of the actual goings-on at Water World, the sea life theme park that's located right here in San Diego."

"If you have sensitive viewers," I finished, "you might want to change the channel now. Some of what you're about to see may be a little upsetting."

And with that, the producers rolled the story. The segment Troy and I had spent the last six months putting together. Featuring interviews with ex–Water World employees, marine biologists, veterinarians, and animal rights activists. And most importantly, an undercover video revealing it all.

Yes, in the end we'd gotten our video. Not in the dead of night, led by a whistleblower, but right out in the open, using our phones as our cameras, as if we were just tourists. Each day we'd consult the DVD footage Ryan had given Troy that we'd shot five years before, then we'd go out and try to duplicate those shots now. Then we took both shots and edited them together so the people of San Diego could see these atrocities had been going on for years. That these animals had been suffering a very long time.

It hadn't been an easy story to put together. We didn't have much time to work on it, after all, with our News 9 jobs taking up a lot of our time and Troy doing his intensive therapy to combat his PTSD. He'd also started volunteering at a local veterans' hospital, working with soldiers who had just returned home and were trying to acclimate to life back in the US. After all, he knew how hard it could be to try to find a new normal, something he, himself, still struggled with at times.

He wasn't cured. But he'd come to terms with the fact that he might never totally be himself again. He might always jump at loud noises or have nightmares wake him in a cold sweat. Sometimes he got angry, too. But now, thanks to his therapy, he knew how to combat that anger. To better analyze his feelings and figure out the cause of his distress so he could better manage it. Instead of withdrawing and feeling guilty over his lapses, he knew now he could come to me to share how he was feeling. I wasn't going to judge him or think less of him. In fact, admitting weakness seemed to me like the bravest thing in the world.

I was so proud of how far he'd come. And how far he was determined to go. He wasn't the boy I'd fallen in love with five years ago. But he was the man I wanted to be with now. We'd taken it slow. Learned to trust each other again. And now we would finally have our moment. The chance to make a difference as we had always hoped to do.

And the best part? We were doing it together.

The segment ran many more times. On stations around the country and all around the world. Not long after that, the government launched a full investigation into Water World that ended with them being shut down forever. The animals that could safely be reintroduced to the wild were set free and the ones that were unable to transition were transferred to sanctuaries to live out their days. And other investigations were launched against similar parks, to see if similar atrocities could be found.

"So, Miss Martin," Troy began, cuddling up to me on our blanket on the beach one afternoon about a week after the story had run. We'd fled down to Rosarito, back to our favorite beach hotel. We were pretty much celebrities after the story ran—even more so than before—and it was difficult, some days, to find peace and quiet for our much-needed alone time. "You've finally saved the whales. What are you going to do now?"

"I'm going to Disney World?" I quipped, then grinned. "Though, come to think of it, I might be too busy for a vacation. After all, there are a lot more animals out there, needing to be saved. Not to mention children, and the environment, and—"

"And . . . you're not going to have any time left over for

your poor, neglected boyfriend," he teased, poking me in the ribs. "Though," he said with a contemplative nod, "I suppose you already went and saved me."

"Nah. I'm pretty sure you saved yourself. I was just there for the hot sex."

His eyebrows waggled. "It was, indeed, hot sex. Still is, for that matter."

I laughed. "You aren't sick of me yet?"

"God, I could never get sick of you. I could never even get half of what I want from you." He crawled on top of me, kissing me on the mouth. I kissed him back, feeling chills run up and down my arms. I knew very well what it was like to never get enough. Luckily we had a lifetime ahead of us to satisfy those cravings.

"Maybe we should get back to that hotel room," I suggested. "Before we get arrested on the beach."

He nodded. "Actually, there's something there I want to show you."

"Is there now?" I teased, raising an eyebrow.

He laughed. "Not like that. I mean, definitely like that. But there's . . . something else, too."

I cocked my head. "What is it?"

He shrugged, looking a little sheepish. "The first chapters of my book."

"What?" I stared at him. "But I thought—"

"I know. I never thought I'd get to the point where I'd want to write it, either," he agreed. "But my therapist said it can be therapeutic to write it all down. Get the story out of my head and onto paper. At first I wasn't thinking about publishing it—it was just for me, really. But the more I thought about it, the more I wanted to go ahead and take a publishing deal. I think it might be able to help people see what's truly going on over there. Not just my story. But all the stories I saw while I was there." He gave me a rueful smile. "I went over there to make a difference, after all. Maybe this was how I was supposed to do that, all along."

I smiled at him, my heart soaring at his words. I knew how hard it must have been for him to take this step. But he was taking it. Just like he was learning how to take control over the rest of his life.

"I'm proud of you," I said, leaning over to cuddle against his shoulder. "This is a big step."

"Yeah, well, there's one more big step I'm hoping to take as well," he replied, his face flushing as he spoke the words. "You see, they gave me a pretty big advance for the book. And I thought maybe I'd spend a little bit of that on you."

I watched, breathless, as he reached into his pocket and pulled out a small box. I stared down at it, my eyes widening. Shyly, he got down on his knees before me, opening the box, revealing a huge diamond ring.

"You are the most amazing woman I have ever met," he said in a choked voice. "Not to mention the most patient. The biggest mistake I ever made was to let you go. And I'm going to make sure you never have the chance to get away from me again."

"Oh, Troy . . ."

"I'm not a perfect guy. I'm still screwed up in the head— I probably always will be. But I promise you, I will keep working on that. I'll never stop working on it." He smiled at me, a smile that tore my heart in two. But also mended it all at the same time. "Will you, Sarah Martin, do me the greatest honor? Will you agree to become my wife?"

I smiled through my tears. "Are you sure you can handle that? A simple life with a simple girl?"

"You are the furthest thing in the world from a simple girl," he teased. "But you're absolutely wonderful all the same. A partner, a confidante, a best friend. My best friend. And I can't think of a more Hollywood happily ever after than having you agree to stay by my side."

"Well, then roll the credits," I declared, grinning from ear to ear. "And let's you and me go walk off into the sunset, once and for all."

Turn the page for an excerpt of the first
Exclusive Romance from Mari Madison

Just This Night

Available now from Berkley Sensation

JAKE "MAC" MACDONALD

M ommy! Mommy! *Mommy!*"
  I jerked up in bed, swinging around, my feet hitting
the floorboards before my mind had a chance to process the
movement. For a split second, fighting the fog of deep sleep,
I didn't know where I was. What time it was. Why I was here.

"Mommy? Where are you, Mommy?"

But I knew that voice. And the rest didn't matter.

"I'm coming, Ashley!"

Bolting from the bedroom, I dashed down the hall, bursting into her room like some kind of superman on steroids.
Ashley was sitting up in bed, hugging her grubby stuffed
lion—the one I'd bought her from the hospital gift shop the
day she was born, four years ago last month. Tears streamed
down her chubby little cheeks and her thumb was firmly
lodged in her mouth.

Dropping to my knees I pulled her into a fierce hug,
forcing myself to be gentle and not squeeze too hard as my

heart thumped wildly in my chest, working overtime to rid my body of the excess adrenaline her cries had unleashed.

She was fine. She was safe. She was okay.

"Shh," I whispered. "Daddy's here, baby. Are you all right? Did you have a bad dream?" I could feel the sweat dripping down her back, soaking through her thin princess nightgown as she snuggled closer, pushing her head against my chest as if she was literally trying to crawl inside of me and hide. My heart squeezed. Poor little thing. Was she actually shaking?

"I was scared," she whimpered. "I woke up and I didn't know where Mommy was."

I could feel her head lift off my chest and realized she was looking around the darkened bedroom. As if her mother might magically appear out of thin air at any moment.

Sorry, kid. No magic in the world was that strong.

"We talked about this, sweetheart," I reminded her gently, the bile churning in my stomach now. "Mommy has an important job to do far, far away. She can't be with us right now."

"I don't want her to do her important job," Ashley sobbed, dropping her head to my chest again. "I want her here, with us."

Closing my eyes, I forced myself to draw in a heavy breath. "I know, baby, I know. You and me both." I stroked her hair, leaning in to kiss the top of her head. "Now why don't you lie down and I'll use the magic pixie dust on you, okay? So you can fall back asleep."

Ashley whimpered. "What if I have another dream?"

"If you do, it'll be a good one," I assured her with a confidence I didn't feel. "That's the great thing about pixie dust." I reached for the tub of glitter-infused baby powder sitting on her nightstand. "It only allows for happy dreams about princesses and puppy dogs and hungry little caterpillars . . ."

I turned the tub upside down and squeezed, releasing a puff of powder. The glitter dusted her skin and she smiled, snuggling against her stuffed lion again and looking up at me with wide brown eyes. Her mother's eyes. Which was so unfair.

"I love you, Daddy."

"I love you, too, baby girl," I managed to say, my emotions swelling. I leaned down to kiss her cheek. "More than anything ever."

"Anything ever . . ." she repeated sleepily, her eyes fluttering closed. "Hey! I think the magic pixie dust is . . ." She trailed off, drifting back into sleep.

For a few moments, I didn't move. I just sat there, watching her. She looked so tiny in the giant king-sized bed that took up most of my sister's guest room. So sweet and fragile and precious. How could anyone willingly walk away from this little girl? Hell, I would rather die a thousand times over than leave her for just one night. But her mother. Her own goddamned mother . . .

I realized I was clenching the sheets with white-knuckled fists. Forcing myself to release them, I rose to my feet, the churning anger making me sick to my stomach. I stormed from the room, shutting the door behind me a little too hard, and I paused for a moment, listening, making sure I hadn't woken her. But the magic pixie dust had done its job and the room remained silent. My princess was asleep.

"Is she okay?"

I looked up. Lost in my tortured thoughts I hadn't seen my sister, Sadie, hovering at the landing, dressed in an oversized Padres jersey and boxer shorts. Her long brown hair hung down her back in a tangle of curls and her face was washed clean of all makeup.

I sighed. "She's fine. She just had a bad dream."

Sadie gave me a sympathetic look. "Poor kid. Moving can be tough. And then being in a strange house . . . I'm sure she's going to feel a lot more adjusted once you guys get all unpacked and settled in your new place."

"Yeah," I stared down at my feet. "Probably so."

I could feel her peering closely at me. "What about you? Are you okay?"

"I'm fine," I said quickly. Probably too quickly.

Sure enough, Sadie raised an eyebrow. "No offense, bro. But you don't look so fine from here."

I sighed. She was always too perceptive, my sister. "I'm just . . . frustrated, I guess," I admitted. "I mean, I want to be a good dad, you know. But no matter what I do I can't give her what she really wants. And it makes me feel so fucking helpless."

My voice broke and Sadie moved to wrap her arms around me. But I shrugged her off. I didn't need her pity. It was already bad enough I was practically a charity case, moving cross-country to San Diego to take advantage of her offer of free babysitting while I was at work. I'd offered to pay her, of course, but she had argued that she was already staying home with two kids—how hard could one more be? And like the pathetic broke bastard I was, I allowed myself to believe it to be true.

Sadie, to her credit, didn't try to press me. Instead, she smiled. "I'm going to go make myself a sandwich. You want one?"

"Sure," I reluctantly agreed. It wasn't as if I was going to get back to sleep anytime soon anyway. Then I looked down at my current getup. I'd been in such a rush to reach Ashley's side I'd forgotten I was bare-chested, only wearing a pair of ratty boxer shorts. Not exactly good houseguest attire. "Let me grab a shirt and some pants and I'll meet you down there."

By the time I reached the kitchen a few minutes later, Sadie had already gotten out all the sandwich supplies and was currently spreading a thick layer of mayo on my ham and cheese. I sat down at the breakfast bar, scrubbing my face with my hands, trying to banish the memory of Ashley's frightened eyes from my mind. Her cries for "Mommy" that would never be answered.

God, I hated lying to her. But what else could I say? The truth?

The bitch left us, baby girl. She's not coming back. But trust me—we're much better off without her.

"Is this some kind of brother and sister secret powwow or does a poor, hungry husband stand a chance at scoring a sandwich, too?"

I looked up, stifling a groan as Sadie's husband, Joe, stepped into the kitchen wearing a black Batman bathrobe and bare feet. Great. Ashley must have woken the whole house with her screams.

"What, are your hands broken? You can't make your own?" Sadie shot back with mock grumpiness. But I caught the adoring looks they exchanged when they thought I wasn't looking.

"Hey! I'm just saving my strength for that extra-long back massage I plan to give you once we're back in bed," Joe said with a sly wink. My sister laughed.

"Oh, fine. Just this once. But it better be a damned good massage." She grabbed two more slices of bread from the bag and tossed them on the counter. Then she caught my look and her smile faded. "Are you sure you're okay, Mac?" she asked worriedly.

Joe turned to look at me for the first time. "Yeah, man. You look like hell. No offense."

I groaned. "Why thank you. I'll be here all week."

To my annoyance, he continued to study me. "You know what this guy needs?" he asked, turning to Sadie. "To get out of the house. A night on the town. That would fix him right up."

"Uh, no," I interjected before my sister could answer. "I'm good. Really."

Joe turned back to me. "When's the last time you went out?" he demanded. Before I could reply he added, "And, no, Chuck E. Cheese does not count."

"Joe . . ." Sadie said warningly.

"What?" Joe asked, holding up his hands in mock innocence. "I'm just saying. A man needs a night out with grown-ups every once in a while." He grinned wickedly. "Think about it, Mac. Endless lines of tequila shots, pretty girls, maybe some sexy, sexy times?"

"Joe!" Sadie's voice rose.

"Okay, okay! Jesus." Joe snorted. Then he turned back to me, lowering his voice. "You know I'm right though. Right?"

I sighed. I had to admit, the idea did sound pretty awesome. I hadn't had a night away from Ashley since *that* night. And that night was pretty much a lifetime ago at this point. Just the idea of sitting at a bar, having an adult beverage as I people watched. It sounded like a little slice of heaven.

It was also impossible. I wasn't that guy anymore. I mean, I probably was, deep down, but I had other priorities now. My life was not my own.

"Dude!" Joe cried, slamming his fist against the counter, as if something had just occurred to him. Though I had a pretty good idea he'd been working up to this from the moment he'd started in on me. "I've got a great idea!"

I could see my sister shooting him another disapproving look, but he ignored her, rushing in before she could interrupt. "I'm supposed to check out this new club for my company's Christmas party tomorrow night. You could totally come with me. They say it's a hot spot for reporters—News 9 is right down the street. So it'd be perfect." Joe nodded enthusiastically, as if he'd already gotten me to agree. "We'll have some drinks, take in the sights . . ." He waggled his eyebrows. "Maybe even find you a little hotness for the ride home."

I rolled my eyes, waiting for my sister to jump in and save me again. Instead, to my surprise, I found her nodding slowly. "You know, that's not a terrible idea," she said. "I could watch Ashley while you were out."

"No, thank you." I shook my head firmly. "No way am I just going to go and take off and leave Ashley to go clubbing."

Sadie frowned. "Uh, Mac, you do realize you're going to be forced to quote 'take off' on her every day once you start your new job, right? Consider this a trial run—not to mention a good lesson for the both of you. Like, you learn it's still possible to have a life in addition to being a good father and Ashley learns that when Daddy goes away, he always comes back. It's kind of perfect, actually."

"It's completely perfect," Joe agreed. "In fact, you'd be a terrible father to stay home and deny your daughter this all-important life lesson. And I know you don't want *that*."

I sighed, looking from one expectant face to the other. They weren't going to drop this, I realized. And I was sick of arguing.

"Fine," I said. "I'll go. But," I added before they could break into celebration, "don't expect me to bring home anything but a hangover." I'd go to their club, I'd have some drinks, but when it came to picking up women? That was off the table.

Joe snorted. "No problem. I'm sure Sadie can hold off picking out china patterns a few more days." He paused, his playful face fading. "But seriously, bro, keep your options open. I mean, no pressure or anything—just see what's out there. After all, it's not fair to write off the entire female race just because of what happened with Victoria."

I cringed. And there it was. The name that, spoken aloud, still had the power to send a cannonball of hurt straight through my gut. Hell, they might as well have put my balls in a vise and started cranking the handle.

"Look, I said I'd do this nightclub thing," I ground out, forcing the lump back down my throat. "But we have to make a rule right now. From this point on no one ever, ever mentions that bitch's name in my presence again." I paused, then added, *"Ever."*

I pushed back on my stool as I rose from my seat, the force of the movement causing it to crash to the floor. As I turned to pick it up I could feel my sister's and Joe's pitying stares burning into my back. Which, if I was being honest, was worse than their teasing.

I wanted to turn around and tell them I was just fine. That Ashley and I did awesome on our own and I didn't need some stupid female to complete me. But I knew if I even started down that rabbit hole, I'd look like I was protesting too much. And in the end, it was better to just drop the whole thing all together.

The bitch was gone. I was still here. And evidently I was going clubbing.

It's just one night, I told myself. *What could happen in just one night?*